PAYNE'S CURSE

BROOKE BRAUNEIS

ISBN- 979-8-9878460-0-1

Cover and Interior Design by Natalia Junqueira | Dawn Book Design

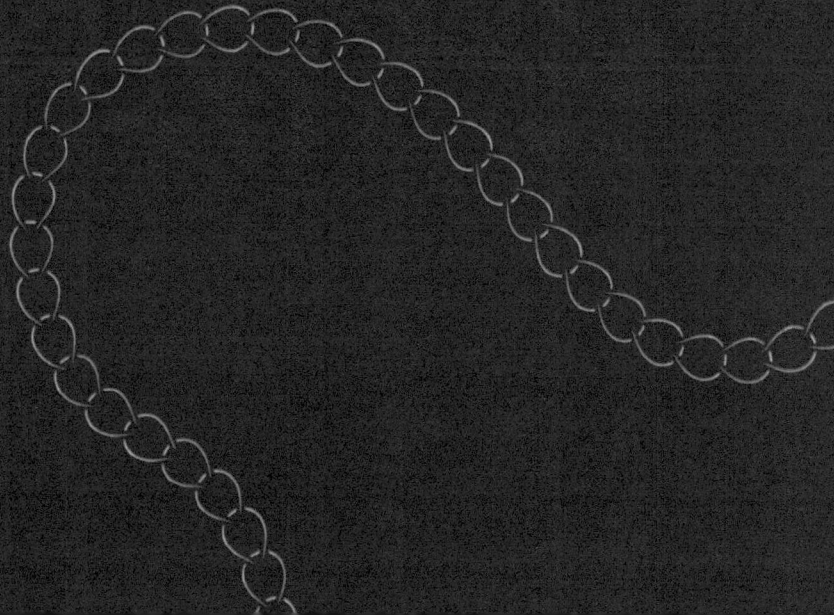

To my sweet friend, Lacey.

You have supported me from the birth of this story.
You have endured countless revisions and endless edits,
and through it all, have encouraged me to never
stop writing.

This story is for you, friend.

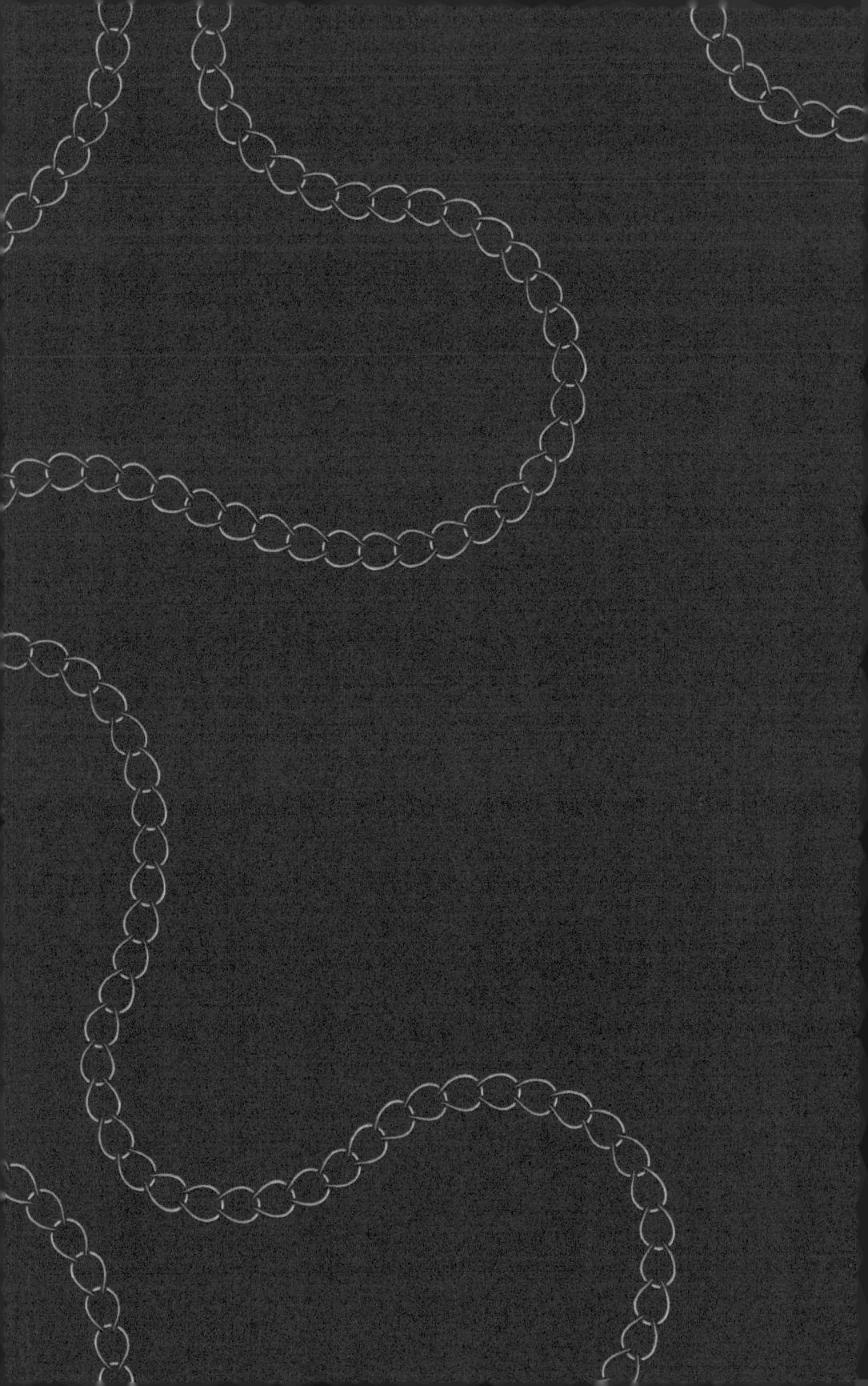

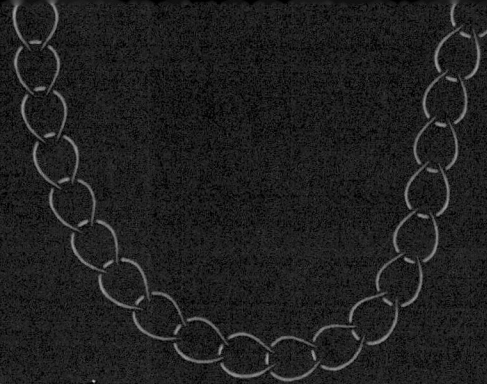

Dear readers,

If you have stumbled upon this story, I'd like to tell you, you have stumbled upon a jem hidden among the hordes of books that fill our world.

But this story is merely the accomplishment of a dream of mine that started nearly eighteen years ago, when I was still a little girl at the ripe young age of twelve.

At that point in time, I believed I would one day be a world-famous authoress.

And here I am, years of writing, changing plot lines, developing characters, scraping paragraphs and starting over and over, again and again.

Is it perfect? No. But my twelve-year-old self would be proud, proud that I finally finished a story and had it published, my name—finally—written on the bottom of a book.

So, this story is for all the dreamers out there, dreaming of becoming something big one day.

Don't stop believing in yourself and never give up on your dreams.

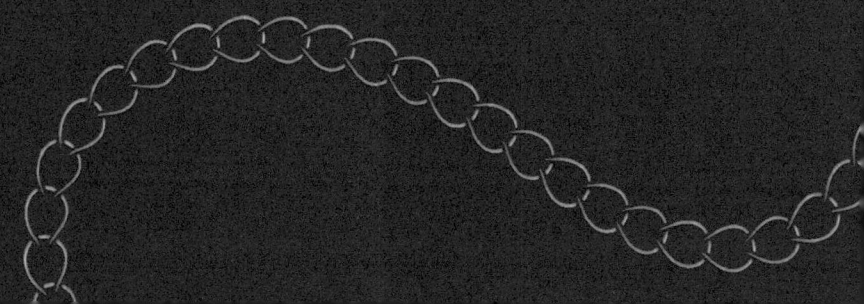

The Beginning

The sea raged, a creature unlike any other, as though Oaran, the god of the sea, himself had woken from the deep, his wrath had been kindled. In a tempest, dark waves turned into a billowing beast threatening to swallow everything whole and return any lives to Asta, the goddess of death. But these kinds of storms do not suddenly appear. They churn slowly in the deep and when least expected, they rise. Only those who've experienced Oaran's wrath sense the shift in the air and water. Waves no longer roll softly to shore but crash dangerously against the earth. Dark clouds gather on the horizon with distant thunder and lightning foretelling of the storm's true intent. The scent of rain hangs in the air, mixed with the ever-familiar tang of sea water. The sea is unlike any other creature, his storms are what make his waters feared among men.

A few smaller vessels were still making their way to the docks. Crews scrambled to get the ships secured to the docks. The larger ships were already moored, expertise had allowed them time to weigh anchor with some peace of mind, before the storm had even begun. The *Sea Jewel*, the largest of the vessels, was tucked away at the

1

furthest dock along the port, avoiding unwanted attention. Her crew had long since descended upon the town ravenous for any source of entertainment they could find. By the time the storm had reach the port shores, they were five ales deep, swapping tales and sharing laughs with any who cared to listen.

Two men of the *Sea Jewel's* crew however did not join in the ramble but sat quietly in the tavern's back room. There was some resemblance of silence for the two men, but it was overshadowed by the jovial shouts coming from the heart of the tavern. One of the men was young, handsome, and untainted by the salty sea life and booze. He sat, enjoying a single beer, not at all interested in the partying beyond his table. He could have joined in the laughter and brawls of the other young men but remained where he sat. Storm grey eyes twinkled mysteriously as he watched the lively tavern around him.

The young man's companion was different. His companion sat rigid, unsmiling as he watched the tavern life unfold before him. His jacket, once deep crimson, had now faded, resembling aged wine. Deep lines covered his brow and creases wrinkled the corner of his eyes, years of squinting into the sun. Countless hours at sea had aged him, but instead of wisdom behind his eyes, there was something cunning and sinister. But what set him truly apart from his younger companion was a ghastly scar that ran from his temple down to his chin. It was that scar that set him apart from any found at the tavern. That scar revealed his true name and explained the cautious glances his way. He'd earned this scar and in turn had made a name for himself.

Rumor was an old nemesis had etched the scar on his face after some sort of mysterious treasure. He had gotten the scar, but the treasure remained a mystery. Most prayed they would never see this man, let alone cross paths with him. If they were so unlucky, most prayed they would live to tell the tale. A tale of an encounter with the most feared pirate of Oaran's waters, Captain Atherol Payne, but those who dared to sail with him, called him simply Captain Payne.

Silence sat between the captain and his young companion. But neither seemed inconvenienced by the lack of conversation. They waited patiently, both eyes trained on the tavern's front doors. The captain clamped his lips in a painfully tight line across his darkened face, their guest was late. Suddenly, the tavern door opened with a bang. A gaunt man scurried in, eyes darting uncomfortably, searching the room. The little man was out of place, the way he snatched his cap in his hands, twisting over and over only confirmed his discomfort. Payne raised a brow, glancing at his young companion.

"Our contact." The young man muttered, standing quickly, gesturing to the nervous little man. When he did not notice the gesture, the young man made his way over to the willowy man and introduced himself with a whisper, pointing to the table and his companion. Captain Payne smirked, watching the scene unfold. The young man loomed over the childlike man, who shrunk away as though he had been stung by a jellyfish. The young man had the uncanny talent of intimidation, an ability that had proved to be useful. It was the reason why Payne had made him his second in command, even at such a young age. His second in command offered the man a chair across from Payne. The man's eyes fluttered from the captains to his scar before his face turned ashen.

"Dr. Boswick, I presume." Payne purred; the little man nodded wringing his hands together.

"Nervous, doctor?" Payne gestured to the motion, "There is no need," a smile formed on his lips, "unless, of course your information is incorrect, then you would have every reason to be nervous." Dr. Boswick dropped his hands, licking his lips, before taking a seat.

"Tell me what you know." Payne demanded.

"The girl is here, she lives on the north side of the town, in the business district." His voice, nasally and somewhat shrill, grated painfully on the captain's ears.

"And her father?" Payne mused.

"Gone." The doctor paused, "He's a merchant, absent for weeks—months—at a time." Payne smiled, slightly, just as he had expected. Payne glanced at his second in command, an invisible source of tension rose between them. The doctor glanced from Payne to the younger man warily, also sensing the rising tension in the room.

"Does anyone look after her?" Payne asked, shifting in his chair. But instead of answering, the doctor dared to eye the captain with a sense of deliberate scrutiny.

"For a time, she had a governess, a Ms. Bloomington. Now, it is just her and the estate staff." The doctor finally answered. Captain Payne clapped his hands together, causing the doctor to jump. Payne's black eyes twinkled with sinister delight.

"Excellent! I trust you will be able to give my second more specifics of the estate location, staff, and any other information that may be valuable to our mission." It was not a question, Payne gestured to his second, he expected all information to be conveyed.

"And what of my payment?" Dr. Boswick asked, his voice held a faint glimmer of courage. The captain glanced with a smirk at his second, who nodded slightly.

"You will be paid in full, as per our agreement. Once we receive the information we need." The doctor shivered but nodded. "You have been most helpful, doctor." The captain purred a wicked glimmer spread over his face.

Dr. Boswick nodded nervously, "What are you planning to do?" The captain rose from his chair, the wicked gleam glowed in his eyes.

"I plan on paying her a friendly visit." Payne grabbed his glass and took a generous swig, "and then I plan on destroying her."

Chapter 1

The streets of the business district of Whaeldrake were alive and bustling. The various shops that lined the streets were opened for business and the usual traffic of men and women who visited them came and go at their own leisure. Carriages of all shapes and sizes ran up and down the streets, adding to the familiar sounds that filled Dover Street.

Dover street was known for holding a few established, well-liked businesses, but it was mostly home to some of the wealthier families of Whaeldrake. The house at the end of the block was the largest estate, sitting up on the hill overlooking the rest of Dover Street, and the ongoing clamor of all the shops and people that visited them. It was the only estate on the street that had a lush, green garden adorned with a beautiful quaint courtyard. It was a slice of the country smack-dab in the middle of a bustling port town, a little piece of heaven. Over the years, the estate had become somewhat of an attraction for the people of Dover Street and all Whaeldrake. But despite the beautiful grounds belonging to the estate, the inhabitants of the estate were a mystery. All anyone knew was that the estate kept a well-paid staff, responsible for caring for a young lady who oversaw the staff. It was said that the young lady's father was a well-known merchant but was seldom ever home.

The young women sat in the front drawing room, watching the streets of Dover below. It was her usual morning past time, providing her with a different change of pace from the loneliness that had become part of her daily routine. She sat alone; a book perched in her lap. The woman's golden locks were gathered in a fashionable bun, piled on top of her head, a few loose strands framing a delicate slender face.

The drawing room was completely opposite of the streets below, quiet, and unassuming. A grandfather clocked ticked away, calmly behind her, reminding her of time ticking aimlessly away. But then it chimed, bringing a frown to the young woman's face as she glanced behind her at the face of the clock. Margaret, one of the estates servants, was late with her breakfast. But just as though she had summoned her but mere thought, Margaret flung the drawing room door open and rushed in. Her apron was crooked and her cap was nearly falling off her mound of black curls. The lady watched her rush in like a flurry, clearly unamused with her servant's lack of diligence.

"You're late Margaret." The young women remarked coldly, fixing steel blue eyes on the frazzled maid.

"I beg your pardon, Miss Wynnefred." Margaret curtsied slightly before rushing forward with the tray of food, another servant following in behind her with a cart of coffee. Wynnefred, or Wynne as she preferred, eyed the maid carefully as the tray of food was set before her.

"Coffee Miss?" Margaret offered, doing everything to avoid Wynne's gaze.

"Please." She nodded. Margaret quickly poured a cup of delicious black coffee, before nearly dropping the pot and causing Wynne to jump in her seat.

"Oh!" cried Margaret, "A letter arrived this mornin', Miss, from your father." The maid revealed a sealed envelope from her pocket and set it on the table before her. Wynne eyed the letter, but made no move to open in.

"Thank you. That will be all Margaret." Margaret curtsied and slipped from the drawing room. Wynne barely noticed her leave; her eyes were fixed on the envelope before her as she took a tentative sip from her coffee. The black liquid made her toes curl, she should have added some cream and sugar, but the bite of bitter coffee helped to curb the apprehension that suddenly welled inside her stomach. Her father's elegant handwriting stared up at her. Carefully, Wynne took another sip then retrieved the letter; it was heavier than she expected. Had he sent something to her in addition to a letter? She held her breath as she pried open the seal. Instantly a golden locket slipped out onto her lap.

Strange. She thought, her father had never sent her anything before when he was away on his journeys, why send her something now? Maybe his letter would explain the unexpected gift. Momentarily setting the locket aside she opened the single paged letter and frowned. He had hastily scrawled a single line on the page.

Payne is coming. Meet you at the Keep.

Frowning, she read the message again, but it didn't make any more sense than the first time. She didn't know anyone named Payne and knew nothing of a Keep let alone where it might be. Irritated, she examined the locket, hoping something about the necklace would help her uncover the meaning behind her father's words.

The locket was beautifully crafted, not much larger than a coin. The golden face was decorated with intricate golden filagree surrounding a center of blue jem stones. In the center of the blue stone lay a single trident. Wynne tried to open the locket but couldn't find the latch and she didn't feel like prying the beautiful piece open, risking damage to the necklace. But then she noticed very dainty handwriting along the outer rim of the center, where the trident lay. She squinted but couldn't make out the words. It looked like a different language, but she couldn't quiet tell. She pursed her lips, why on earth would her father send her this locket with a note that made absolutely no sense?

The drawing room door opened and the butler, Henry, hurried in, wheeling a small cart in front of him. He hurried to her little table and began clearing away her breakfast dishes, though she hadn't had a chance to really eat her food. Though, even if she wanted to, she was not hungry.

"May we be expecting Mr. Hunt soon, Miss?" Henry inquired, noticing the envelope on the table.

"It's the strangest thing," Wynne mused, handing the letter to the butler, "Maybe you can make heads or tails of his message." The butler raised a brow but took the letter. Wynne studied him closely as he took in the words.

"Do you know what he's talking about?" She asked quickly as soon as he returned the note to her.

The butler shook his head, "No Miss."

"Henry," Wynne warned, "If you know something, you must tell me." The butler met her stare with resilience that only a man of serving fifteen years in their household could muster. Wynne knew she did not scare him, to him she was still the rambunctious five-year-old, not a twenty-year-old woman sitting before him.

"I'm sorry Miss, your father must've had his reasons for sending the note." He replied curtly. Wynne nodded, though she did not believe him. She watched him clean up the rest of the dishes, noting the glance he made to the locket that sat on the table. She was sure he recognized it, but how? He left the drawing room quickly, leaving her alone, yet again.

Wynne sat in the silence, staring at the locket, and mulling over her father's note. Maybe she should send a response to her father, asking for some explanation and clarification? She decided against the idea. Henry, despite her annoyance with him, was correct in his summation. Her father had his reasons for everything that he did, and asking for clarification sometime was more daunting than just accepting his words, however obscure. But this was also one of the reasons she always felt so isolated. The only people she really socialized with was the house staff and Ms. Bloomington. But even then, Wynne could not help feeling resentment towards her father for always leaving her behind. He was out traveling the world, and what was she doing? Stuck on Dover Street, watching everyone else live, while her own life ticked away to the beat of the old grandfather clock. She felt restless and agitated, she needed a diversion.

Ms. Bloomington, her former governess, was the only person in town she knew well enough to call on. Her mind was made up, she stood quickly leaving the cryptic note behind but taking the piece of jewelry with her. She would figure out the meaning of the necklace on her own, cryptic note or not.

Her room was situated on the second floor of the estate and was the largest bedroom in the house. After her father and her had moved in, he had insisted she take the room, wanting her to be the most comfortable in their new home. But Wynne new the real reason, her father was never home and had no use for a large immaculate room. He wanted to make her happy so she wouldn't feel lonely in his absence. Unfortunately for him, she did feel lonely, and the larger room did nothing to sway her resentment or her loneliness.

Wynne rang for Katherine, or Kitty, as the maid preferred to be called. Kitty was an older woman, who had been with their family for ages. She had been her mother's maid before her passing and after she died, she had insisted on staying, to care for Wynne. Over the years, Wynne had grown fond of Kitty, she was the closest thing she had to a mother in many ways. Thinking of her mother, brought a wave of sadness. She had only been five years old when her mother had died. The memories Wynne had of her mother were few and far between. At one point, when she was younger the idea of not being able to remember what her mother looked like, sounded like even, had terrified her. But now, she had learned to live with the grief that her memories would indeed fade, but the love that her mother had always expressed towards her would remain. That love could never fade or forgotten.

"You rang Miss?" Kitty asked stepping into her room.

Wynne smiled, "I am going to pay Ms. Bloomington a visit this afternoon." Kitty nodded and moved for the closet to pick out a dress. Wynne had no shortage of fine clothes; her father had seen to it that she had ample allowance to buy anything she pleased. And although she purchased a new gown from time to time, Wynne spent most of her allowance on growing her library.

When they had moved in her father had commissioned a well-known carpenter to fashion beautiful wall to ceiling shelves in her room. Ever since then, she had made it her mission to fill them with as many books as she could get her hands on. Books of all shapes and colors lined the shelves and every one of them held a spot in Wynne's heart. Books for her was a chance to learn and escape her little world. In the pages of a book, she could see anything, be anything she wanted to be. Books had taught her languages; she had already mastered three. Books had taught her about the weather, about science, history, art! Books were the way to her heart and her soul, and without them she was not sure she would have been able to survive her drab, quiet life in Whaeldrake.

"The blue or green dress today, Miss?" Kitty asked, eyeing two of Wynne's gowns. Wynne glanced over her shoulder at the dresses Kitty was deciding between.

"The blue one." Wynne nodded to the navy blue one, it would bring out the blue in her own eyes. Kitty nodded in agreement, of all her dresses, blue was the predominant color in her wardrobe. In Wynne's mind, it was the only color that brought out her eyes and made her blonde hair sparkle.

Kitty helped her into the dress, making sure her corset was snug. After Ms. Bloomington retired from her post as governess, Wynne had stopped wearing corsets altogether, much to Kitty's consternation. But when she did go out, Kitty was adamant that proper society norms must be followed to the letter. Wynne grumbled and argued, but Kitty always won the arguments, despite Wynne's best efforts. Once dressed, Kitty moved to Wynne's hair, knotting it into an intricate braid and pinning in up in excellent fashion.

"Ms. Bloomington will be pleased you've come to see her." Kitty smiled, glancing in the mirror as she pinned back a few loose strands.

"I should say so," Wynne laughed, "It's been a few weeks since I last visited."

"I believe her niece just got married." Kitty mused. Wynne pursed her lips, vaguely aware of Ms. Bloomington telling her all the details of the wedding when she had gone to visit her before. She had not remembered the date Ms. Bloomington had told her though.

"I will be sure to get all the details when I see her then." Wynne knew Kitty would enjoy hearing of the wedding. More recently, Kitty had been more vocal about her excitement for when she herself was to be married. Wynne laughed the idea off merely because she had no long line of suitors. In fact, she frowned, she had no line of suitors. Her father was always away and had no time to find any suitors for her. It was socially unacceptable for her to find one on her own, so she was stuck waiting. Secretly though, Wynne was waiting for the day when Kitty would have the gumption to confront her father about his duties as a father. She smiled to herself at the thought, that was something she wanted to witness. Kitty had a spunk about her and had a knack for speaking her mind. It was what had made her a favorite of her mother's all those years ago, and consequently now Wynne's favorite.

Wynne picked up the locket and slipped it around her throat. The gold sparkled against her skin, offsetting the beautiful navy blue of her dress. Kitty spotted the necklace, she squinted, and frowned, taking a quick step closer before raising her eyes in surprise.

"Where did you get that?" She asked quickly.

"It came in a letter from my father this morning." Wynne turned to face the maid.

"Your father sent this to you?" She gaped.

Wynne nodded, feeling her own confusion rise, "Do you recognize it?"

Kitty nodded fervently, "It was your mother's." Wynne felt like the rug was pulled out from under her feet.

"This locket was hers?" She glanced down at the locket, willing any memory of the locket to surface, but there was nothing.

Kitty nodded, a sad smile crept onto her face, "She wore that locket every day, it was her favorite." But the sadness changed to confusion, "After she died, though, the locket disappeared." The maid's eyes fixed on the locket.

"Father must have taken it." Wynne thought, Kitty nodded in agreement. It was the only thing that made sense. Her father had been devastated when her mother had died, keeping something of hers that had meant so much to her made sense.

"Do you know what the words in the center mean?" Wynne asked.

Kitty frowned, "Words?" She shook her head, "No miss, I don't know what the words mean, I didn't even know there were words on it." Wynne believed her. Kitty was brilliant but reading and writing were not one of her specialties. Wynne bit her lip, there was a book shop on the edge of town, outside of the business district that she visited frequently, maybe the shop owners would recognize the words. They would also have a book that might help her decipher the strange text. Wynne mulled over the idea; it was a thought.

"Well, thank you Kitty, for clearing up that mystery for me."

Kitty smiled, "She would have wanted for you to have it anyways, Miss." Yes, Wynne had no doubt that her mother would have wanted her to have it. But why had it taken so long for her to even get the locket in the first place. If her father was here, she would have hounded him about it. But he wasn't, so she would have to be content with waiting for answers to her questions. Or, she thought, she could get the answers herself. She smiled, that sounded like a much more exciting plan.

Chapter 2

Ms. Bloomington did not live in the Business District, but instead lived five blocks away in what was once called the Garden District. It had once housed some of the most beautiful gardens, but in recent years, many of the tiny homes and gardens had fallen by the wayside. Ms. Bloomington's home, however, was one of the few that still cared to preserve the beautiful gardens. Ms. Bloomington, after retiring her post, moved there, and decided to grow flowers, selling them to many vendors that sold in the Business District. She had since earned a reputation for some of the best grown flowers in all Whaeldrake.

Wynne walked up the cobble stoned path, inhaling a deep breath of all the lovely blooms that lined the path. The rose bushes were in full bloom and the deep rich smell of rose blossoms filled her nose. The roses were by far Ms. Bloomington's favorites, though the bushes that lined her walkway were never cut, they were for her enjoyment and for all those that stopped by for a visit.

Wynne knocked, waiting patiently to hear signs of life on the other side of the door. She didn't have to wait long before Ms.

Bloomington's butler, a Mr. Cooper, opened the door. He ushered her in immediately before hurrying away to fetch the lady of the house.

"Wynnefred!" Ms. Bloomington cried, flying into the parlor, a bright cheery smile fixed on her plump face, hands held out in warm greeting. Since her resignation, Ms. Bloomington's once stiff mannerisms had loosened becoming more friendly and open. Gone were high society mannerisms and were replaced by something warm and genuine. Still refined and polished, but also relaxed and natural.

"I hope you do mind a visit from one of your old students." Wynne remarked, taking her hands, and squeezing gently.

Ms. Bloomington laughed, "Mind? I do not mind you calling, ever!" She squeezed Wynne's hands in return before gesturing for her to have a seat.

"And what do I owe for this lovely visit?"

Wynne shook her head, "Merely your company. I received a letter from my father today and needed a pleasant distraction."

Ms. Bloomington's smiled faded slightly, "How long has he been gone?"

"It will be five months, next Thursday." Wynne replied simply, but Ms. Bloomington's eyes could read the pain in her face and eyes.

"Did his letter give any indication when he will return?"

Wynne scoffed, "No. It was a single cryptic line and this locket." Wynne remarked showing the women the beautiful new locket that hung from her throat. "I'm beginning to think he won't ever come home."

Ms. Bloomington cooed, "Nonsense my dear! Your father travelled just as much when you mother was alive."

"Yes, but he took her along with him! She got to travel and see the world, but me, he just leaves me at home."

"That is because the sea is no place for a lady." Ms. Bloomington chided.

"Neither is staying at home with no connections or social atmosphere."

Ms. Bloomington raised a brow, "You can't fault your father for no social atmosphere, my dear, not when I have invited you to plenty of social gatherings."

"Which I come to." Wynne argued, half-heartedly.

Ms. Bloomington laughed, "Not as often as I would like for you to." Wynne shook her head, though she knew Ms. Bloomington was correct. She was the only one that invited her to any social events, and she did go, on occasion, but she never fit in with any of the other guests in attendance. The few times she did go, she would merely stand around awkwardly, attempt to make some conversation, fail, and then leave early.

"Why don't you come to more of my parties?"

Wynne sighed, "You know why I don't."

The women shook her head, "Please, explain it to me again, dear, for my sake."

"Because I'm an anomaly, I don't fit in with anyone. Finding some sort of common ground with anyone is virtually impossible!" Wynne cried, to which Ms. Bloomington just smiled warmly.

"You're not an anomaly, your life—it is just different than everyone else's." Ms. Bloomington's voice was soft and comforting, but it only made Wynne feel patronized.

"Yes, and no one understands that difference, nor do they even care to try."

"Because you don't let them." Ms. Bloomington concluded; Wynne knew she had lost her foothold in the argument.

"I will do my best to come to more of your parties." Wynne conceded.

Ms. Bloomington smiled, "I promise, my dear, the social parties will be worth your while. And who knows, you may even make a new friend!" Wynne smiled, biting back her doubtful retort. She knew Ms. Bloomington was right, but in the back of her mind, despite all her resentment towards her father, wished that she was out with him, traveling the world, living the life she read about in all her books.

Tea was called for and promptly served and the conversation shifted towards Ms. Bloomington's niece's wedding. Her niece, Annabelle, had married a man in the imperial army, an admiral who came from a prestigious family. The admiral was from Triura, to the northwest of Gallanmar, and that is where they both were now stationed after they married.

The wedding had been large, the gifts had been extravagant, and her dress was unrivaled by any other wedding dress that had ever been or ever would be created. The guest list was extravagant, with even some royals from Triura attending. Wynne listened to all of Ms. Bloomington's exaggerated details with a smile, some nods, and occasional coos of excitement. But beyond that, Wynne's mind wandered to the locket and the errand she would be running after lunch.

Wynne had a hankering that the words scrawled on the locket were Avanthian, but she couldn't be sure. Her grandfather had known Avanthian, and she remembered a brief time when he had wanted her to learn, but then, for some reason, he had dropped the matter entirely. Her grandfather had been a sailor as well but had been extremely educated. He was the reason for her love for books and for language, encouraging her to read as much as she could and to absorb as much knowledge possible. He believed knowledge was power, the and the written word had so much to offer, but only to those willing enough to dig and find it out.

The thought of her grandfather brought real pangs to her chest. Once her mother had died, he had stayed behind to help see to her education while her father continued the business. When she got older and Ms. Bloomington was employed, her grandfather once again returned to the sea to help her father and his growing business. But then word came that he had died at sea and Wynne was yet again faced with grief. To this day she did not know how he had died, her only comfort was that he was out at sea, which was where his heart had always been.

"Wynnefred!" Ms. Bloomington's voice called, shaking her out of her thoughts. The memory of her grandfather receded from her mind. Wynne blinked and found Ms. Bloomington watching her carefully, waiting patiently for her response. Wynne blushed, embarrassed by her blunder.

"I'm so sorry Ms. Bloomington, what was it you said?"

Ms. Bloomington smiled, "Your future husband must be warned that you tend to drift in and out of daydreams." The woman responded with a gentle chide.

"My future—husband?" Wynne questioned, clearly confused by the conversations sudden change in topic.

The woman nodded, before frowning, "Your father has still not set up any suitors for you, has he?"

Wynne shook her head, "I am not sure when he has the time to do so."

"Tsk." Ms. Bloomington shook her head, woefully, "It is unacceptable for a young women of your age and rank to be without a proper suitor."

"Maybe Admiral Reed has a cousin who is single?" Wynne offered, but Ms. Bloomington just frowned.

"This is not a joke my dear. Marriage is what every women strives for." Wynne held back the urge to roll her eyes.

"But what if a woman is not inclined to marriage."

The woman's brows raised, "Not inclined? Why would a woman of high, respectable breeding, not be inclined for marriage?"

"What if she wants to travel the world, experience an adventure or two, instead of marrying? Would she not be able to do as she pleases?"

"No." Ms. Bloomington said firmly, sensing the direction of the conversation.

Wynne laughed, "And why can't a women do as she pleases with her own life?"

"Because it is not proper!" Ms. Bloomington exclaimed.

"My mother did so, and I believe she was still as proper as any other young lady who had stayed at home and found a husband."

"Your mother, Estris rest her soul," Ms. Bloomington remarked pointedly, "Was a wild creature and was only tamed by your father, she had a completely different life before she met your father!" Wynne smirked; she remembered the stories well from her grandfather, stories of her mother and father when the first met and how they had fallen in love.

"And," Ms. Bloomington added, not giving her a chance to say anything contradictory, "if your mother was still alive today, Estris rest her soul, would agree with me. And," Ms. Bloomington continued forcefully, "she would be helping your father set up a suitable match for you." Wynne smiled, though she knew Ms. Bloomington was wrong.

From what she knew of her mother, her mother had never been conventional. She had enjoyed doing things differently than the way society dictated them. Had her mother been alive today, she would have continued in her ways of thinking, she would have trained Wynne up to believe the same things. Wynne would have had an ally for her uncanny thoughts, instead of trying to fight everyone who forced societies norms upon her.

17

Chapter 3

Lunch passed in a similar fashion with Ms. Bloomington's not so subtle hints of Wynne's need for a social lift and the importance of finding a suitable husband. Wynne smiled pleasantly and took the conversations in toll, but secretly she was counting down the minutes till she could depart and carry on with the rest of her plans for the day. For her part, Ms. Bloomington did not notice Wynne's sudden quietness and small smiles, which was a relief. Finally, when the moment was just right, when her departure seemed the most obvious choice, she leapt at the chance.

The book shop lay just on the outskirts of the Business District tucked away in a corner of the district, away from all the clatter of carriages and chatter of people. It was what made this book shop one of Wynne's favorites to visit, because it had a certain ambience, quiet and peaceful, among all the chaos that existed outside its walls. Her father had always disapproved of her visiting this book shop, because it was so far from the Business District. But, Wynne reasoned, with her father not here, she could go anywhere her heart pleased. Who was going to stop her?

Wynne pushed open the door, a sweet bell announcing her arrival. The familiar smell of worn pages and the subtle notes of must hit her nose, it was a welcome smell. The shop had a few patrons lining the shelves, scouring the shop for something unique to read. But the clamor from the streets outside instantly melted away and a gentle calm filled Wynne. The book shop was indeed a book shop, but one of the owners allowed customers to use the book shop as a library of sorts.

"Good afternoon, Miss Wynnefred!" A deep voice called out to her; his Levanian accent thick and gruff. She looked up and found Mr. Schmidt, one of the shop owners, glancing her way. He was a small in stature but made up for it in size. He was a large man, looking more like a ball with stubby legs than anything else. The other shop owner, a Dr. Boswick, stood beside him and eyed her as well. Dr. Boswick, was a willowy man, pale and sickly looking. His face was hallowed and the glasses perched on his nose just accentuated the dark circles under her eyes. He was a nerves and fidgety man, that made Wynne uncomfortable. For the most part, she only ever talked to Mr. Schmidt.

"Good afternoon, Mr. Schmidt." Wynne nodded pleasantly, "Dr. Boswick." She added, nodding curtly to the other gentleman. Dr. Boswick's eyes fell from hers, his gaunt face looking more ghostly than alive.

"What brings you to the shop this afternoon?"

"I was wondering if you could point me in the right direction for deciphering some text." She asked, stepping forward. She slowly removed the locket from around her neck and held it out for the man to examine. Dr. Boswick leaned in, curiously, but said nothing.

"A family heirloom?" Mr. Schmidt questioned.

Wynne nodded, "My mother's actually."

"May I?" He asked before taking the locket from her. He slipped on his glasses and examined the locket under the lamp light.

"It is very detailed for a piece so small." The shopkeeper remarked, before squinting his eyes slightly, "This is piece is quite exquisite." He mumbled, studying the illuminated locket, turning it over to examine both sides thoroughly.

"The detail is stunning, and the craftsmanship is as intricate as they come." He glanced up at Wynne, she noticed the look of admiration sparkling in his dark eyes.

"Look here Boswick," Mr. Schmidt gestured, holding the locket out for the other man to examine. But Dr. Boswick did not take the locket, merely peered over his shoulder, nodding along.

"That is Avanthian, is it not?" Mr. Schmidt questioned. Dr. Boswick adjusted his glasses, before squinting at the text scrawled onto the brim of the locket.

"It appears to be." He whispered before retreating behind Mr. Schmidt.

Mr. Schmidt nodded, beaming, "I thought so!" He took one more look at the locket before returning it to Wynne, "We have several Avanthian language books that you might find helpful, but I would also suggest checking out the book of Avanthian folklore."

"Avanthian folklore?" Wynne questioned as she slipped the locket back over her head.

The shopkeeper nodded, "That trident in the center is a sign of the Avanthian god of the sea, Oaran."

"Our patron deity?" Wynne questioned.

Mr. Schmidt nodded, eyes twinkling, "You know Avanthian mythology?"

"Not as much as I should know." She admitted, somewhat embarrassed of the lack of knowledge she had. She recognized the deity, but other than that she did not know too much of Avanthian folklore. The Avanthian's were an ancient people group that existed when Taeren was a united country. But then the division happened, and five territories were created and the laws, practices, and customs of the Avanthian's had been separated out among the territories. Over time, many of the old ways had been replaced by new and improved practices.

"Do you also have some Avanthian history books as well and maybe a pen and paper?" She questioned with a knowing smile.

He chuckled, "We have more than we know what to do with." Mr. Schmidt grabbed some paper from under the counter and a small pencil then hurried out from around the counter and led her to a shelf close to the back, "Any of these on this shelf, should help

21

you decipher the locket and give you some insight into Avanthian history." He winked and left her standing there, examining all the books in peace.

Wynne set to work immediately; she would only have a couple hours before she would need to return home. But where to begin? She had no idea the significance of the locket, if there was any, other than that it was her mother's prized piece of jewelry. She grabbed several grammar books, an Avanthian artifacts book, history book and a book on Avanthian folklore before retreating to a small nook tucked in a corner at the back of the shop. There was a small table and chair there, which had not always been there, but after a few visits of her leaning against the shelves and once going as far as sitting in a deserted isle, the chair and table and magically appeared. She knew Mr. Schmidt had set up the chair and table for her and she had yet a way to show him her appreciation for the sweet gesture.

Wynne started with the Avanthian grammar book. The Avanthian language was made up of symbols, not letters. Which made the language beautiful when written, but somewhat more difficult to decipher. First, she started with copying the alphabet and the combinations of symbols that made up certain vowels. Once that was done, she carefully copied the letters from the rim of the locket and began to translate the words. It took longer than she expected, since she had to continuously reference the grammar book for rules regarding language structure of the archaic language. But, after some time, familiar words started to form before her, but it was still not a coherent sentence. She dropped her pencil and stared at the page before her. This language was more difficult than she thought.

"How is it coming Miss Hunt?" Mr. Schmidt's gruff voice sounded, startling her from her page of absolute nonsense.

"It's not. I have only been able to decipher a few words, at best, and they don't even make sense." She grumbled, shoving the paper she had been pouring over forward towards the shopkeeper.

"Let me take a look." He mumbled; brows furrowed as he took up her page of scribbles. "You have translated the bigger words but are struggling with the fillers?" He smiled as Wynne grumbled her confirmation.

"Sea, chaos, heart, reign—it makes no sense!" Wynne cried, letting her frustration bubble over her.

"Let me see that book." Mr. Schmidt nodded to the open grammar book beside her. She handed him the book, secretly wishing the man luck. He studied the book, flipped through h a few pages, and then glanced at the page with all her scribbles.

"I think, I have gotten it," He set the book down, "Oh daughter of sea and chaos, let your heart reign true." He said slowly, as if the words were stumbling over his tongue. Wynne frowned, how had he managed to get that so quickly.

"I didn't realize you were an expert in translating Avanthian Mr. Schmidt."

He chuckled, "An expert, I am not. But, in my grade school years I studied the Avanthian language. The rules of their grammatical structure are difficult to decipher, and I never cared for their symbols, so I dropped my studies of the language altogether." He added scrunching up his nose. Wynne nodded; she wasn't really surprised that the shopkeeper had some knowledge of the archaic language.

"But what does it mean and why is it on a locket that my mother owned?"

Mr. Schmidt shook his head, "I do not know why you mother had this locket, but the phrase does ring a bell." His brow furrowed in concentration as he scanned her book filled table. After a moment, he spotted the title he was looking for *Avanthian Folklore: Tales of Old and Glory.* He opened the book, quickly scanning the contents before finding what he was looking for.

"Here is it!" He cried, jabbing a finger on the page proudly before handing it over to Wynne to examine for herself, "Oaran, god of the sea, was also said to be god of chaos because of the nature of the sea." Wynne peered at the page before her and did indeed see what he was referencing.

"But what of the rest?"

Mr. Schmidt shook his head, "It could have been a popular phrase said among women to honor Oaran?" Wynne pondered, studying the page before her.

"The Avanthian's served four gods, correct?"

Mr. Schmidt chuckled, "Five," He corrected, setting a map down in front of her to view, "After the Division of Taeren, the five territories were formed with each god becoming a patron of each territory. The territories are the same ones we have today." Wynne nodded, she was familiar with the territories of Taeren, though not as familiar with each of their patron deities, except that of her own territory. Gallanmar was the territory of the south, with Whaeldrake being one of the largest and major seaside ports of the entire country. Ebrus, directly north of Gallanmar, was famous for their banking and investment opportunities for business in all Taeren. It was where her father's business headquarters sat, with his business partner in charge of keeping their investors happy. Triura was to the west of Ebrus, Athana was directly north and Oflein to the east. These three territories were the farming industries of Taeren. But Triura held a more prominent head of the three, but only because they were home to the ancient head temple of the Avanthian's.

"So, it's safe to assume it may have been a popular phrase among the women of Gallanmar."

"Possibly. Some towns may have had their own phrases to honor the god." Mr. Schmidt mused. Wynne bit the inside of her lip. Her mother had been raised in Gallanmar and as such, it would not have been odd for her to have a necklace, honoring their patron deity. But Wynne too had also lived her entire life in Gallanmar, specifically in Whaeldrake and she had never once heard the phrase. Maybe in a different region or different port city, it was a familiar phrase? But there could be no way of knowing for certain.

Just then, the clock chimed at the other end of the shop. Wynne groaned, it was five o'clock, she had managed to let the entire afternoon slip by, and it had done so in what appeared to be only a couple of minutes.

"I am so sorry Mr. Schmidt!" She cried, gesturing to the mess of papers and books before her.

He smiled, "Tis no trouble Miss Hunt."

"But your books,"

"Tsk, tsk" he shook his head, "never you mind that, I will put them away in no time." He smiled as he pressed the folklore book into her hands, "Take this as well."

She shook her head, "Oh, no—"

"I insist! You still have many questions; I can see that in your eyes and this book will give you some answers. It will serve a greater purpose with you than just being stuck here on this dusty old shelf, not being read." She gripped the book in her hands and held it close to her chest.

"Thank you." She smiled, gripped the man's arm tenderly, "I must be off!" She clutched the book tightly to her chest as she hurried out of the shop. Information buzzing at the back of her brain. Avanthian folklore lay at the heart of the very territory she lived in, but she did not know much about the Avanthian's and their history.

Yes, Oaran was the patron of Gallanmar, but beyond that she did not know or understand much of the history revolving around the development of the individual territories. It was not that she was not educated, she had received the best education that money could afford, but the Avanthian history had become more of a legend than anything and many of the ways and traditions that once were had become archaic and forgotten over time. As Wynne clutched the book to her chest and moved through the streets, she felt a sudden flood of determination wash over her. What if uncovering Avanthian legends helped her to understand why her mother had the locket and why she now possessed the locket.

Pressed for time, she decided to take a short cut. Her father would not be pleased with her taking back-alley ways, but he was not here to voice his displeasure. Wynne started down the street, book tight to her chest, head held high, her pace confident and steady. She had taken this way several times, never this late in the evening, but she had just as much right to be here as anyone else. As she crossed the tiny street a grimy hand appeared from the shadows, grabbing her wrist. She let loose a scream yanking her hand free. Glancing maliciously at the owner opening her mouth to yell but faltered when she saw the man's face.

"Mr. McNeely?" The look of recognition filled the man's face as he stumbled towards her.

"Miss Hunt?" he slurred, stepping out into the light. She nodded, taking a cautious step away from him and angling herself in the direction she needed to go.

"You have grown so much!" He cried, loudly. Wynne smiled and nodded again, glancing nervously around her. The stench of alcohol was strong, and the slurred speech told her enough to know that he had been indeed drinking. As she moved around him, he cried out and grasped for the locket at her throat.

"Oh no, no, no!" He screamed "To Asta's arms!" he swore, loudly, clasping the locket tightly in his hands.

"Mr. McNeely, please!" Wynne yelled, yanking the locket away from him and cradling it protectively in her own hands.

"Miss, you awl' right?" A man came up beside her, concern filling his face as he studied the swaying drunk before her.

"Yes, I am fine." She smiled politely, moving away from both men. Mr. McNeely jumped at her, grabbing her shoulders violently shaking her. As soon as he did, however the other man stepped into intervene.

"You have to get out of here!" Mr. McNeely screamed.

"You're drunk!" The man yelled, holding him back away from Wynne who stood frightened, watching everything unfold before her.

"He's coming for you!" McNeely cried, terror filling his face.

"What?" She started, "Who's coming for me." He leaned towards her, against the other man's grip.

"He's coming for you!" He hissed.

"Who?" She demanded, forcefully.

His eyes widened, "Payne." He hissed. Wynne took a step back in shock. How did he know that name?

"That's enough old man." The other man grumbled, pulling McNeely further away from Wynne.

"What do you know about him?" Wynne demanded, taking a step towards him.

"He's coming for you!" He yelled. Wynne felt her nerves shake and suddenly noticed the crowd of people that gathered around them, looking at the commotion with curious gazes. It was the kind of attention that would start people talking and that was the last thing she wanted or needed.

"He will find you and kill you!" McNeely wailed, "Except for the curse," he fought against the men holding him back, "Oaran's curse will be the only thing to save you!" The crowd was growing, but

Wynne had heard enough, she was already moving. Eyes trailed her as she hurried from the alley way. These people had heard everything, and their eyes held looks of judgement. They could tell, no doubt from which district she hailed from, and it would only be long before they put together the pieces of who she was, and rumors would spread. Wynne felt sweat beading at her back, her heart thundered in her chest. She didn't trust herself to stop the entire way home and it took everything within her to not run home. Wynne hurried up the front walk and threw the door open, closing it quickly behind her. Once the door was closed behind her, she inhaled a sharp breath, her entire body felt shaky.

"Miss Hunt!" Henry cried; she could clearly see the alarm on his face, "We were wondering where you had gone—" He paused, eyes narrowing with concern at her trembling frame, "Are you alright miss?"

It was a question she could not answer, would not answer. This was the second warning of a man named Payne, coming for her. But now— now, she had learned that this man was going to kill her. She inhaled a shaky breath, before forcing a smile on her face, a weak one at best.

"I am fine Henry." She pushed herself off the door and forced herself to stop shaking, "I got stuck at the bookshop longer than I wanted and had to rush home. I am merely out of breath from walking so fast across town." The butler nodded, though there was a look of doubt on his face. Wynne ignored the look, hurrying past him.

"Please send my dinner to my room this evening and have Kitty come attend me at once." She commanded over her shoulder. If Henry acknowledged her command, she did not know. Her mind was consumed with the threat of some impending doom heading her way.

Chapter 4

Daniel McNeely, the last time Wynne had seen him, she had been twelve. At the time, McNeely has been her grandfather's navigator and had been quite skilled, if memory served her correctly. He had been kind to her, taking time to teach her the inner workings of a ship's navigator. What had happened to him? She never remembered hearing he'd been dismissed sometime after her grandfather had died.

His words echoed ominously in the back of her brain. He had recognized the locket; she was sure that it was the locket that had set him off. But why? What was so special about this locket that warranted a death threat! And why was some mysterious man looking for her? And what was this about Oaran's curse? Wynne shook her head, she could blame his outbursts on intoxication, that he had drunk too much and was out of his mind. But there was a deep nagging feeling in the pit of her stomach that told her, he was coherent enough to make the statement. Which led her back to the question, why?

Thunder rolled in the distance accompanied by a flash of lightening. The rain had come so suddenly, tapping relentlessly against the windows. But it was the rumbling thunder that made Wynne jump in her chair. It was as though McNeely's ominous warning had also brought about the weather. Her nerves were jumpier than ever and not even a nice cup of tea or warm food could ease away her nerves.

Kitty had come not long after she finished her dinner armed with a barrage of questions. And though Wynne answered them to the best of her ability, she was not able to bring herself to mentioned McNeely, the locket, or the ominous warning. What could Kitty have done even if she had told her? Wynne shook her head, no, the only thing that Kitty would have done would have suggested a call to the police. But what would the police to do? Nothing.

So, Kitty had done as Kitty had always done when Wynne had done anything she shouldn't have. She scolded her and reminded her that she was to be more careful and to bide her time and not lose her head in books! Wynne bore all the reprimand with more patience than she knew she possessed. She bathed and retired early for the evening, claiming the excursion for the day had taken more out of her than she realized.

But in the confides of her room, she was left to her own thoughts and her mind wandered. Thunder rumbled louder, almost like the storm was now overhead, threatening to shake the very walls of the house down around her. She sat perched in her armchair, staring at the Avanthian folklore book before her. She wanted to open it, she knew it would give her mind the distraction she needed, but there was just a hint of hesitation, a nagging feeling that if she opened the book and dived deep, she would find things she'd regret. She took a deep breath and opened the book and slowly began to read.

In the beginning, Taeren was a beautiful and undiscovered world, until the Avanthian's arrived from the sea and claimed Taeren for their own. They settled the land and gradually overtime they became a large, unified people spreading throughout all Taeren. The Avanthian's were unified unlike any other continent, which made them strong and more powerful than any other.

Unlike any other people group, the Avanthian's were known for serving five deities: Cadona goddess of the sun, Estris the goddess of the sky, Oaran the god of the sea, Rhaesis the god of the earth, and

Asta the goddess of death. With unity of the people and unity among the gods, Taeren prospered.

But one day, the kings of men became greedy, and they sought power above their means and instead of gaining power they succeeded in creating wars, that plundered the land of Taeren. In an instant, the peaceful unity that had once dominated the people was lost. Families were turned asunder; homes were destroyed, and once powerful kingdoms had crumbled, falling victim to human greed. Everything that had made Taeren great, went up in smoke, the peace they had fought so hard to maintain, was now washed away in the blood of the people who had fought so hard to maintain it. Chaos ensued, and tyrants relished in the terror that had befallen the land and her people.

At first, the deities stayed their hand, thinking that the kings of men would prevail and would right the wrongs they had committed. They let the human wars play out on their own, hoping Taeren would be restored in time. But as the wars raged, the kingdoms of men continued to crumble, it grew apparent that if the deities did not intervene, all of Taeren and the Avanthian ways would be lost. So, together the deities, led by Cadona, put an end to the wars among Taeren. They then carved out five territories, one for each deity. They were to become that territories patron and would govern their territory according to the Celestial Laws. Each patron deity chose a family to rule their territory and though war had waged for so long, peace was restored to Taeren.

Cadona goddess of the sun, named her territory Triura, establishing the high temple in the capitol city of Calenia. Estris, goddess of the sky, named her territory Athana. Oaran, god of the sea, named his territory Gallanmar, but chose to keep his residence under the sea, in his palace, Thalatia. Rhaesis, god of earth named his territory Oflein and Asta, the goddess of death, named her territory, Ebrus. With the territories of Taeren established, peace was restored to the continent and the Avanthian heritage continued and Taeren reached a new height of power among the all the continents.

Wynne set the book down, the folklore was not far off from what she had learned in her own history classes and matched everything that

Mr. Schmidt had mentioned earlier. There indeed had been a war that had divided Taeren into five territories, and each had claimed a certain god for their territory's patron. This was all information she was familiar with, even with its archaic origins. Her eyes skimmed the page, until something popped out onto the page at her.

> *The children of the deities are gifted with god-like abilities, but limited by their human forms. Allures are children of the sea, Etheri are children of the sky, Kerei are children of the earth, Necros are children of death and Auris are children of the sun. All patron deities have children, but only their sons and daughters, those with the essence of the deity, can be given the birthright. The birthright of a patron deity is the promise of inheriting the throne, the seat of a god's power when they choose to pass onto Iteala.*

Wynne's brow furrowed. This was something of Avanthian mythology she had not heard before, and most of it she wasn't sure she believed in its entirety. It was all so farfetched, deities having children with humans, and those humans having god-like capabilities? And the deities themselves having sons and daughters, who they themselves had the essence of the god? Wynne shook her head, no, it was something she'd expect to find in one of her adventure books, but not in real life.

Thunder crashed overhead; she glanced warily out her window. She could have sworn she had heard a different sound mixed in with the thunder. Carefully, she rose and moved for the window, peering out into the blackness. She saw nothing, but an empty, wet courtyard. Lightning flashed illuminating a figure standing in the courtyard that had not been there a moment ago. He was standing there, staring up at her window. Wynne gasped, but in a moment the courtyard was once again empty. She moved away from the window, feeling her heartbeat pounding in her chest.

What was going on? Wynne fled her room, leaving her lamp behind and hurried to her father's study. She crept slowly to the window, peering down below. Five men stood outside, watching— waiting. Fear rushed through her, she forced herself to swallow the scream that was forming in her chest. She retreated into the hall, heart pounding furiously in her chest. Who were those men? A heavy hand clamped down on her shoulder. She shrieked, whirled around but found Henry standing there.

"Henry!" She cried, resting a trembling hand over her chest, "You scared me."

"Hurry, we don't have much time!" He hissed just as the front door crashed in and Wynne heard shouts from the entry way, thunderous footsteps echoed throughout the house. Whoever was outside, was now inside and Wynne had a sinking feeling she knew who they had come for. Henry reopened her father's study door and pushed her inside.

"To the stair-well!" He directed. The stair-well was the estates only secret passageway that led to a hidden door out to the courtyard.

"Once you get to the courtyard, you must run." He instructed, quiet calmly, despite the shouts and thundering footsteps nearing.

"Where am I supposed to go?"

"Find your father, go to him. He will know what to do." He urged, slipping his overcoat over her trembling shoulders.

"Whatever happens," he whispered pressing a coin purse into her hands, "don't let him find you."

"Who Henry?" She demanded, "Payne? Is that who is here now?"

"Now is not the time!" He snapped, "Now go!" He scolded, pushing her down the stairs and closing the door behind her. He had never snapped at her before. She fled down the cold steps and halted at the bottom. Shouts echoed followed by wood splintering. A gunshot spliced through the silence followed by a hallow thump. Wynne pressed a hand over her mouth, stifling her cry. There could be only one thing that had made that sound and the thought made her stomach queasy. Footsteps and shouts filled the stairwell, they had found the passageway. She needed to move, now!

Wynne threw herself out into the rain and tore through the courtyard. She ran out through the garden and down the dimly lit street. She knew these streets well but traveling them at night and in the rain was discomforting. Where should she go? She glanced at the coin purse; the ideas started pouring into her mind. She could rent a room, but the taverns were down by the docks. She was alone, dressed only in her night gown and Henry's overcoat. She shook her head, no, she needed a safer place to go, a place she could trust. Ms. Bloomington, she thought, would be the safest option and it was someone she trusted, someone who would keep her safe until she could figure out how to get to her father.

Filled with some relief and a rudimentary plan, she hurried down the street. As she traveled down the soaked streets, she kept her head on a swivel, searching every nook and cranny in the streets for her pursuers or anyone that seemed suspicious. But as she walked along, she found no signs that anyone was following her, and slowly she felt her shoulders relax. It wasn't long before she made it to Ms. Bloomington's home, the curtains were drawn, and the house was black. She swallowed, a sudden feeling of guilt coming over her, she was about to wake the entire household.

The gate moaned in protest as she pushed it open, splitting the silence in an ear splintering creak. She glanced warily behind her, but the street was still empty. She hurried up the walk and pounded on the door, waiting for any signs of life behind the door. It wasn't long before she heard just that, and the door was flung open revealing Mr. Cooper's angry face. He looked like he was going to shout, but when he saw Wynne standing before him his face softened before twisting into confusion.

"Miss Hunt, what are you doing here?" He exclaimed, taking in her apparel with growing concern.

"I am so sorry Mr. Bradley, I am in trouble and—" she glanced behind her to empty streets and sighed, "may I please come in?"

"Of course!" He cried, opening the door wide. Wynne hurried in, grabbing the door quickly behind her and shutting it. A quick glance at the street revealed a man, turning down the street. He appeared to be alone.

"Are you alright?"

Wynne nodded, feeling relief swell through her, "Yes, for now, I believe I am."

Chapter 5

Wynne sat in the parlor, snuggling deeper into the armchair, a heavy quilt draped over her shoulders. The fire had been stoked, tea had been called for and promptly served. Ms. Bloomington had been awoken and now sat across from Wynne, wearing a worried expression on her face, Mr. Bradley stood guarding the parlor door.

"Now, tell me again, the message from your father." Ms. Bloomington prompted, waiting for Wynne to set her cup down.

"Payne is coming. Meet you at the Keep." Wynne repeated, letting the warm liquid soothe her dampened limbs.

"But who is this Payne? Someone your father might know?"

Wynne shook her head, "I don't know." Her brain whirled, trying to figure out the identity of the person named in the note, but nothing had come to mind.

Mr. Cooper cleared his throat, "If I may." He stepped forward, holding the local paper out before him, "This may be something." He handed it to Ms. Bloomington, who snatched it up immediately. Mr. Cooper directed her gaze to one article, which she read quickly.

"I don't understand Cooper." She shook her head, "This article is about a pirate that has been spotted here in Whaeldrake," She waved her hand nonchalantly.

"Keep ready my lady." Mr. Cooper coaxed, stepping forward again, taking the paper and pointing to one spot Ms. Bloomington had missed.

"He is an infamous pirate, my lady." Mr. Cooper said quietly. Ms. Bloomington's eyes narrowed as she read the sentence Mr. Bradley was pointing to. Wynne waited, holding her breath as she watched Ms. Bloomington's eyes widen in shock and confusion.

"Etheri above," Ms. Bloomington whispered, sitting back in her chair, face pale before the fire light.

"What is it?" Wynne demanded, feeling the color drain from her face as well.

Mr. Bradley's head dipped slightly, not wanting to look Wynne directly in the eye, "Captain Payne is the pirates name, and his ship, the *Sea Jewel* has been spotted docked here in Whaeldrake."

"That can't be." Wynne whispered. There was no way that was the Payne her father had been referencing in his note. But at the same time, it was a coincidence Wynne couldn't deny.

"This is very serious, my dear." Ms. Bloomington whispered.

"We don't know if he's really the one who my father wrote about." Wynne protested, weakly.

"Then who else would he be warning you about?" Ms. Bloomington argued. Wynne bit her lip, the conversation with Mr. McNeely replaying in her brain. She hadn't told Ms. Bloomington about that encounter, and she knew that if she did it would only confirm their suspicions that a notorious pirate was after her. But the biggest question that nagged at her, was why was a notorious pirate after her? Could it be something that was tied to her father and his merchant business?

"Why on earth would he be coming after me?" Wynne finally asked the question out loud, not really expecting a response. But Ms. Bloomington shifted slightly in her seat and suddenly seemed more interested in the carpet beneath her feat that meeting Wynne's eyes.

"You know—don't you?" Wynne whispered, which brought Ms. Bloomington's attention back up to her face.

"Nothing concrete." She offered faintly.

"Then what do you know?"

"Only that I had heard the name mentioned once or twice right after your mother passed."

Wynne raised a quizzical brow, "And you remember mere the mention of his name?"

"It was a conversation with your father and grandfather, the name meant nothing to me at the time and the only reason I remember it at all was because they had been arguing, quite loudly I might add." Wynne frowned, she never remembered a time when she heard either her father or grandfather raise their voices, let alone argue with one another. But maybe the stresses had been high between them after her mother had passed. The old familiar emptiness returned to her chest, she had been young when her mother had passed and no doubt that had put strain on her father and quite possibly even her grandfather.

A thunderous knock sounded at the front door, causing Wynne to jump in her seat. Panic took over as she flew from her seat to the window. The rain was coming down in a steady stream, showing no signs of stopping. But it wasn't the rain that caused her breath to hitch in her throat, but the man standing at the door and the two others pushing through the front gate.

"Damn!" Wynne hissed, "They're here!" she stepped away from the window.

Ms. Bloomington grabbed her hand, "We must get you out of here!" She pulled Wynne into the hall, "Cooper, ensure all the doors are locked." The butler nodded and moved toward the hall but stopped dead in his tracks when the front door splintered open and in rushed shouting men.

"Quick Wynnefred, this way!" Ms. Bloomington cried, opening the library door, and shoving her inside, "Hide wherever you can!" She cupped Wynne's cheek in her hand, stroking her jaw with her thumb, "Be brave." She whispered before fleeing from the library, making as much noise behind her as possible.

Wynne surveyed the room, searching frantically for any place that would hide her. In a moment of last-minute desperation, she dove under the covered table. Shouts echoed in the hallway, followed by the door to the library being flung open. Wynne flinched as she heard footsteps in the library, she fought to keep the scream in her throat from slipping out.

The footsteps slowed to a gentle, deliberate pace, as they moved about the room. It was as though Wynne could feel eyes roaming the room, searching high a low for any signs of life. The footsteps came closer to the table, and she fought to keep her breath swallowed in her throat. She could feel eyes staring at the table, she waited for the horrible moment when the tablecloth would be ripped up and she would be revealed, but to her amazement, the footsteps retreated from the room, and she heard the library door click closed. She let the breath loose on her lips and waited a minute before crawling out her hiding space.

"I thought that looked like a good hiding place." A voice hissed behind her. Wynne spun and found herself face to face with a beady-eyed man. Acting on instinct she threw the first object her hands landed on. The book, however, did not faze him, dodging it effortlessly, laughing. Was he amused?

"You've got spirit." He chuckled, "The captain will like that." He purred. Wynne felt her stomach drop but managed to turn and run. The man lunged after her, catching her by her skirts and then a boney arm wrapped around her, throwing her to the floor. She screamed, lashing out as hands descended on her. Determined not to be taken, she scratched and clawed herself free. The man desperately tried holding her back, but the attempt just fueled her rage.

Movement caught her eye; she stopped just as Ms. Bloomington brought a vase down on his head. To her relief the man's grip loosened enough for her to wiggle free and spring to her feet. Together the two women fled from the library, the man's groans of annoyance echoing after them. The blow Ms. Bloomington had delivered had not been enough. It had stunned him yes but had also accomplished annoying him more than anything.

"Run Wynnefred!" Ms. Bloomington yelled. Wynne took off down the hallway, her heartbeat pounding in her ears. At the dining hall, she finally stopped and glanced behind her, expecting to see Ms.

Bloomington there beside her, but the hall was empty. Dread settled over here, where had she gone? Slowly Wynne attempted to calm her breathing, straining to listen for any sound of Ms. Bloomington behind her. But the house had suddenly gone eerily silent. Groaning, Wynne crept out of the dining hall and tip-toed back towards the library. Suddenly she heard voices off to her left, in the great hall. She crept up slowly and peeked in through the crack in the doors. There she saw Ms. Bloomington standing, as resolute as possible, in front of the beady-eyed man and two other men standing a ways behind him.

"You've caused me some trouble." The beady eyed man grimaced, rubbing the back of his head where Ms. Bloomington had brought down the vase.

"You dare speak to me about trouble." Ms. Bloomington huffed, "I believe this is my home you've invaded." Wynne had to smile at the sass in her voice. She was not going to let them believe for a second that she was intimidated or afraid of them.

"Tell me where she is then, and we will be on our way." The man hissed, taking a step towards her.

Ms. Bloomington frowned and crossed her arms across her chest, "Over my dead body."

The beady-eyed man whipped out his pistol, quicker than Wynne could register, "That can be arranged." He growled before a gunshot split through the air, echoing through the house. Wynne flung a hand to her mouth, holding back her scream as she watched Ms. Bloomington fall to the floor, landing lifelessly in a pool of blood, her blood. Wynne felt the corners of her vision blur and her fingertips went suddenly numb. The sound of a door slamming open echoed around her, but she seemed to be miles away. Forcing herself up, she glanced back in the hall and saw a young man strut into the room. He was younger than the rest, but the way he walked in the room told her, that he was in charge and by the look on his face, he was not happy.

"What did I say?" The young man's deep voice split the echo around her and brought her back to the present moment.

"Oaran's deep," he swore, "Spare me your lecture boy. It was a necessary loss." The beady-eyed man sneered, shrugging his shoulders nonchalantly. The young man moved quickly, effortlessly, and like a snake, grabbing the beady-eyed man by the throat and pinning him to the wall.

"Your little stunt cost us!" The man growled, "Now the girl's gone and we have bodies." The beady-eyed man's eyes bulged as the young man's hand tightened ever so slowly around his throat, "You disobeyed orders, again." His deep voice rumbled, the tension slowly mounting in the room.

"Like Payne cares ab-about a but-ler and a-an old ha-ag." The beady-eyed man rasped, stuttering through the choke hold. But the younger man lashed out slamming him against the wall once more, causing the paintings to shake.

"Follow orders, Haddox." The young man growled, "Or the next bullet will be in your chest." Wynne watched the younger man, holding the beady-eyed man up against the wall, letting his threat hanging the silence. Then, just as fast as he had grabbed the man, he released the beady-eyed man. Wynne could see the rage light in his eyes. He stood slowly, grabbing his throat, and rubbing some life back into his already bruised neck. He took a step towards the younger man pointing a finger.

"What makes you think you're so special boy?" Haddox spat, "You think, just because you have the captain's favor that you can give orders as you see fit?" Wynne watched as the younger man clamped his eyes closed, his shoulders tensed ever so slightly. Haddox, however, was not finished with his verbal assault.

"Whose bullet is it going to be Caspian, huh, whose bullet?" The man sneered. To Wynne's horror, the young man, Caspian, spun around in one fluid motion and shot Haddox right, square, in the chest. The shock was evident on the man's face as he peered down at the gaping hole in his chest. Then he slumped back against the wall and fell, a single crimson hole growing on his chest.

"Mine." Caspian whispered. Then glanced at the other men standing in the hall, watching, "Get to the ship." He holstered his pistol, "I'll find her myself."

Chapter 6

Wynne had slipped out the back before anyone remaining in the house had discovered her. She ran down the streets, listing her options of places she could go to hide. However, there were not many and the few she had thought of were less than ideal. She decided to find a tavern and rent a room for the night. It would allow her time to get her bearings and come up with a better plan of evading capture. Her plan was not ideal, however, because it meant her traveling alone and that was more conspicuous that anything, but what else was there for her to do. Two people, maybe even more than that, were dead. She choked back the bile that gathered at the back of her throat as images of Ms. Bloomington's lifeless body flashed before her eyes. She had been the cause of the woman's death, she would bear the blame, along with all the others that had died. Henry, she winced, he had died trying to save her. Ms. Bloomington too, had died trying to protect her. She choked back tears and felt the sobs tearing at her throat. She could not stop now, not when people close to her had died for her.

Though her adrenaline was coursing through her veins, she also felt dread and confusion weighing her down. Confusion because the

reason for her pursuit and capture remained a mystery and dread because she had a feeling, deep down in the pit of her stomach, no matter
what she did or where she would try to hide, they would find her, and
she shuddered to think what they would do to her when they eventually would. But none of that was important now, now all she really
needed to think about and focus on was getting to a tavern and laying
low. Maybe, there was a chance she would be able to send word to her
father. She turned onto Harper's Ferry, which led straight to the docks.

She slowed to a walk and kept her head down. The least amount
of attention, the better. Her teeth chattered uncontrollably, she
needed to find a warm place to get out of her sopping wet clothes.
To preserve whatever warmth, she had left in her body, she hugged
her arms around her waist, trying to seal in any warmth. But the rain
continued in a steady stream and showed no signs of stopping any
time soon. But before the comforting ease of knowing she had lost
her pursuer could settle in, she felt an itch at the back of her neck,
followed by an unwanted shiver. Slowly, she glanced over her shoulder at the street behind her. She spotted the man in an instant, Caspian, was not ten yards behind her and closing in. Fear surged through
her, urging her to run as fast as she could away from him. But no, she
needed to think, he was calculated, but so was she.

She ducked into an alley way and forced her weary legs to sprint.
But as she ran, a fire broke in her chest, spreading throughout her
body and limbs, warming up the numbness that had threatened to
swallow her. With the new warmth brought a surge of new energy.
Footsteps echoed behind her; she didn't dare look back. At the end of
the alley, she leapt out into the street and sprinted for the next alley
way, risking a quick peek over her shoulder. Caspian was barreling
towards her with a speed far greater than her own. But it didn't matter, she could lose him, she was confident in her ability to do so.

This alley was, however, much narrower than the last one and
it was filled with stacks of boxes and crates. Using them to her advantage, Wynne ripped a few stacks as she passed, sending an entire pile of crates toppling over her behind her. That would hopefully, slow him down some and would buy her more time. She turned
again, finding herself in an even narrower alley, but pushed forward

sprinting to the end before jumping out into the adjoining alley. But the ground was wet, and just as her foots landed, she felt her world slipping beneath her. She crashed to her knees and slid several feet along the uneven cobblestones. Not only was she rain soaked, but she was now covered in a fresh coat of mud and grim from the streets. But now was not the time to worry about appearances. Adrenaline pumped through her veins and drove her to her feet, pushing her to continue through the sting in her knees and hands. But the adrenaline was ebbing, and in a sudden panic she turned down another alley way but stopped dead in tracks.

"No!" She gasped, she was at a dead end, staring at an unmovable brick wall. She needed to back tack before she was caught. Turning quickly on her toes, she moved to sprint back into the alley she had just come from but froze in her tracks. Her pursuer, Caspian, stood ten feet away, blocking her only way out of the alley. His chest was rising and falling, gently, compared to her own that was rising and falling so violently, she was sure she might topple over. They stood staring at one another, Wynne's eyes and mind searching for any sign of an escape route.

"He said you'd run, but I didn't think you'd actually be dumb enough to do it." He remarked in a tone that seemed somewhat amused and exasperated at the same time. Wynne refused to acknowledge him, but instead focused her attention on the stack of crates to her left. They were piled high, high enough to reach the top of the wall. Her mind whirled with the possibilities, she just needed to move slightly to her left.

"You can't blame me for running." She said at last, taking a careful step towards the stack.

He smirked, "Bold to assume you'd actually get away."

Wynne frowned, "I don't know who you are, or what you even want with me." She took another careful step, not much farther, "I had to try."

"Just come with me and I will promise your safety." He offered, which made her pause. Why on earth would he promise her that? Was he not just chasing her through the rain after storming through two homes to get to her?

"Bold of you to assume I'd even trust you." Wynne barked back, but it only resulted in making him smile, slightly.

"Don't do anything I will regret." He warned, voice low, as if he sensed she was about to do something drastic.

"I'm not one to follow orders." She smiled back, then launched herself towards the stack of crates. The stack swayed with her weight as she scurried up the crates. But before she could even make it halfway, the stack swayed violently backwards, and she felt herself falling to the ground. Crates rained down on her as she landed on the cold ground, pain exploding into her bottom and up her back. Grumbling, she shoved the cracks aside, exhaustion weighing down her arms and leaving her with myriads of aches and pains. A hand grabbed her and yanked her to her feet. With as much strength and dignity she could muster she defiantly looked up at Caspian.

"Are you finished with your lousy escape attempts?" He questioned, rather smugly. Wynne frowned, holding her head a bit higher.

"For now." She replied, wirily. He studied her for a moment, before gripping her arm tighter and forcing her down the alley way.

"Let's go." He grumbled.

"Where are we going?" She demanded, shaking her arm, his grip held firm.

"Ferryman's Tavern." He grumbled, "There is someone there who would like to meet you." He met her eyes, but she couldn't read a single emotion there. Instead, she swallowed the fear the now bubbled in her throat. He didn't need to tell her who she was going to meet, and she didn't have the stomach to even ask. Now, she just needed to figure out why the most notorious pirate had gone to such great lengths to find and kidnap her.

Chapter 7

The Ferryman's Tavern lay several blocks away from where Caspian had trapped her. It wasn't long before she saw the small tavern, glowing in the dark before them. The tavern itself glowed with warm lantern light, ultimately a welcoming sight to any looking for a warm place to stop in for food or drink. Laughter and clanky music filled the air as they neared the tavern. But Wynne only felt dread the closer and closer they came to the tavern. What was going to happen to her once she stepped into that tavern? She prayed no harm would come to her; but the closer she got to the tavern, the more fearful she became. Caspian, gripping her arm firmly, pushed her inside.

Thick plumes of smoke from pipes to cigars filled the great room in a visible cloud and swallowed her. The thick stench of ale clawed at her throat so that she choked. Men, of all ages, some rough with age and others still untainted by the sea sat around the room, laughing loudly, and sharing their tales. Women flocked around the room, seemingly unphased by the catcalling and wandering hands that sought to catch a feel for them as they passed, carrying trays of mugs filled to the brim with ale. Wynne suddenly felt very out of place, she did not belong in a place like this.

Eyes locked onto them as they walked by, well, they locked onto her. Caspian, belonged in a place like this, she did not. It was evident enough by her mannerisms, and evident even more by the clothes that she was wearing. The sound in the tavern seemed to die down, painfully so. Wynne was suddenly very aware of her breath and heartbeat as she continued walking. She felt her cheeks burn in embarrassment as snickers and whispers rose as she passed. Caspian ignored the glanced and stares and pushed her to the counter. Then, just as quickly as the noise had stopped, the hum of conversation began again.

"She's a might too fancy fer' yah, aye Caspian?" The bar tender piped up, studying Wynne sidelong. Several others around them chuckled in agreement.

"She's here for the captain." Caspian cried with a smirk that caused all the men around them to guffaw in laughter. Caspian glanced down at Wynne, his smile faded slightly when he saw the heard pressed look in her eyes and the disdain on her pursed lips.

"She's a bit dirty." A man to the side of them commented, looking Wynne up and down, bringing all the attention to her muddy, rain-soaked clothes. Caspian grabbed two big pitchers of ale, and took a swig from one, turning fully to face her and study her with a look of cautious scrutiny.

"A little dirt never hurt anyone." He mused and carefully reached over and rubbed a smudge of dirt from her cheek. Wynne smacked his hand away, which only resulted in hoots and hollers rolling between the gruff men around them.

"Aye, but she do have spirit!" Another man beside them yelled, brushing stray fingers along her jaw. Wynne jumped, smacking his hand away as well and feeling the heat rush to her face. But the man just merely leaned back and bellowed with laugher, taking a swig of his ale and moving on to the next girl, who was more than willing to have his roaming fingers graze more than just her jaw. Caspian downed his ale, leaving the empty jug on the counter, and with his free hand grabbed her arm and moved her quickly away from the counter.

"Blushing," he leaned down and whispered in her ear, "will only make it worse." He pushed her deeper into the tavern, towards a back room. When they reached the closed door, he knocked once, then without even waiting for a response back, shoved her inside.

It took a moment for her eyes to adjust to the darkness of the room, but when they finally did, she found herself in as small but quaint little room overlooking the port. It was a grand view of all the ships travelling in and out, and yet was still out of the way to ensure any onlookers could observe and go completely unnoticed. Her eyes snagged on a broad-shouldered man that stood facing the window. He was a burly man, with peppered gray hair that hung to his shoulders and was tied back with a leather strap. At the sound of their entrance, he shot a quick glance over his shoulder, eyes falling on her as she stopped in the center of the room.

"Good evening, Miss Hunt." The man greeted, "So nice of you to join us, please, have a seat." He gestured to the chair on the other side of the table. She had every intent to decline, but a hand on her shoulder forced her into her seat. Darkness engulfed her, there was one little candle at the center of the table, but even that candles light seemed to dim in the presence of the pitch black. Cold leeched into her skin and she shivered, would she ever get out of her wet clothes?

"Your silence if most intriguing." The man, who she could only assume was the captain, moved toward the empty chair across from her and took a seat. The absence of proper light did not allow her to make out any facial features. The dim candlelight cast uneven shadows on his face, revealing what looked like a horrendous scar that tore into his jawline. He stared at her with dark penetrating her eyes, waiting for her to respond.

"Did you expect me to grovel?" She demanded at last, finally finding her voice. And to her credit she delivered her statement with much more bravado than she felt.

"Quite frankly, Miss Hunt," He smiled, "yes, I did."

"I am sorry to disappoint you then."

"You look just like her." He whispered.

"Who?" Wynne questioned.

"Your mother." He grumbled, suddenly frowning at her, this wistfulness in his eyes was replaced by something dark and utterly sinister.

47

"You knew my mother?" Wynne questioned, though the idea of his having any sort of acquaintance with her mother was utterly absurd.

"Your mother and I were quite close, many, many years ago." His tone was wistful, his eye distant as though he was remembering a fond memory.

"You must be mistaken." Wynne objected, shattering the peaceful look from his eyes, "My mother would have never associated with the likes of you." She stated, firmly. But the captain did the unthinkable. He leaned comfortably back in his chair and laughed, a deep bellowing laugh. It seemed so odd coming from his mouth, and it took Wynne by surprise.

"It seems like she never told you about her early years and about the many adventures we shared in together." His smile faded, "I'm not surprised. Nerissa always had secrets, even from me." His eyes narrowed. The sound of her mother's name on his lips made her squirm uncomfortably.

"So, you had your men break into my home, kill my butler and my dear friend just to tell me you knew my mother?" Wynne demanded through clenched teeth as tears pooled in her eyes. The captain looked surprised by her statement. His eyes snapped to Caspian, who stood silently by the door, watching, and waiting.

The captain's eyes darkened, "The butler and friend?" He questioned with lethal calm, it sent shivers down Wynne's spine, but Caspian did not seem altered by the sudden shift in the captain's demeanor.

"Haddox got a bit trigger happy." Caspian answered, carefully. The image of Ms. Bloomington flashed before her eyes, and she felt her stomach drop and a hot tear run down her cheek as she looked up to the captain. He, however, was not looking at her. Instead, his eyes were pinched closed as he held the bridge of his nose, tightly in his fingers.

"I thought I made my orders quite clear." The captain ground out through clenched teeth, sending more shivers down Wynne's spine.

"It's been dealt with." Caspian replied, with secret emphasis, which made the captain nod, approvingly. Apparently, Caspian dealing with people was something the captain was familiar with and recognized the truth behind those simple words. Wynne closed her eyes, but only saw the dead people that now flooded her mind. She felt a gasp escape her lungs as her eyes snapped open. The captain was staring at her, studying her. She forced herself to sit upright and sniffed back the tears that still threatened to pour down her face.

"No one was supposed to die Miss Hunt, I am here for you, and you alone." He declared, quietly, as though those words were to repay her for the lives that were lost by an extension of his very own hand.

"What should I expect from a man with no honor." Wynne snarled. No number of sorry words were going to bring back Henry or Ms. Bloomington. He had robbed them of their lives and had stolen them away from their families. Wynne thought of Henry's wife, they had been married for nearly fifty years, she would be devastated when she learned of what happened to her husband. Ms. Bloomington did not have children of her own, but her many nieces and nephews were just like her children. Wynne bit her lip, they would be broken hearted when they learned what had happened to her. Would she ever get the chance to apologize to them? Would they even want to hear her words of apology? She sniffed, if she even made it out of this, she wasn't even sure she'd survive this herself.

But the captain ignored her. All remorse was gone from his ragged face as he stood from his chair. Slowly he prowled towards her, which made Wynne stiffen in her chair. He took a careful step around her chair and circled behind her; she didn't dare follow him with her gaze. Suddenly, she felt cold fingers at the back of her neck. She jumped but forced herself to not swat his hand away. His fingers trailed beneath her collar and grabbed at the chain hanging from her neck. A sudden sense of dread flooded her as he pulled the chain, revealing the locket.

"Well, well, well—what do we have here." He mused as the locket was revealed. She felt a sudden urge of panic and in one quick motion she swiped the locket up in her hand and stood quickly, turning towards the captain, and backing away from him towards the window.

"It was my mother's." She sputtered, clutching the locket tight in her hand.

"Yes," he drawled, "I know. Please, have a seat, Miss Hunt." He commanded, there was no room for objection. Wynne slowly, sat back down, but her hand remained clutched around the locket, sealing it from his dark eyes.

"But, I wonder, Miss Hunt if you even know what power you hold clutched in your fingertips?" He stood before her, back straight and hand clasped carefully behind his back.

Wynne shook her head, "It's just a locket."

The captain scoffed, "You know nothing of what it is you hold and even more," He leaned forward, "you know nothing of the women who gave it to you." Wynne felt her voice get stuck in her throat. She wanted to protest, stand up for her mother and the legacy that she left for her, but there was something in his eyes that made her pause. The captain, smiled, then waved a hand towards Caspian.

"Take her to her room." He commanded, "Give her some clean clothes as well," he glanced back at her, "we sail at first light." Caspian grabbed her arm and hauled her to her feet.

"What?" She gasped, they were taking her with them, but why?

"I am afraid, I still have use of you, Miss Hunt." He moved slowly back towards the window as Caspian pulled her to the door. But Wynne dug her heels in and forced him to stop.

"What do you need me for?"

The captain looked back out to the darkened bay beyond the window, "A curse can only be broken with all the right pieces."

"What are you talking about, what curse?" Wynne demanded. The captain glanced over his shoulder.

"You accuse me of having no honor, but I wonder what you'll say when you learn your mother had none either."

Wynne felt her face flush, she gritted her teeth, "She had more honor than you'll ever have!"

He chuckled, "Secrets, Miss Hunt, all of your precious memories of her were built on dark secrets," he turned back to the window, clutching his hands behind his back, "and all secrets come to light, eventually."

Chapter 8

Wynne was led to a back hallway with stairs that led straight to the second floor of the tavern. Many of the taverns along the docks were two stories, because having rooms to rent for the evening meant even more money coming in. They passed a few doors before Caspian stopped her and pulled a key from his pockets, gesturing to the door.

"This is it." He muttered, sliding the key into the lock, and turning quickly before shoving it open. Wynne peered inside. It was a simple room, with a window a bed and a small writing desk with a side table that held a wash basin. But the one thing in the room she was eager to explore was the window. Caspian must have read the expression on her face because she heard him sigh.

"It's locked." He motioned to the window, nudging her forward before leaving her standing in the small room.

"Here," He handed her the lamp he had been holding, "Don't do anything stupid. There's a guard outside your door." He added, quietly before shutting the door and locking it behind him. Just for good measure, Wynne tried the door once she heard his footsteps retreat down the hall and down the stairs. The door was securely locked and wasn't going to budge. Wynne then hurried to the window and tried the glass, she muttered under her breath, Caspian hadn't lied. The window was locked tight. She was, to her horror, sealed shut in this tiny room.

A knock sounded at her door, startling her. The door unlocked and swung open to reveal two tavern women. She noticed one of them from downstairs, who had been waiting on tables. Wynne studied them carefully as the hurried into the room, she caught a glimpse of a big burly man standing outside the door. So, that must be the guard Caspian said, would be guarding her room. No matter, she focused her attention on the two women instead. Maybe, they would be able to help her or in the least give her some more information.

One of them carried a wash bin, the other carried a large bucket and what looked like a stack of fresh clothes. But beyond that, the women made no efforts to introduce themselves or even try to appear friendly to her. Instead, they were so focused on their designated tasks, it was as if Wynne was not even there.

"Do you know why I am here?" Wynne ventured, questioning the one who had just set down the wash bin. But she ignored her completely, turning to retrieve water from the wash basin.

"Surely," Wynne moved to the second woman, "you must have heard something." Wynne prodded sweetly. The second woman was not so downright rude, she at least glanced at Wynne. Granted it was a nervous look, but Wynne felt a twinge of hope that she might win the girl over. But, before she could open her lips, the other woman cleared her throat, and she scurried off to refill the bucket for more water.

"Won't you even try helping me?" Wynne demanded to the first woman. But this time, the woman looked at her, square in the eyes.

"We do not question the captain." Her voice was clipped and somewhat harsh, "His requests are never to be doubted or challenged." She poured the last bucket into the basin and gestured for her to get in, "You will wash. Once you are finished you can change into the fresh set of clothes we brought." The two then turned toward the door, rapped on the wood frame three times before the door opened quickly. They hurried out and in an instant the door closed behind them and was once again bolted shut.

Wynne stood for a moment in the silence, eyeing the water in the tub. She was not fond of cold baths, but better to be clean then covered with grim from the streets and rain. She stripped off her nightgown and lowered herself, gingerly, into the tub. The cold sting of the water made her hiss, as she slowly settled in, letting the coldness seep into her. She set to work immediately, feeling her teeth begin to chatter. She grabbed the soap and started to scrub. She scrubbed every nook and cranny she could find. Once she scrubbed her body raw, she turned to her hair, delicately massaging the soap into her long locks. Now for the part she dreaded the most. She took a quick breath, then without thinking, dunked herself under and rinsed the soap from her scalp. Once she was done, she wasted no time getting out of the cold water and wrapping herself into the warm towel. She rubbed herself dry, bringing the warmth slowly back into her arms and legs.

She eyed the clothes; the women had left for her sitting on her bed. There was a cotton tunic that seemed rather too large for her delicate frame. Instead of a skirt, there was a pair of black trousers with a very worn leather belt. She half wondered if these clothes had belonged to some poor man who no longer needed them. She swallowed and tried not to focus on the origin of her new clothes. At least, she thought with some consolation, there was no corset among the items. There was also a soft pair of shoes that reminded Wynne more of a pair of slippers instead of actual shoes. But these were dry, and they were better than walking around completely bare foot.

Once the dry clothes were on, she turned her attention to her hair. The tavern women had not left her anything to tend to her curls, which meant she would need to use her fingers. She groaned, her curls were thick and tended to have a mind of their own. But after a few struggling moments of combing through her wet hair, she managed to detangle her long blonde strands. She had no intentions of braiding her hair, but preferred to let it air dry, it would dry faster than if she braided it. Sighing, she smiled slightly, more out of relief instead of happiness. The weariness from the night's events had suddenly settled on her and her body felt heavy.

Wynne lowered herself gently on the edge of her bed and the memories of what had transpired only hours before became to trickle in. Facts, information, blood curdling images swarmed her mind, some unwanted and others though provoking. Fear slowly crept up on her, and her heartbeat quickened in response, her palms became sweaty. Muffled laughed, below, cut into her thoughts. The people downstairs knew nothing of what was going on with her, normal life went on seemingly undisturbed. She clenched her fists and took a deep breath trying to steady her nerves.

Everything is going to be fine. She whispered internally.

She exhaled, taking another deep breath. Her nerves were still jumpy, and she felt jitters tingle their way through her body. She closed her eyes and forced herself to take another deep breath and exhale.

"Everything is going to be fine." She whispered. She inhaled once more and exhaled through her nose, but instead of feeling relaxed her throat constricted as she choked back tears. Carefully, she breathed deeply again, her throat bobbed as a tear slipped onto her cheek.

"You are going to be fine." She whispered forcefully but choked on the words. Hopelessness, the feeling that nothing no matter what she did or how hard she tried, permeated her soul. It fed her quaking fears and brought new, hot tears spilling onto her cheeks. Wynne tried desperately to hold back her sobs, but they came so quickly. She buried her face in the pillow, practically swallowing it as she attempted to squelch her sobs. The facts loomed before her, only making the sobs worse.

She had been kidnapped by a pirate, and not just any pirate, Captain Payne. But the reason behind the kidnapping was still unclear. He had mentioned knowing her mother, which could be a lie, but he could also be telling the truth. He had named her by name, had mentioned secrets, dark secrets. Of her mother? She shuddered, her mother had been a saint, granted an adventurous spirit, but she could not in good conscience believe that her mother had purposefully hidden things from her. And even if she had, why hadn't her father told her about them? It made no sense and made her head hurt if she thought too long and hard about it.

Captain Payne had also mentioned a curse, but what curse? And what did she have to do with any of this? Wynne's father and even his own crew man, Daniel had both given her warning, cryptic ones albeit, and neither warnings had been enough to help keep her from being kidnapped. So here she sat, alone and afraid in the upper room of a tavern with no idea what was going to happen to her. What were they planning on doing to her? The possibilities whirled, leaving her feeling dizzy and nauseated.

Surely, the authorities had been notified, and would send word to her father of her capture.

"Meet you at the keep."

Those had been the words written to her from her father. What did they even mean? Was that a place? She felt a sudden swell of panic, no one would be able to find her! The likely hood of someone in the tavern remembering her was remote and highly unlikely that they would even disclose any information even if they did remember. The maids' words echoed back to her, "His requests are never to be doubted or challenged." The likely hood of someone admitting that she was there and with the captain were very, very slim.

She was alone.

Sitting up, Wynne wiped her tears from her cheeks. She couldn't cave now; she was made of more gumption than most young ladies her age and rank. There was still an opportunity for her to escape. Her only chance would be in the morning before she was escorted to Captain Payne's ship. Her chances of escape would decrease drastically as soon as she boarded his ship. So that meant a very small window, but an escape was still plausible, if she developed a fool proof plan. Slowly, she felt her fear melt away, slowly being replaced by a steady feeling of hope. Sniffling, she tucked her legs up onto the cot and scooted under the thin cover. She needed to rest as much as she could.

But sleep toyed with her. One moment she was lost in sleeps warm embrace only to be jolted awake by a shout of a peel of laughter from below. It was the longest night she had ever endured. And just when the noise had quieted, the first slivers of sunlight peeked through the small window. It crept into her room like an unwanted visitor and settled uninvited on her cheek. The thought of escaping still on her mind, despite the underling feeling of exhaustion. Aching from the stiff bed, she rolled off the bed and splashed come cold water onto her face. The cold, mercifully, sent a jolt of energy through her, waking her up.

She had formulated her plan in the wee hours of the morning but decided in the early morning light to run over her plan once more. Satisfied, Wynne scanned the room for the lantern. The tavern maids had left it in her room the night before and had never returned for it. Smiling, she grabbed the lantern, it was now or never. She dropped the lantern, the glass shattering instantly over the floor. There was a loud snort outside her door and a flood of fresh curse words. There was a loud groan and a shuffling sound followed by the familiar jingle of a key being inserted into a lock. Frantically, she grabbed the largest piece of glass and sat down on her cot, just as the door opened. A giant man lumbered instead; his face scrunched in a scowl. Wynne shriveled back at the sight of him, but the bite of the glass cutting slightly into the palm of her hand, reminded her that there was no going back. She took a deep breath and smiled up at the man.

"What happened?" He grumbled, taking in the sight of the broken lantern at her feet.

"I—I'm a bit clumsy." She shrugged, smiling sweetly. He frowned and mumbled stepping towards her. Just as she thought he would, he grabbed her arm and forced her to her feet. Inhaling, she counted to three and then swung her free hand sinking the shar piece of glass into the man's cheek. He let loose a torrent of profane screams and let go of her. She ran, fleeing down the hall. The man's bellows echoed behind her, followed by a large crash.

Wynne tore down the stairs to the main room, her eyes finding the front door. But just as she moved for the door and for freedom, it was opened, and Caspian walked in. He saw her and his eyes widened. She yelped and retreated, making her way towards the back of the tavern. There had to be another door towards the back. She stumbled through a door and found herself in the kitchen and just as she thought, there was another door.

Big meaty hands wrapped around her neck, and she felt her body fly and slam against the wall. Wynne choked as fingers tightened around her throat, the air pushed from her lungs. Wynne found herself staring at the bloodied face of the man she had stabbed. Rage filled his eyes as he glared at her.

"Gods damn!" He shouted, clutching his fist tight, "You little wench!" He growled.

Wynne slugged a fist against his arms, but that only resulted in his grip tightening against her throat, choking even more air from her lungs. She opened her mouth, desperately trying to get some air, but nothing came. Black spots filled her vision, and a loud buzz sounded in her ear. Her throat was on fire and the pressure in her head was unbearable.

He squeezed tighter.

Pressure exploded behind her eyes. Her entire face felt as though it was going to explode. He squeezed harder and her focus was gone, this was how she was going to die. Something fuzzy, in the corner of her vision caught her attention. There was a shout, but the words were warbled. Then, she felt a rush of air as her body fell. A cold shock spliced through her as she felt her body land on the floor. Her mouth opened as fresh air flowed through, so fast, she started choking uncontrollably. Grey blue eyes found her, before everything went black.

Chapter 9

Wynne's eyes fluttered open; she was staring at a wooden ceiling. Turning, she winced, where was she? The room was small with bare walls and no window. Slowly, she felt herself drop, then roll back. She knew that feeling and dread settled into her gut. She was on a ship.

The door opened sending streams of bright light pouring in. She flinched, glancing towards the light only to find a dark silhouette entering and moving towards her. She blinked, but all that she could see where orange and yellow spots. The figure came closer, casting a shadow across her face. She blinked and saw Caspian staring down at her beside her cot.

"Hammer was going to kill you." He stated, flatly. Her mind whirled, Hammer? Visions of a bloody face flooded her memory. She inhaled sharply, her failed escape plan.

"You're lucky I found you in time or he would have." Caspian remarked. Was he reprimanding her? Caspian extended his hand, and Wynne found him holding a cup. She eyed the cup suspiciously.

Caspian rolled his eyes, sighing, "It's just water." He remarked, reading her mind, "Can you sit up?" When she made no point to answer, he sighed again reaching for her, but she jerked away from him.

"I can do it!" She rasped; pain flooded her throat as the words came out too forcefully. She could hardly even recognize her own voice.

"Careful." Caspian commanded, this time his voice was reprimanding, "He practically crushed your throat. Speaking isn't going to be easy for the next couple days." Wynne forced herself to nod, though she had a string of sarcastic remarks she was dying to give instead. She took the cup and pressed it to her lips, suddenly aware of how thirsty she was.

"Steady." Caspian whispered. Wynne closed her eyes, her head had started to spin, the room moving along right with it. Slowly, she tipped the cup back and spilled the smooth cool water down her throat. It ached as she swallowed, but the refreshing cool feel of the water soothed some of the itchiness in her throat.

"Here." Caspian handed her a few cloth bandages and a small jar of ointment, "For the cut on your hand." She glanced at her hand, noting the large patch of dried blood. She opened her hand and winced, the glass she had been holding at done a number on her hand. Though, she thought, probably not as bad as Hammer's face.

"Did Payne send you?" She whispered, choking on her own voice. He glanced at her then back to the floor, something had flickered in his eyes, but it was too quick for Wynne to decipher.

"No." He turned quickly and moved for the door, "Don't' make him mad, it will only make things worse." And with that he opened the door and quickly shut it behind him. Wynne stared at the closed door, wishing he had stayed for just a moment longer. Her head ached, what was happening. For a moment, she thought she had seen concern on Caspian's face, heard it in his voice as he spoke. But no, she shook her head, the pounding only getting worse. She was delusional.

She worked quickly to mend her cut hand. The ointment did little to sooth the slice, at first, but once she got past the initial sting and wrapped it securely with the bandages, the throb in her hand slowly started to fade. She would carry this scar with her forever, there was no going back. Ms. Bloomington would pitch a fit when she saw the scar on her hand. Wynne's hand fluttered to her chest, no, she thought. Ms. Bloomington would never see the mark on her hand. She lay back on the cot as she felt the sting of tears rush to her eyes.

No, Ms. Bloomington would never again pitch a fit about anything that she did or didn't do and that realization brought a wave of fresh, painful emotions. Guilt, sorrow, pain, anger—all of them came with a force Wynne had not realized. Tears accompanied them and she found herself curled up on the cot, letting those emotions loose. She did not know what the captain wanted from her, but she would not let Ms. Bloomington's death, nor Henry's be in vain.

Hours passed before she door to her room opened again, "Captain would like to see you." Caspian declared, interrupting her nap. He helped her up from her cot and kept a firm hand on her arm as he led her out of her room. The sun greeted her, kissing her cheeks with a warmth that brought some comfort to her. The smell of salt filled her nostrils and lingered on her lips. The sky was bright blue, almost blinding her as she walked out on to the main deck.

The crew working the deck didn't stop as she was led past them, though she did notice them staring at her as they passed. She wasn't sure what they had been told about her, but judging from the curious, lingering stares, they had not been told much. Which was telling, whatever the captain needed her for, the crew was not privy to that information or quite possibly where they were even going.

Caspian didn't say a word as he led her to the captain's quarters where she was instructed to sit and wait. From her perch, she observed the room. The captain's quarters were beautiful. It was obvious he loved the finer things in life. Gold trim sparkled against the backdrop of deep, rich, navy-blue walls. In the middle of the room sat a giant wooden table covered with little nick-knacks and papers. Windows reached from floor to ceiling, letting in so much sparking sunlight that made the room glow. His room overlooked the bow of the ship with nothing but open sea and clear blue skies. How had this room belonged to a fearsome, blood-thirsty pirate? And better still, who was his cabin boy? Wynne couldn't help but credit the immaculate room to the unseen cabin boy and not the captain. The room itself would make even her maids stunned. Not even her own fathers captain was this clean or pristine.

The door opened, interrupting her moment of grand rapture. The captain waltzed in, followed by the guard, Hammer, who now bore several stiches in his cheek. Caspian, she noted, was nowhere to be seen. The guard was glaring at her as he entered, his face scowled when she met his eyes. He took up his post by the door, slowly folding his arms over his broad chest. Wynne turned around back in her seat and swallowed. She had not inclination, whatsoever, to move from her chair. Not when all three men bore stern, almost venomous gazes.

"Do you know what happens to prisoners who try to escape?" Captain Payne questioned. The room suddenly grew deathly quiet.

"I was under the impression; I was your guest."

The captains gaze went dark, "You disregarded that privilege the moment you maimed one of my crew members faces." Wynne shifted slightly in her chair, though she did her best to maintain eye contact with the captain.

"So, I will ask you again, Miss Hunt." He spoke slowly, "What happens to prisoners who try to escape?" Wynne felt the color drain from her face. She didn't want to know what his punishments were for his prisoner's. Given how feared he was, she couldn't only imagine his punishments fit his reputation.

"They get shot." Captain Payne snapped. Wynne trembled as the color completely drained from his face, "But, since I need you alive, that would not be a suitable punishment." He sneered, "I need you alive," He repeated, staring at her, the dark glimmer remained pressed over his facial features, "But that's it."

"What are you going to do to me?" Wynne whispered; her voice barely able to get out the words she was almost too afraid to ask.

He ignored her, "I didn't think you possess the courage," he remarked, a momentary impressed looked passed over his face, "it's apparent you have more of your mother's spirit than I thought, and you will, no doubt, try again." He stared at her, studying her with complete indifference. Wynne could hardly hold his gaze; his black eyes reminded her of an abyss.

"Ten lashes with the whip."

She croaked, "What?" practically falling from her chair.

"Ten lashes with the whip." He repeated, emphasizing each word before gesturing to Hammer. The guard moved towards her and grabbed her arm, pulling her from the chair to her feet.

"You can't do that!" she cried, pulling her arm free.

The captain laughed, "Ah, but I can!" He strutted forward, stopping inches before her, and forcefully grabbed her chin in his hand.

"Next time you will think twice before escaping."

"But Captain—" she started but was cut off when his hand tightened on her jaw.

"You won't try escaping again," he mused, a wicked gleam flickered in his eyes, "and you will have the scars on your back as a reminder." He shoved her jaw away from him in disgust and a hand clamped down on her forearm, dragging her away. Wynne tugged but the grip on her arm tightened. Caspian pulled her out of the room, despite her pitiful screams of protest.

Frantically, she dug her heels into the ground pulling harder, but her efforts were in vain. Men, all around her stopped to watch as she was dragged out to the deck. Wynne saw Caspian pushing through the growing crowd. He seemed confused but made no effort to find out what was going on, what was about to happen to her. Hammer threw her down before the mast. She had no time to catch herself and tumbled painfully to her knees, splinters pricked at her palms as she fell forward, catching herself before completely face planting the deck.

Before she could recover, hands descended on her, holding her fast. She squirmed and thrashed, trying to escape, but no matter her efforts, she was held tightly in her place. Her arms were forced above her head and bound to the mast. Chains were then shackled to her ankles, forcing her into position to receive her punishment. She swallowed, her back completely exposed. She began to cry, her body started to shake beneath the fear that now settled in on her.

The captain moved through the crowd, making his way before her at the mast. He looked down on her with callousness and a hardness she had not yet seen on his face before. This was the man who had made the fearsome legends, the man was said to have no feelings and who showed no mercy.

"Captain Payne, please!" She cried, her voice splintering as her throat screamed in protest. There was enough fear and desperation in her eyes and face that any sane man would have stopped, would have given her a lighter punishment. The captain's face frowned, and he sauntered towards her, grabbing her chin once again in his calloused hand.

"I will break you." His whispered, delicately into her ear.

"Please." She whispered, tears streamed down her cheek, "Please, don't do this."

"Welcome to a world of men with no honor." He sneered, pushing her away.

"Cedric, ten lashes for Miss Hunt." He cried; a hush fell over the crew. Wynne screamed after him as more tears poured from her eyes. A big man lumbered forward. A black whip hung, like a snake, from his hand. Over her shoulder, Wynne watched as he slowly approached.

"Please!" She pleaded, looking back at the captain. But she could see it in his eyes, his resolve had been set. He would not relinquish and break her indeed he would do. Wynne hung her head and braced herself for what was about to come. She felt her breath hitch in her throat, waiting. Every muscle in her back was taught. She gripped the ropes binding her wrists righter, bracing herself for the worst.

The whip cracked. Fiery hot pain ripped through her, like a hot poker being dragged across her back. She screamed, searing pain ripped through her bruised throat. The second lash sent a wave of bone breaking pain surging throughout her entire body. She felt herself fall forward on the mast, the bite of cold harsh wood pressing into her skin. Her scream turned into a wail as tears flooded her tightly closed eyes, spilling out onto her cheeks. The third whiplash sliced her open, exposing her to the malicious salt air. Hot scarlet blood poured down her back. The tang of iron filled her nostrils, the taste of blood lingered on her tongue.

How many lashes would she be able to endure? This pain was unlike any other pain she had ever endured. Part of her wondered if she would even survive to remember the scars being branded on her back. The whip cracked again, and pain struck her like a venomous snake, shattering her soul from her very body. Her vision blurred; the rims of her vision darkened. She felt her body sagging under the tremendous weight of pain, the very weight of her body. Everything was going numb, she couldn't feel her hands or feet bound to the mast, still holding her upright, baring her back to her punishment. Before the next blow, she let the darkness embrace her like an old friend and slipped into the abyss.

Chapter 10

Wynne was surrounded by fire. Her skin was alight in searing pain and no matter where she turned, she could not escape the torment. How had she gotten here? The pain radiated throughout her body; all her senses numb to anything but the pain she felt. This wasn't a dream; this pain was real. The fire tearing across her back, was real. Her eyes fluttered open; she blinked trying to clear the fog from her eyes. She blinked a few times as the room slowly came into focus. She was lying on her stomach, her head facing the door. No, not a door, bars—she swallowed, this was a cell.

Wanting to sit up and see more of her new surroundings, she tried to move her arms under herself to prop herself upright. Piercing pain shot through her back, she sucked in her breath and froze, hoping the pain would stop. But it lingered, slowly, gently she lay herself back down on the cot. She would not be attempting to move for some time, she would have to be content with the little view she could get of her new surroundings.

She shouldn't be surprised that she had been moved to a cell, but she had hoped that the captain would have some shred of decency left in his body to give her the tiny room back. She guessed she had squandered that shred when she had maimed Hammer. A tear streamed down her face; she couldn't help but think that it had been worth it all. If she had been allowed to do it all over again, she wouldn't have stabbed him in the face.

There was a gentle click, followed by the screech of rusty hinges. Wynne didn't even dare move her head as she heard footsteps enter the cell behind her. When the footsteps paused, Wynne could feel eyes watching her. After a moment of silence, waiting for whomever it was who had come to see her announce himself, Wynne forced herself to turn her head to the other side.

Caspian stood at the doorway. Wynne didn't have enough strength to scowl, but she could feel the dread shake through her bones. Why was he here? He was just standing there, staring at her— staring at her maimed back.

"What do you want?" She ground out, her voice still raspy and not entirely her own. The sound of her voice seemed to bring him out of his trance. He straightened up and moved quickly from his spot at the door to her side, kneeling beside her cot. Wynne felt her entire body recoil, but unfortunately couldn't make herself move away from him. She was pinned to her spot by a severe burning sensation and if she moved it would only make the sensation more prominent. It was then that she noticed he had not come empty handed. From under his arm, he produced a small satchel.

"I'm here to patch you up." He said softly.

Wynne laughed bitterly, "Did Payne send you?" She flinched as his fingers, cool as ice grazed against her raw skin. A raw tingle of unfamiliarity shivered down her spine.

"No." He answered, again softly, "If it were up to him, he would let you rot down here."

"He needs me alive." Wynne remarked, recalling the words the captain had spoken to her.

Caspian frowned, "Alive, yes, but he doesn't care what state you are in." That made her stomach tremble.

"And you do?" Wynne scoffed. But when Caspian met her eyes, she saw in them a gentle gaze, that was softened and almost saddened.

Why did he look sad? Hadn't he been the one that had captured her in the first place and brought her to this madman. Was it remorse that she saw in his eyes? But that was the only answer he gave her to her question. Wynne sucked in a sharp breath as he peeled away what was left of her tattered, blood-soaked shirt.

"Why are you doing this?" Wynne asked through clenched teeth, trying not to squirm as he gently cleaned the wounds on her back.

"I didn't think he'd actually do it." He replied, his voice barely above a whisper. His answer confused her even more. Her brows knit together as she watched him over her shoulder gently washing her wounds.

"So, you're helping me to ease your conscience?" She mumbled, earning her a cold side glance.

"I'm helping because," he sighed choosing his words carefully, "I'm the only friend you've got on this ship." He whispered, running a cool cloth along her back. She hissed as the cold bite nipped at the raw wounds.

"Since when did kidnapping people become a sign of friendship?" Wynne admonished, not caring in the slightest at how loud she had spoken.

"Since yesterday." He grumbled, "This is going to sting." He added before smothering her back with some sort of ointment. The ointment was smooth against her skin but felt like pinpricks all along her back.

Wynne hissed again, "Shit!" She cried under her breath, feeling her entire body seize up in discomfort. She saw a quick smile on Caspian's face, but it was quickly gone when he applied the second coat of the ointment, earning him another hiss from Wynne.

"Are you done torturing me yet?" Wynne ground out, but just as the he applied the last little bit of ointment, she felt a gentle wave of coldness flow across her back, numbing the throb of her wounds. She sighed and for the first time, she felt the muscles in her back relax and the fiery throbbing ceased.

"You will have to leave it uncovered for a while." Caspian stated, inspecting his work. Wynne nodded, not entirely liking the idea of her back being completely exposed but the idea of putting on a shirt over her fresh wounds did not sound any more appealing.

She flinched as Caspian's hand came to rest on her forehead, "You have a fever." His chair screeched across the floor followed by the same rusty creek of door hinges, Caspian's footsteps fading from ear shot. Wynne strained to hear something, anything, but all she could hear was the familiar sound of the ocean, crashing against the ship and the creaking of the ship as she moved with the undulating water. Then, she heard his footsteps hurrying back down the hall and the door opened once more.

"Drink this." He commanded, kneeling beside her head. She frowned at the small bottle but nodded. Gently, he helped her sit up, slightly. He held her up with a sturdy arm as she downed the content of the small vile. A warm liquid rushed down her throat, tasting somewhat of honey and salt. It smoothed out the scratchiness in her throat and settled the ache in her stomach. When she finished, he helped her lie back down and checked her back. That simple movement had zapped what energy she had left in her, and she felt exhaustion swell over her. In a moment, she lost herself to sleep and for a little while she felt the pain melt away.

The sway of the ship was familiar and comforting to her. It reminded her of a time, long, long ago. A time when her mother was still living, a time when she felt loved and cherished by both her mother and father. But that time was gone, and this ship was not her fathers, but that of a monster. She suddenly found herself standing in the middle of a vast ocean, alone. She glanced around her, how had she gotten here? Where had the ship she had just been on gone? An island sat before her in the distance. Fog, dense and thick, surrounded it like a shroud, and yet something about the island was calling to her. Had she seen this island before? She couldn't remember.

"Wynne." A voice whispered beside her. She jumped and found a woman standing beside her.

"Mother?" Wynne questioned. The woman beside her, turned her head and nodded gently, smiling slightly. There was a faint glow and when Wynne looked down, she saw her mother's locket glowing at her throat.

"Find me in the looking glass." She whispered, reaching a hand towards Wynne's cheek. Wynne felt her touch, though it felt more like the kiss of sea breeze. The locket around her throat began to pulse in response.

Wynne frowned, "What?"

"He hunts for me!" She cried, her mother's eyes turning black. The sky around them darkened, and Wynne felt herself being pulled away from her. Wynne watched as her mother raised a hand, and a wave rose at the command.

"Who?" Wynne shouted, trying to run to her mother, but something unseen held her back.

"Find me!" She commanded before disappearing into the swell of a giant black wave.

"Mother?" Wynne cried, but her voice echoed along the black water. She was alone, standing and facing the island. The water still as glass and the wind gone completely. Wynne felt a sense of heavy dread weigh down on her and her chest felt like it was being crushed. She felt like as though she would drown under the weight.

Wynne jerked awake; her heart thundered in her chest. Something around her neck was burning, the locket. She glanced down quickly and thought for a moment that the locket was glowing. But before her eyes could adjust fully the burning feeling went away and the locket was no longer glowing. Had she made it up? Wynne felt fidgety, she needed to get up and stretch her legs. Gritting her teeth, she pushed herself up. Her back and shoulders protested beneath the strain, but she ignored it and learned over her knees, trying to alleviate some of the pressure in her back. Gasping, she fought to take a deep, steady breath, trying to quench the swell of nausea that now gripped her stomach.

"What are you doing?" A deep, familiar voice questioned. She winced; Caspian stood in the doorway, watching her.

She scowled, "What are you doing here?"

"You were screaming." His eyes drifted from her to the locket. Paranoid, she gripped it in her hand. Had he also seen the locket glowing?

"I was not!" Wynne snapped, wishing she had more strength to stand. The firmness in her voice and statement was no doubt meaningless when she couldn't even hold herself upright.

He folded her arms, "And you weren't going to stand either."

"Why do you care?" She countered, her voice raising in anger. His gaze hardened, but he made effort to move from his post. Wynne sighed and rubbed her temple; her head was pounding.

71

"Where are you taking me?" She demanded. Her need for answers had been compounded by her very strange and vivid dream.

"The Keep." He answered. She glanced at him, surprised he had even answered her. But she was also surprised because it was the same place her father had mentioned in his note to her.

"Where is that?" She questioned, hopping that she would get more answers to the many questions she had.

"It's an island." He replied. Wynne felt her breath get stuck in her chest. She had just dreamed about an island. Had that just been a coincidence, or was it something important?

"Do you know the secrets about my mother, the ones Payne mentioned?"

Caspian shifted slightly, "Now's not the time."

"Not the time?"

"You're not ready for the answer to that question." He countered, firmly.

"And who are you to say?" Wynne felt her temples throb as her anger swelled.

"It's not the right time." Caspian stood his ground, not wavering at the sound of anger on her tongue.

"When will the right time be?" Wynne questioned, her anger seething.

He met her eyes, "When you are ready." Wynne felt her anger bubble once more but before she could thing of a sarcastic response, he was gone. Why had she thought he would answer her questions in the first place?

I'm the only friend you've got on this ship. Those had been his words the night before. She had been tossing them around in her mind, weighing their validity. Did she really believe he was her only friend? She wasn't sure, but what she was sure of was, she would do what she needed to do to prove their worth, to prove his worth.

Chapter 11

Several days, she wasn't exactly sure how many, passed before the ship sailed into bad weather. Fortunately, her back was on the mend and the pain was not too great to allow her time to stand and walk her cell. But the cry of the storm bells, made her sick with worry. The lookout had spotted the storm on the horizon, calling the crew to action with the clanging of a bell. Footsteps echoed on the wood above her as the crew members flocked to their stations, preparing for the oncoming storm.

The winds picked up first, starting to howl around the ship. The smell of rain hung in the air, leeching through the wood. Wynne could almost see the billowing black clouds gathering on the horizon and it sent a shiver down her spine. The ocean beneath the ship started to swell, rocking the ship back and forth. Wynne felt her stomach drop as the ocean suddenly dropped, taking the ship with them. She had never cared for the fluttering feeling and swallowed his discomfort, mentally preparing herself for what was to come.

The first few drops tapped on the deck above, but soon, heavier drops followed, creating a symphony of thunderous pelts, pounding violently against the deck. Then she heard the first rumbled of thunder and felt a tingle of awe, as she felt the vibrations of the thunder beat against the hull of the ship. Storms were a majestic power she admired, from a distance. Storms on land were one thing, but storms on an ocean, she swallowed, they had a way of turning her admiration into fear.

Waves crashed against the ship, seeping through the cracks, soaking every surface. The ship was tossed back and forth like a child's toy. Wynne found herself gripping the edge of her cot when as much strength as she possessed. Her entire body was tense as she tried to resist the violent rock the ship was now subject to. She couldn't shake the gut feeling that this storm was only going to get worse.

More shouts sounded above, barely making it over the howl of the wind. Wynne thought she could hear the bell still clanging, but she couldn't be sure. She glanced towards the stairs and saw water pouring down them. She swallowed, she was in the lowest part of the ship and during a storm, that was the worst place to be.

In answer to her fear, footsteps thundered down the stairs. Two men she had never seen before came into view and went straight for the pumps. Together they started pumping, relieving the ship of some of the water that that was starting to flood into the ship. But it didn't matter how fast they pumped though; the water continued to rise.

"We're taking on too much water!" One man, the younger of the two, shouted frantically.

"Aye, tell Caspian!" the older man cried, still pumping, his face contorted in fierce concentration. The younger man did not hesitate, he turned and rushed up the stairs, taking them two at a time and disappearing to the deck above.

The ship pitched starboard side, catching her off guard and sent her careening into the wall. She yelped as the shock of the fall reverberated through her bones, sending a flash of pain through every wound on her back. Wynne gritted her teeth and tried to correct her mistake but was tossed to the other side before she could grab onto the cell door. She was tossed carelessly to the floor, instantly soaked. Groaning, she pushed herself up, trying to pick herself up before she was tossed to another corner of her cell. She was unsuccessful and felt herself crash against the opposite wall, landing right on her back. She moaned, every wound along her back felt like it had reopened, she could feel the sting and trickle of fresh blood. Gritting her teeth, she grabbed for the cell bars, the only thing anchored into the floor and pulled herself up to her feet, bracing herself against the door.

Thunder crashed above her and rumbled beneath her. It was followed by footsteps, crashing down the stairs. She glanced towards the stairs and saw that it was the captain. His face was twisted in rage, his expression was dark as he flew towards her cell. Wynne spotted Caspian, following him, his attention was solely on the captain.

"This is your doing!" the captain yelled, pointing a finger in her face. Wynne took a slight step away from the cell door, not entirely sure how she should respond. Was he talking about the storm? When she didn't respond, he fumbled wildly with his coat pocket before pulling out the key to her cell. Wynne watched as he struggled to the get the key in the lock, before unlocking and throwing open her cell door with a violent clang. In two strides he was in her cell and had his hand against her throat.

"You will fix this!" He shouted, shaking her.

"Captain," Caspian yelled behind him. Payne scowled and dragged her out of her cell and up the stairs. He moved so fast Wynne had little time to get her feet under her. She stumbled, but Payne did not stop, her shine beat painfully on the wooden steps. He dragged her up to the main deck and Wynne was greeted by a howling wind and pounding drops of rain against her face. Black clouds, above, swirled in the sky as black waves, no, walls of water, rose all around her.

"Captain!" Caspian shouted behind them, but Payne did not stop. He dragged her to the upper deck, a wide-eyed crew man at the helm stared at them, briefly before returning his attention to the storm and the ship in his command.

"Control the storm!" Payne shouted, as he threw her down before the helm. What was he talking about?

Wynne stared up at him, "What?" She cried, confused. He was mad, utterly mad. There was no way she could control any kind of weather, let alone this ragging storm. And what's worse, was he thought she could!

Rage, red hot, flooded his face, he reached down and slapped her, "You have her blood!" He spat, "Control the storm!" He repeated. Wynne shook her head gently before glancing at Caspian, who was looking at the captain. There was a mix of fear and annoyance on his face. When she didn't answer, the captain lunged for her, grabbing her, and holding her up before him. He shook her, gritting his teeth angrily.

"Control it!" He screamed.

"I—I can't!" Wynne yelled. He dropped her and frowned, disgusted with her. He slapped her again before grabbing her numb cheek and bringing her face to his.

"Do it!" He screamed. Wynne trembled and felt a tear trickle down her cheek. If she could do what he was asking her to do, she would, in a heartbeat. But what he was asking of her was impossible. He raised his hand to slap her again, but Wynne saw Caspian step forward and grab the captain's arm.

"Captain!" Caspian shouted, "This is not her storm!" The captain's eyes moved from Wynne to Caspian and the furry that lay in his black eyes made Wynne's blood curdle. But to her relief, he let go of her. She tumbled to the deck, a wave of relief filling her entire body. Payne straightened upright and without any hesitation swung a meaty fist, connecting with Caspian's jaw. Wynne gasped as Caspian took a step back in shock, grabbing his jaw. Payne lunged for him, grabbing his shirt in his fist.

"Don't ever challenge me again!" He snarled, "Or I will kill you!" He spat, then shoved Caspian aside. Payne stormed from the helm back down to his private quarters, ignoring the clamor among the crew members hard at work to keep the ship from being swallowed whole. Caspian wiped a hand across his mouth, Wynne spotted a trail of blood along his fist. He looked at her, she froze, his eyes were filled with icy rage, but not at her, towards the captain. He reached for her, and gently grabbed her hand in his, pulling her to her feet.

"Are you alright?" He shouted.

She nodded, "Is he insane?" She shouted, gently feeling her now swollen cheek, a fear lone tears trailed down her cheeks.

"Only during storms." He replied. He led her down to the main deck and they made their way back down the stairs and to her cell.

Wynne had never been more relieved in her life to be locked back in the cell.

"Why only during storms?" Wynne asked, clutching the cell bars.

Caspian met her eyes slowly, "It has to do with your mother."

Wynne raised a brow, "One of her dark secrets?"

He nodded.

Wynne bit her lip, "You're not going to explain it to me, are you?" She mumbled, stopping him with a piercing gaze.

"One thing at a time." He said quietly, "Storm first." He added. Wynne nodded, feeling somewhat foolish for demanding answers here, and now. The crew needed him, especially since Payne had barricaded himself in his quarters.

"Thank you!" Wynne cried after him. His paused briefly on the steps, looked over his shoulder, nodded slightly and for the briefest moment she saw a smile spread over his face. Then he turned and disappeared up to the main deck.

"I'm the only friend you've got on this ship."

She pursed her lips in thought. She wasn't sure why he was helping her, but this was the third instanced where he had helped her in some small wall. But what did it all mean? What was his motive? What did he have to gain in helping her? She allowed herself to entertain the idea that maybe—just maybe—his words held some truth.

Chapter 12

The storm had passed as quickly as it had come, but not before battering the ship and her crew. Still, it had been a long night, but when dawn finally broke, Wynne felt the waters beneath the ship relax and the wind died down. The rain turned into a lazy drizzle as an absolute calm washed over the ship and entire crew. Peace, Wynne could feel it from within her tiny cell. And in her relief, she fell back onto her cot and closed her eyes, exhaustion filled her.

But she wasn't asleep for long. Wynne awoke to knuckles wrapping on the door of her cell. She sat up, wincing, and found Hammer glaring at her through the bars. He didn't say anything as he passed. She shivered; he did this at least two times a day. She had thought the storm would have worn him out, but apparently, she was wrong. The first couple times he had done this, she had awoken to find him standing at the door, staring at her. Not really knowing how long he had been standing there watching her.

She remained on her cot until he slinked away. When she could no longer hear his footsteps, she allowed herself to sigh. Gingerly, she sat up, careful not to jar her back. Last night's little stroll had opened some of her wounds, in addition to making her back more tender and sorer than ever.

Footsteps echoed outside her door; she glanced up to see Caspian standing outside her door with a tray of food. She eyed him suspiciously as he opened the door, hurrying in. Wynne noticed that he had not locked the door behind him. Was he testing her? Even if he was, she had no desire to escape, not until her back as healed. He took a seat beside her, setting the tray carefully on her lap. It was filled with enough food to quench the hunger pains in her gut. There was hardtack, some dried meat, figs and what looked like some sort of beans. Her eyes flickered from the food up to Caspian, who was watching her carefully, quietly.

"It's not poisoned, is it?" She asked, picking up the hardtack, examining it carefully.

He chuckled, "I'm not in the habit of poisoning young ladies."

"No, you'll just kidnap them." She retorted, eyes narrowing before taking a tentative bite of the hardtack. No suspicious tastes, just the dry taste of hardtack.

"Are you going to sit there and watch me eat?" She demanded after swallowing.

"Does it make you uncomfortable?" He mused, with a slight smirk.

"I wasn't aware watching others eat was an enjoyable pass time."

His smirk grew to a slight grin, "When the subject is as beautiful as you, it's easy." He purred. Wynne snorted, beautiful indeed—she could just imagine! Covered in grim, and dirt, her hair was a tangled mess and goodness know what her face looked like. She shook her head; this kind of thinking was not getting her anywhere.

"Well then," she swallowed, wiping the crumbs from her fingers, "while you're watching and enjoying the beautiful view, I hope you'll finally tell me why I am here." She ventured.

"Persistent, aren't you?" He sighed, somewhat exasperated.

"Blame yourself." Wynne remarked, pointing a finger at him as she snatched up a piece of the dried meat, "You're the one who promised."

"I believe my exact wording was, 'When you're ready.'" He mumbled.

Wynne raised a brow, "I'm definitely ready." She wasn't entirely sure what constituted her being ready or not.

"I have a few conditions." He remarked. Of course, he would have some stipulations, Wynne rolled her eyes.

"Conditions?"

"I will tell you what I can, when I can." He announced, firmly, meaning no matter how hard she pressed, he would not give her information until he was ready. But, if it meant getting answers, she could curb her curiosity long enough to wait for him to give her the information.

"Anything else?" She questioned.

"Payne can't know I'm talking to you." He added, "And."

"There's more?" She choked, feeling the dried meat stick in the back of her throat.

He frowned, "You have to trust me."

She balked, "I'm not agreeing to that condition." She exclaimed, "The other two are just fine, but trust you—I can't give you that."

"I won't lie to you." He started firmly, "But to believe me, you'll have no other option but to trust me." Wynne scowled, that was the last thing she wanted to do! But it made sense. She'd have to trust, trust that what he would tell her was indeed the truth.

She bit her lip, "Trust goes both ways."

He nodded, "That's what makes it so powerful and delicate." He looked at her with a funny expression.

"What are you expecting from me?" She muttered.

He smiled, slightly, "Nothing but your trust." She studied him for a moment. There was something so sincere in his eyes, yet she couldn't quite shake the sense of uneasiness. Was it uneasiness because she didn't trust him or uneasiness because she did trust him. She didn't have much of a choice, she needed answers and he was the only one willing to give them to her. He, no doubt, was taking a risk, she would have to do the same thing.

She sighed, "If it means I'll get some answers—I'll trust you." Caspian nodded, smiling, but it wasn't a happy one. He seemed saddened that had agreed to trust him, but why? Before she could ponder the reason, the expression was gone, like a vapor.

"What is the Keep?" she started.

"I told you, it's an island." He answered. So, he hadn't been lying about that.

"Yes, but what does it have to do with my mother?"

"She hid something there," he started, "something Payne wants."

"And what would that be?" She asked, trying not to lean forward with anticipation.

"A chest."

"Like a treasure chest?" Caspian nodded.

Wynne frowned, "That's it," she said slowly, "a treasure chest?" her confusion was mounting, "What does that have to do with me?"

"He needs you to find it." He replied simply, as though the answer was obvious.

"Why can't he find it himself?" Wynne's voice rose in irritation, "Why does he need me to do it?"

"You're the only one that can find it." He said emphatically.

"Why me?" She asked.

"He can't find it on his own." Caspian replied.

Wynne frowned, "You are not making this very easy." She protested, feeling her irritation rising, "Why can't he find it?"

Caspian sighed, rubbing his eyes, "Because he's not meant to find it."

"And I am?" Wynne questioned.

"Correct." Caspian confirmed, thought it did more make Wynne relieved. This made her position to Payne valuable, but also meant Payne would be more dangerous. If this chest was something he wanted desperately, he would do whatever it takes to get it. But what would that mean for her?

"What's in this chest?" Wynne prodded, but Caspian looked at her slowly. It was the first time he had paused since their conversation began and Wynne had a feeling, she was not going to get an answer. In confirmation of her suspicions, he stood quickly and hurried for the door.

"I have to go." He announced.

"Wait a minute!" Wynne cried, grabbing his arm, "You can't leave!"

He chuckled, "I can't?"

"No!" She exclaimed, "You have to answer my question!"

He smiled, "All in good time." He whispered then ducked out of her cell. She remained where she sat, the information tumbling around in her mind. She ran a hand through her hair, trying to process everything he had told her. Payne was under a curse, and he was looking for a chest. She swallowed a chest that only she could find. Caspian had answered her questions, freely, but in doing so, had also created new ones. But, she thought, it was a start at least. For the first time, since she had been taken in the alley way, she felt a small spark of hope bloom in her chest. Maybe, just maybe she would make it out of this alive.

Chapter 13

The days passed slowly, merging into one long stream of nothing-ness. Fortunately, the extra time gave Wynne's back a chance to heal, but ridges now scared her entire back, a permanent reminder of Payne's cruelty. Gingerly, she ran a gently hand over the ridges, the ones she could feel, and bit back tears. Wynne swallowed her tears, reminding herself that it could have been so much worse.

Caspian visited her often, but rarely stayed long enough for them to chat in great length. Wynne was starving for a long conver-sation, burning with the need and desire to ask him her questions, but he never relinquished any extra time. They had agreed to trust one another, but they had not had any lengthy conversations since their first talk. In desperation, Wynne had tried poking and prod-ding him into staying and talking to her, but he'd either ignore her or glare when she prodded too much. She had to give him credit for being as resilient as he was.

The other person who made a consistent effort to see her was Hammer. His visits, however, were merely to fulfill his own perverse desire to get a rye out of her. Wynne tried her best to ignore him, it never lasted long, but when his visits became more and more, she finally had reached her limit. She lashed out, snapping violently at him, but that would only result in him leaning back and bellowing in pure sadistic delight. The sound of his laughter grated against her nerves. So, when he came down for the second time that day, her patience was worn thin. Wynne eyes him gloomily as he strutted up to her cell and draped his large meaty arms through the cell bars.

"And how is our caged beauty?" he crooned. Wynne turned her back, hoping he'd take the hint.

"What?" he gasped, nonchalantly, "No response?" She refused to look at him, hoping he'd just leave her alone. Pain, suddenly, exploded from the back of her head, as she tumbled backward off her cot. She screamed, grabbing the back of her head, and launching herself to her feet, ready to fire off the stream of insults she had been holding at bay. But she stopped short when she saw the cell door swing open. The blood suddenly drained from her face as Hammer took one slow step inside her cell. He stood there, leering in the doorway, the cell door key dangling from his meaty fingers.

"You have they key." She whispered, her voice trembling. Slowly, she backed herself into the corner. Hammer pressed forward, laughing.

"I thought we'd have some fun today." He snarled.

"Hel—" Her scream was cut short, by his meaty hand clamping down on her mouth.

"Now, now Miss," he sneered, "we don't want ya' spoiling our fun now, do we?" She lashed out, her foot connecting violently with his shin. He winced, and cursed before shoving her against the wall, knocking the wind from her chest. There was a glint of silver and Wynne froze as she felt cold, sharp steel pressed to her throat.

"I thought we would find a way to make your pretty face match mine." He lifted the dagger from her throat and flashed it before her eyes. Her eyes wandered to the fresh red scar on his own face, the one that had put there. He dragged the dagger lightly over her cheek, the feel of steel bit into her cheek.

"Mmhmm," he purred, "I think it will be a nice addition, don't you?"

Wynne squirmed, "You're a monster!" she hissed. Hammer frowned and grabbed her jaw, pressing his blade to her cheek. She felt the sharp edge bite into her flesh.

"Name calling will only make me mad." He chuckled, pressing the blade deeper into her cheek. She whimpered, as her cheek lit up with a raw sting. She felt a drop of blood pour out onto her cheek. Hammer's eyes widened as he saw the drop of blood trickle onto her skin, he squeezed his hands tighter against her jaw.

"So," he purred, "the sea witch does bleed red after all." He remarked, glancing at the thin line of crimson that now coated his dagger.

"I will enjoy watching your pain." He sneered. Wynne couldn't move but groaned as she felt the dagger dig deeper into her skin. But then, she felt herself falling away from the wall, warm hands grabbed her, lifting her to her feet and then they covered her face. Grey blue eyes, Caspian, found her own, searching for the wound. His eyes lingered on the mark on her cheek, his face lighting up with rage.

"Out of my way Caspian!" Hammer growled, as he wiped blood from his nose. Had Caspian hit him?

"You're not supposed to be down here." Caspian growled, turning towards him, pushing her behind him.

"On whose authority?" He sneered.

"Mine." Caspian's voice thundered in response.

Hammer snorted, "I heard what you did to Haddox." He snarled, "I only take orders from the captain." Without warning, he lunged for Caspian, but Caspian dodged him easily. Not deterred by the failed attempt, Hammer spun, lunging again with lightning speed. Hammer's elbow caught Caspian's jaw, sending him crashing into the wall. Gleaming in triumph, Hammer turned back towards her.

Wynne jumped for the open door, but Hammer beat her, grabbing her and throwing her back against the wall like a rag doll. But Caspian, had also recovered, and tackled Hammer from behind, the two crashed to the ground. Wynne backed herself into the corner, as far away from the skirmish as possible. Hammer threw Caspian off, but he sprang back like a cat. Hammer swung but only hit air as Caspian dodged then planted his fist on Hammer's jaw. Wynne grimaced at the crunch. Hammer stepped back, dazed, and blinked several times. But he was not quite finished yet. He attached again, but this attack was too slow. Caspian side stepped easily, connecting his fist with Hammer's nose. Blood spewed all over Hammer's face.

Dazed, Hammer took a single step back. His shoulders sagged, and blood mixed with sweat, ran down his face. He spit, raising his fists in one final attempt. It was a desperate attempt, one that didn't even make Caspian flinch. Caspian connected the final blow and Hammer crumpled to the floor. But Caspian wasn't finished. He grabbed Hammer's shirt, yanking him to his feet. Wynne could see the furry blazing in his eyes.

"Never lay a finger on her again." He growled, "or I will kill you." Caspian shoved Hammer out of the door. He stumbled down the hall and disappeared up the steps. Caspian didn't watch Hammer disappear before turning towards her. His face was flooded with emotions—anger, concern, fear. He reached for her face, and she felt his fingers brush across the cut on her cheek.

"How long?" He asked quietly. Wynne bent her head, as the tears welled, clouding up her vision.

"Miss Hunt—Wynnefred," his voice was so soft and gentle, she lifted her eyes to his, "how long has he been coming down here." He repeated.

"Since we left port." She whispered, her lower lip trembled, "but, he's never had a key before." Fresh new tears fell down her face.

"Damn it." He seethed, under his breath, "Wait here." He muttered, then ducked out of her cell. She sat carefully on her cot, shaking slightly. He returned a minute later with a cup and a few bandages. Without a word, he sat down beside her and poured some of the water onto the cloth before tenderly wiping the blood from her cheek. She winced as the movement brought a sharp fresh sting.

"I think you'll have a scar." He muttered. She didn't say anything, though. Her body had already gained numerous scars from unspeakable horrors, what was one more?

Chapter 14

Wynne lay on her back, staring up at the ceiling. The ship was quiet as it tipped back and forth in a methodic rhythm. It was soothing in a way, but she could feel the despair of being cooped up for days on end, confided in a small room. She was on edge and could feel the incessant fidgety feeling creeping into her limbs.

"Are you alright?" Caspian's voice cut through the darkness and into her thoughts. She sat up and saw him leaning outside her cell.

"How long have you been there?" she demanded.

"Not long." He admitted.

"Hammer won't be bothering you anymore." He declared. It was something in his voice that told her, Hammer would not be bothering anyone anymore. Wynne raised a brow, but Caspian just folded his arms, resolutely.

"Why did you help me?"

"I told you," Caspian sighed, "I'm the only friend you have on this ship."

"You also chased me down an alley and kidnapped me." She snapped.

He rubbed the back of his neck, "I had to." he muttered, avoiding her gaze.

"Why?" She demanded, "So I can find some mystery chest my mother hid on some crazy island?"

"Yes." He met her eyes, but his gaze was surprising soft, "There was no other way."

"For what?" she demanded, standing up and stepping towards the cell door where Caspian stood. He turned towards her and grabbed the bars, fixing a penetrating gaze onto her.

"To keep you safe." He whispered. She stepped back, slightly, studying his face for a glimpse of insanity. But his face was void of anything but deep concern and complete transparency. To her surprise and confusion, he was sincere in what he was saying.

She shook her head, "Caspian," she gestured to her cell, "how is this keeping me safe?" At this, his eyes fell to the floor. He was wrestling with an emotion she couldn't quite put her finger on.

"You have to trust me." He said at last, looking back up at her.

"How can I? You have hardly told me anything worthwhile. The things you have told me have only resulted in me having more questions."

To her surprise, he nodded, "I know, I have to be careful." She sighed and slid to the floor, resting her back against the wall facing Caspian. Caspian, in return, crouched. The only thing separating them was the cell bars.

"There are things you need to know." He whispered, "but I can't risk telling you here." She nodded, but pulled her knees to her chest, trying to contain the swell of emotions suddenly building in her chest.

"What can you tell me?"

"Payne did know your mother," he proclaimed, his voice no longer a whisper, "he keeps a portrait of her on his desk." He added. Wynne made no effort to hide the disgust on her face. Did her father know? Surely, her mother wouldn't have kept a secret like that from him. But she was struck with doubt, the more Caspian told her the more she felt like she did not know who her mother really was.

"What is in the chest?" Wynne whispered.

"I don't know for sure," he began, "Everything I've heard had been here-say."

"Payne hasn't told you?"

Caspian shook his head, "Not entirely. He trusts me, but it only goes so far."

"So, what have you heard?"

Caspian sighed, "Have you heard of an Allure?" Wynne frowned, why on earth was he bringing up an Avanthian mythology? The fact that he even knew anything about the Avanthian's also surprised her.

"Of course, I have." The Allure, were legends, widely spread among the people of Whaeldrake. They were good omens, and a sign of success for any merchant, but they were nothing but a legend, a myth told by old seamen. But the look on Caspian's face made her assumption of a mere myth fade.

"It is said that your mother was an allure, and a very powerful one too." Caspian added, his voice barely above a whisper. Wynne sat back, letting his words sink in. According to Avanthian legends an Allure was a child of Oaran. They were said to hold power over water, it was a gift from the god himself, to the ones he treasured the most of his patrons. Each division of Taeren had their patron deity and each patron deity had their children that they bestowed powerful gifts to.

Wynne frowned trying to remember the information she had read in her books. Estris was the goddess of the sky, and her children were called the Etheri. Rhaesis was the god of earth, and his children were called the Kerei, and lastly the goddess of death, Asta whose children were called the Necros. They were said to look just like any regular human, but their heavenly gifts set them apart in so many other ways. They were revered individuals, and usually held great esteem and privilege according the Avanthian legend. But there was the tiny detail that they were a myth and legend—passed on through the ages, surviving the division of Taeren, to become wonderful children's stories, nothing more.

Wynne felt her jaw drop, "You can't be serious?" She demanded.

Caspian's lips were pressed tight and resolute as he met her gaze, "There are a few crew members still on board that remembered her and confirmed her abilities."

Wynne shook her head, "Wait—wait just a minute!" She held up her hand, waving him to stop, "There are men on this ship that actually remember seeing her—actually remember her? And they also say that she had these—abilities?" Wynne felt a pang of jealously sweep through her. Her mother had died when she was five and not a day had gone by since then that she had wished that her mother was still a part of her life. She envied those around her who had the opportunity to know her and remember her. And in addition to seeing her, interacting with her, they had seen her with these supposed abilities? It was too much to believe all at one time.

Caspian nodded, "The stories started to swirl the moment you were brought on board."

"What kind of stories." Wynne questioned somewhat apprehensive of the answer Caspian would give her.

"Your mother could control the seas, making her quite beneficial for Payne's quest for gold and ultimate power." Caspian started slowly, "She was fearless and unrelentless, and quite powerful. She sailed with Payne years before she met your father." Caspian paused rubbing his hands together, like he was nervous about what he was going to say next.

"It's said, she loved Payne—had given him her heart."

Wynne held up a hand, shaking her head violently, "No." she cried, "You don't really expect me to believe that do you?"

It was his turn to frown, "I promised I wouldn't lie to you."

"I wasn't expecting you to tell me Avanthian folk lore and that my mother was some illusive legend much less tell me that she was also the lover to the most feared pirate of the sea." Wynne pressed her fingertips against the bridge of her nose.

"That doesn't mean I am lying to you." Caspian remarked softly.

"You may not be lying, but that doesn't mean I am going to believe you either." She snapped, "This is ridiculous!" She cried, folding her arms across her chest, as if in doing so, she would somehow protect herself from the words Caspian was delivering.

"I know it is a lot to take in."

"No!" Wynne shouted, shaking a finger in his fac, her calm façade dissipating, "You have no idea what it's like to be told you mother is assumed to be some mythical allure and," Wynne drawled, "to be the ex-lover of you kidnapper and personal torturer!"

Caspian's head dropped, "I'm sorry." Was all he mumbled, and unsurprisingly it did not make Wynne feel any better. If anything, it made her feel angrier.

"Well don't be." Her words full of the bitterness and anger she felt.

"I believe it's true." He whispered, adding more sting to her wounds.

"Of course, you do." Wynne sighed.

"I've seen things in my time travelling with Payne—things that make no sense." He countered, his voice growing louder in defense.

"Like what?" Wynne demanded, her voice rising in desperation.

Caspian's brow furrowed, "Superhuman strength, power over nature—over death!" He stood quickly; his fists clenched by his side. Wynne took a tentative step away from him. He was angry—at her, for doubting, questioning what he had seen. The presence of this raw emotion took her by surprise. But before she could counter, he checked his anger quickly, and soon straightened himself upright, unclenching his fists slowly.

He met her eyes, "If your mother wasn't really an allure—would you be here, on this ship?" Wynne met his eyes, slowly, and saw the conviction of truth in his eyes. She didn't want to believe him, but what other explanation was there for her presence aboard this ship? It would also explain Payne's behavior, just days before, when the ship had entered the storm. She pursed her lips; Payne had wanted her to control the storm. What's more, he believed that she could. Wynne shuttered at the thought. The more she thought of her mother, the more questions just surfaced, and it started to make her head hurt. Wynne swallowed, wishing more than anything she had her books here with her, at her disposal. Her mind was whirling with questions and her memory was not doing her justice now.

"I'm still waiting for the part when you tell me this is all a joke, and I am actually just dreaming." She remarked, trying to keep her voice light, and in her own way, letting him know her anger was not directed at him. She saw his shoulders relax, but the stern expression on his face remained.

"I told you; I won't lie to you." He said confidently.

"What if everything you are saying is just that—rumors?" Wynne whispered, one last final attempt to grasp at a straw she knew was not even there.

"Rumors," Caspian whispered, "all have an element of truth behind them." Wynne felt a shiver run down her spine. She didn't hear the door close, or Caspian's footsteps retreating up to the upper decks. Her mind was in a fog, trying to process all the thoughts and emotions running rampant in her mind. She sank to her cot and stared aimlessly at the floor, her head suddenly feeling heavy.

Gently, she laid down, resting her hands on her stomach, her fingers fidgety. Her mind was exhausted, but no matter what she tried, she could not shut off the thoughts that flitted through her mind. Their conversation pooled before her, but she was having a hard time accepting any of it as truth. She inhaled a deep breath, trying to settle the growing anxiety mounting in her chest.

There was no reason not to believe Caspian. Though he had been the reason for her being here in the first place, he had done nothing since but try to win her trust. So, the real issue with his claim, was not the claim itself—but the source of his claim. The Avanthian folk lore. Did she believe in the old legends or not? She remembered a time, long ago, when she relished those stories, and she did believe in them. But at some point, she had just accepted them for what they were—stories. But what if they weren't, what if they were indeed real?

Without warning, her mind went to the one person she was trying not to think of, her mother. Wynne squeezed her eyes shut, as she felt the sting of tears flood her eyes, just as the image of her mother flashed before her. Beautiful long blonde hair, that sparkled like gold in the sunlight, accompanied by a smile that radiated like the sun itself. Deep blue eyes, almost black, looked back at her. If her mother had been an Allure, that would mean the woman from her memories, was not who she had really been. Wynne swallowed her tears, trying to push down the feeling that all her memories of her mother were based on lies.

Her fingers found the locket hanging at her throat. She grasped it firmly and held it up to look at it closer. The trident, the symbol of Oaran, sparkled. It stood out on the face of the locket, like a beacon. Wynne studied the beautiful script written on the outside rim.

Oh, daughter of sea and chaos, let your heart reign true.

Those words now meant something entirely different to Wynne. An Allure was a child of Oaran, gifted with abilities and powers no one could even begin to fathom. They were children of the sea and chaos. And if what Caspian was saying was true, her mother was the daughter the locket was inscribed to.

But something else caught her eye. Wynne squinted, holding the locket up closer to get a better look. It was a hinge! Excitement poured through her. This was no ordinary necklace; this was a locket! And there was a chance it could still open and there was a chance there was something left inside from her mother. How, she had not noticed it before, was beyond her. She didn't have to try very long before, the lid of the locket popped open, and a very small, folded piece of paper fell into her lap. Tentatively, she unfolded the paper and saw a few words inscribed there.

Find my keeper and awaken me in the deep. Journey with me to challengers end to find me in the looking glass.

The looking glass? That was the second time she heard that term before, once in her dream and now on this piece of paper. But what did it mean? And what was all this other stuff about a keeper and awakening? She yawned, information still pooling in her mind, but she was exhausted and could feel the tiredness deep within her bones. Her eyes lids had grown heavy, convincing her that it was alright to succumb to sleep. Clutching the slip of paper, she closed her eyes and let the overpower calm of sleep swallow her whole.

Chapter 15

Teal blue water crashed onto creamy sand, lapping up over her toes. The water was warm, and the sand was soft beneath her feet. Wynne looked up, she was standing in a lagoon, sparkling sea water greeted her. Confusion, however, knit her brow as she searched for answers as to where she was. She wasn't supposed to be her, but just then, someone took a step beside her. It was her mother, eyes sparkling and a gentle but sad smile on her face. Carefully she took Wynne's hand in her own, but Wynne could not feel her touch. Her mother fixed her gaze on the horizon, overlooking the lagoon.

Wynne wanted to speak, had so many questions she needed to ask her mother, but no matter how hard she tried, she could not open her mouth. Panic and desperation set in, she wanted to scream! How was she to know what to do, who she was, or anything, if she couldn't speak!

As if her mother heard her unspoken questions, she turned back to look at her. Her mother's dark blue eyes were sparkling, unlike anything she remembered. There was something different about her, but Wynne couldn't quite put her fingers on it. Her mother smiled but faltered when she saw the locket hanging from her neck. Her expression grew suddenly sad, and Wynne felt the urge to wrap her in a warm embrace, but she couldn't move.

"Find my keeper; awaken me in the deep. Journey with me to challengers end to find me in the looking glass." Her voice pierced her mind, like a sword, flooding her entire body with command and urgency. She winced as the words brought a prick of pain into the scars at her back. Her mother smiled sadly, as though she knew the very pain her words had just caused her.

The lagoon she was standing in, suddenly became fuzzy, the sand beneath her feet, the sparkling water disappeared. In an instant, Wynne found herself standing on the lip of a cliff, overlooking a steep gorge. She felt her stomach drop and caught sight of a bridge spanning the precarious cliff. A gust of wind blew past her, almost knocking her off her feet. There was laughter mixed in with the gust of wind. Wynne looked and saw the figure of a woman, dancing in the wind.

The scene shifted once more, the bridge and gorge whirled past her. She felt dizzy and disoriented as the scene before her cleared. She was now standing in a river, her heart dropped. Standing, armed before her, was a man, taller than any man she had ever seen. Her mother, stepped towards him, he raised his sword to bring it down upon her, but she merely lifted her hand and to Wynne's surprise he melted before her. As Wynne followed her mother, she looked down into the water and saw a man's face leering up at her.

Wynne looked up and she was standing on the shores of a lake. Her mother was walking out onto the water, then stopped, glancing over her shoulder. Wynne wanted to follow her, but thunder stopped her in her tracks. Wynne looked above her, but the sky was clear. Thunder sounded again, Wynne desperately looked at her mother, but she was no longer there.

Thunder sounded again, shouts and echoes sounded all around her. No, she thought it couldn't be thunder. The sky was clear. But there it was again, thunder—no, she thought. It was not thunder; it was footsteps!

Wynne sat up; her heart was racing. She rubbed the sleep from her eyes as the door swung open, a loud creak echoed around her. Caspian walked in, though the grave look on his face, could only mean something bad.

"The captain wants to see you." He announced, not giving her any clues as to the reason for the meeting. Wynne nodded, standing slowly, her anxiety of the seeing the captain made her arms and legs tremble. Caspian said nothing more as he grabbed her arm and led her out of her cell and up the stairs. When had she been to the upper decks last? She swallowed, she couldn't remember, though remembered the sting of the captain's fists against her face.

The sun was just peeking over the horizon, greeting her with warm kisses of sunlight. Wynne squinted, how many days had she been trapped down in the belly of the ship, with nothing my stingy sea water and dusky light to keep her company? She tried to keep the tears of relief from spewing out of her eyes, she wanted to relish the sunlight and the fresh breeze that delicately toyed with her hair.

Several crew members stopped to gawk as Caspian pushed her towards the captain's quarters. They didn't say anything, but she still shrunk under their curiosity and scrutiny. They stopped before the door and Caspian rapped his knuckles, by way of announcing their arrival. They didn't have to wait long, Wynne heard a grunt behind the door, and Caspian opened the door and pushed her inside.

Captain Payne stood at a grand desk, pouring over the maps that were strewn out before him. He looked up momentarily, then grunted again before returning his gaze to his maps. Wynne chided herself for flinching, she would not show the captain any fear, not if she could help it. His demeanor disarmed her. She had expected him to be ravaged with darkness, on the brink of insanity, but his face was clear, calm.

"I want you to look at something." He addressed her, gesturing to the map before him. Caspian gently pushed her forward, Wynne stepped forward cautiously, stealing a quick glance at Caspian. He nodded slightly, a way to encourage her without giving himself away. Steeling her nerves, she peered down at the map.

"It's a map." She replied carefully, doing her best to minimize the sarcasm from her tone.

"I know it's a map, but I want you to tell me what you see." He snapped; his face turned into a scowl. The scar on his jaw was twisted in a way that made him look angrier than he sounded.

"You can't see it?" Wynne remarked.

The captain's black eyes, darkened, "If I could, there wouldn't be any need for you to read it." He clenched his jaw, while he looked at her, "Now, I want you to tell me what you see." The captain remarked, taking a step back and fixing his gaze on her.

"It's an island." Wynne stated, looking back at the map. It was a tiny one too, but unmistakably still an island.

"What else?" the captain prompted, "Tell me everything you see."

Wynne's anxiety was raging, "It's unmarked, the island itself is blank."

"Damn." He swore, his eyes darkening. Wynne swallowed; her palms had begun to sweat.

"There's a legend, but it's just a compass." She squinted, "There are words along the outside though." Wynne added, hoping it would be enough to keep her from getting whipped.

"What does it say?" He replied, leaning in slightly.

Wynne's breath caught in her throat, "Find my keeper; awaken me in the deep; journey with me to challengers end to find me in the looking glass." The same words she had heard in her dream.

"Damn it!" He shouted, throwing a fist down onto the desk, startling Wynne, "Anything else?" He grumbled.

Wynne swallowed, "There are two swords, crossed into an 'X' with," she squinted, leaning forward more to get a better look, "what looks like a serpent's head." At this the captain perked up and stepped back towards the desk.

"Where?" he demanded, forcefully.

"Here." she said quietly, pointing to the spot on the map. He quickly saw where she pointed and pulled out another map, his face was clouded in obvious frustration. Wynne watched him in trepidation, half expecting him to explode in wrath, but it never came.

"Take her to her cell." The captain muttered to Caspian, "Close," the captain muttered, studying the maps, "we're so close." He whispered, as Caspian led her out of his quarters and returned her back to her cell.

"What's happening?" Wynne asked, as Caspian closed the door behind her.

He shook his head, "He won't say for sure, but" Caspian took a deep breath in, "We're nearing the Keep."

Chapter 16

Days passed in utter isolation. The only person Wynne ever saw was Caspian and that was only when he brought her food. She had hoped that he would give her some information about her mother, about the keep—anything really! But the days passed in silence, and she felt more alone now than she had ever felt. To further the feeling of absolute seclusion, she hadn't had any more dreams either. Instead, her sleep had been fitful at best. Her anxiety had soared to new heights and slowly her appetite began to decrease. She reminded herself that she needed strength and nourishment, but over time she lost the desire to even care. Caspian grew concerned and had protested her lack of appetite. But no matter how hard he persisted, her stubbornness won out in the end.

Then, one morning, when she awoke, she found Captain Payne standing in the doorway, staring down at her. There was a glint in his eye, one that reminded her of the delirious man she had encountered that night during the storm. She shrunk away from him, half expecting him to jump at her and rip her to shreds. Movement beside him caught her eye, it was Caspian, and suddenly she did not feel as anxious.

A wave of relief washed over her; however small it may be, was comforting. Caspian stepped around the captain and silently bound her wrists, before helping her to her feet.

"Wouldn't want you trying something foolish." Payne remarked, noting the look of confusion on her face as she watched Caspian bind her. Wynne studied the captain and found his appearance to be greatly altered than the very first time she had met him. Inside of tanned skin, his face seemed grey and stretched thin, strained almost. His eyes, though dark, somehow had darkened and lost their spark. It was as though she was looking to lifeless pits. The sudden change in appearance was so drastic it made her tremble.

"What are we doing?" Wynne dared to ask.

Payne smiled, "It's time." He spoke with an excited tone, though his face remained lifeless. Payne turned and left the way, with Caspian following behind her, keeping a steady hand on her elbow. The sunlight greeted her as she stepped out onto the main deck. It was blinding, but a welcome change to the dark dinginess she had grown accustomed to. A cool breeze, danced across the deck, caressing her cheeks with the fresh scent of salt and brine. She inhaled deeply and felt all her senses awaken. Had she not been bound, preparing to face unknown terrors, it would have been a beautiful afternoon.

But it was not meant to last. There on the horizon, was a thick wall of fog, waiting for them. Wynne felt a sudden shiver run down her spine, the presence of fog was chilling and somewhat unnerving.

"Where are we?" Wynne ventured, studying the wall of fog they were heading towards.

"X marks the spot." Payne announced, as if that would tell her exactly where they were. She thought of the X on the map that she had seen days ago, and fear rippled through her. The X on the map was accompanied by a serpent's head. Whatever lay beyond that wall of fog, was something Wynne was not too keen on finding. The sunlight dimmed as the ship sailed right into the thick wall of fog.

Wynne peered out at the fog that had swallowed them. The sudden lack of sunshine sent a cool tingle up her arms. Something sinister lay beyond, hidden in the mist. Wynne could feel the tension in the air, like it was waiting, ready to pounce on them at any slightest movement. But the ship sailed forward, to some unknown point in the distance. Damp, clammy air chased away the remaining warm sea breeze. Wynne shivered; she would have preferred to stay below deck.

As the ship cut through the clammy air, she heard voices starting to whisper all around her. Straining to hear, she took a step towards the railing, but they flitted away into the fog, just out of reach. Tingles ran down Wynne's spine. She glanced over the side of the ship. A ghostly face stared up at her.

"Beware!" it hissed, then sunk back into the black waters.

"Did you hear that?" She asked, taking a step back from the railing.

"Hear what?" Caspian asked quickly.

"The voice." Wynne whispered. Caspian glanced from her to Payne smiling slightly.

"They're speaking to you." Payne remarked, "Many have sailed into these waters, few have ever returned." Just off the starboard side, something stirred in the water. A sudden feeling of darkness flooded her, searing into her chest like a hot blade. Gasping, she doubled over and clutched her chest. Pain ripped through every limb, straight down to her fingertips. Something, a blackness, tugged at her, drawing her into a deep, dark chasm.

"What's happening?" She huffed. Payne's expression of fear was short lived as he looked from her to the dense fog.

"He knows we are here." Payne whispered. Something warm brushed against Wynne's fingertips, it was a hand. She grasped it, clinging to it as warmth flooded through her body. Caspian helped her to her feet, then released her hand, taking with him the warmth he had shared. But the darkness she felt swelled then vanished, silence, painful and still filled the air. Out of the black depths, starboard side, rose a great sea serpent.

Wynne stepped back; jaw dropped in utter disbelief, as the beast rose to tower high above the ship. She had never seen anything like it. The beast was massive and bigger than the ship itself. The creature was covered in sparkling onyx scales, that fitted together like plates of armor, but glistened like gemstones. Deadly spikes aligned the serpent's spine, all the way up to its head. Wynne felt her stomach drop as the creature opened its mouth and Wynne saw rows and rows of razor-sharp teeth. The great serpent screeched and instantly the men aboard ship started to shout in horror.

"Hello old friend!" Payne yelled, unsheathing his sword, "Where is your master?" He shook the sword in front of him. What damage he through he could inflict upon this beast with his measly sword, was beyond Wynne's imagination, but she had to give him credit. His voice was not quivering, and his face was void of fear. But that still didn't make her feel any safer. The serpent wavered back and forth, momentarily, and then he attacked. The serpent would have destroyed the ship is one fell swoop, but, in one quick moment, Payne had grabbed her and forced her to stand before him. Wynne screamed, but instead of attacking the ship, the beast stopped just short of crashing directly into her. Her breath caught in her throat, as the serpent eyed her carefully. Wynne held her breath as the serpent leaned closer to her, breathing in deeply—as though he was smelling her. Wynne flinched when she saw the beasts' eyes widen.

"Go get your master!" Payne hissed, "We have unfinished business." He added. The serpent slowly rose back up, his eyes fixated on her. The serpent then uttered a guttural scream before diving back under the black water.

"Keep your course!" Payne yelled over his shoulder to the helmsman, "Men, prepare for battle!" He cried. Suddenly off the port side, the serpent's spikes could be seen racing towards the ship. In an instant, the serpent rammed the ship. A big wall of black water toppled Wynne, sending her to her knees. Caspian hauled her back up to her feet.

"Are you alright?" He shouted, fumbling with the binding on her wrists, removing them altogether. She nodded, but the sound of metal clashing caught her attention. She gasped as she saw a battle unfolding on the main deck, but who were they even fighting? Wynne squinted, trying to get a better look. The men were unlike anything she'd ever seen before. They were creatures of seaweed, all of them lurched inhumanly across the deck, attacking all who stood in their way.

"What are they?" Wynne gasped, but Caspian had no time to answer as one of the seaweed warriors descended upon them. Caspian easily maneuvered and sliced the head off the warrior—who crumpled into a heap of seaweed. It was washed away by a wave, as though it had never even been there in the first place.

"Stay close!" he shouted. The serpent continued to ram the ship, but the helmsman stayed the course. When the serpent surfaced again, he wailed, as if calling to someone. Another black wave crashed onto the deck. Wynne gasped as a man appeared from nowhere, crouched, and ready for battle. This man was not like the seaweed warriors but was fully a man. Though, there was something different about him. As the wave receded from the deck, he stood and locked eyes onto her.

"Find my keeper." A voice echoed across her ears. She swallowed, was this man the keeper?

"Caspian!" Wynne cried, but he had already noticed the warrior and had also noticed his attention locked onto her. He pushed her behind him as the man strode towards them. The man's sword was drawn, his gaze was intense. In just a few strides, he was on top of them. He lashed out in furry. Wynne tumbled back and watched the warrior descend on Caspian. Caspian easily met the man's first two strikes, but then the tide shifted. The warrior smirked and spun faster than Wynne had ever seen someone move. He was easily the superior swordsman; every move was filled with power. He moved like fluid, swift and agile. His motions were precise and flawless, it was like watching an elaborate dance, one that he knew like the back of his hand.

In one swift motion, he knocked Caspian's sword from his hand and knocked him to the ground. To her horror, Caspian crumbled to the ground, unconscious. The man turned and moved towards Wynne. But Wynne was already moving, backing away from him, but he was faster. He snatched her up, pinning her to the railing. His strength was unfathomable, as he held her up, effortlessly.

"Hello halfling." He purred.

Wynne frowned, "What do you want from me?" she demanded, her voice trembling ever so slightly.

"You are weak." He stormed, his watery gray eyes searching her face, "You are incomplete." He whispered, picking her up like she was nothing. She screamed, trying to fight him, but it did not faze him. Carefully, he learned towards her. His lips, cool like water, brushed against her ear, sending a shiver down her spine.

"Let the waters of the deep," he whispered, "awaken what's buried deep within." Then he hurled her over the railing. She screamed as she plunged into the black waters below.

Chapter 17

Falling into the water, felt like falling through ice. The frigid water stole Wynne's breath, stabbing into her chest like a dagger. Panic set in as she clawed her way to the surface. But something was holding her down in the water. Whispers stirred all around her. Frantic, Wynne opened her eyes and saw hundreds of ghostly figures surrounding her. Wynne jerked as something grazed her foot, kicking her legs furiously, she had to get to the surface. But, no matter what her effort; she remained suspended in the water. The ghostly figures drifted towards her with whispers hissing in delight.

Wynne was trapped! A cold, bony hand grabbed her arm. A hollow-eyed man drifted in front of her, smiling. She jerked away, but just as she did, another hand grabbed her. Soon, hundreds of hands were grabbing her. Panic seized her as the foul hands ripped at her skin, like they wanted to suck the life out of her.

"Awake!" A deep voice whispered past her, like a cool breeze. A tug, in the pit of her stomach formed, like a weight pressing against her. It steadily grew, stronger and with it the tightness in her stomach increased. Instinctively, she folded her arms over her stomach.

Cold spindly hands continued to rip at her. Then everything around her suddenly calmed. The tug in her gut spread throughout her body and in a moment, she felt herself reaching for a small strand—a string of energy surrounding her. It was hidden in the water around her, all she needed to do was grasp onto it. She grabbed it and light exploded from her chest. All the hands that gripped her melted away. An energy coursed through her body and all her senses exploded. Water ripped past her; every single droplet rolled past her skin. The salt from the black waters left a tang on her tongue. The currents rushed around her, bubbling with delight. She opened her eyes and instead of the hollowed-out ghosts, there was just one figure floating before her.

Wynne did not recognize him. His hair was dark, like the sea, and was suspended in the water around them. He had a beard, but it was long and floated in the water before him. His eyes were black, but they were filled with light, that almost seemed to glow in the dark waters. At his side, he carried a trident.

"Hello halfling." His voice sounded in her head. How was he doing that? And why was he calling her a halfling?

"Speak to me with your mind, child." He chuckled. His lips turned up into a smirk, watching her with amusement. He extended his trident towards her and gently tapped the tip of it to her forehead. Instantly a flood of warmth passed through her entire body, and she felt a hum of energy sing around her.

"What have you done to me?" she shouted in her mind.

"Child of sea and chaos, you have found yourself at last." He announced, opening his arms towards her, but his face was filled with sorrow, *"But it is still not enough."*

"What's not enough?" She demanded.

"Your journey is not yet complete." He floated closer to her, grabbing her arms gently in his hands.

"I don't understand." Wynne yelled back.

"Unleash my curse, retrieve what was lost, and claim your birthright." His voice thundered in her mind, shaking her very core. Wynne felt herself shaking her head. This was too much; she did not understand what he was saying or what even her role in this needed to be. He smiled, faintly and holding her cheek tenderly in his hands. She half

108

expected his hand to be cold, but she felt the hum of warmth beneath his fingertips, like she wasn't floating in water at all.

"Do not let your mother's sacrifice be in vain, halfling." He whispered tenderly, his thumb stroking her jaw. Then he reached back, placed his hand behind the great serpent's head and together the two swam off in the dark. Wynne watched them, could feel them leave, but as soon as she felt them disappear altogether, something darker filled their place. Full forms of ghosts loomed before her in the darkness, hallowed out holes for eyes stared back at her. They hissed at her, they were angry, she could feel their wrath leeching out into the water around her. Frantic, she kicked her legs, forcing herself to the surface, but it was not fast enough. The figures whirled through the water towards her, screeching.

Wynne felt the hum of water all around her and reached for it. She wasn't sure what exactly to expect, but to her surprise, the water answered. Bubbles of water gathered at her feet, surrounding her ankles, she felt power building beneath her. Then just as the screeching ghosts closed in, she unleashed the power beneath her feet and propelled herself to the surface. Sweet precious air filled her lungs as she broke the surface. But her triumph was short lived, the water beneath her was churning, and she could hear the hiss of angry screeches beneath her. They were coming for her again, the blackness beneath her raged.

Wynne still had a slight grip on the water around her, but the ocean was too strong, and she was losing her grip. The darkness beneath her, clamored, trying to grab at her once again. She looked around her frantically and spotted the ship, not too far in the distance. She was close enough for them to throw her a line.

"Help!" she screamed, waving both arms frantically above her head. Had someone seen her or had her voice just been lost in the wind? Wynne started swimming, but the swell of waves tossed her about, making her progress forward taxing at best. Bony fingers scrapped across her ankle. She screamed again, kicking her leg violently, hoping to fend off any of the ghostly creatures closing in on her.

"Help!" She screamed again, louder. Wynne thought she had seen someone looking over the side of the ship; but, before she could

109

take a closer look, a cold boney hand clamped down on her calf. She screamed as she was pulled under completely. Wynne fought tooth and nail, despite her dwindling energy. She tried reaching back out for the strand of energy that she could feel pulsing around her, but exhaustion had set in, and despair had clamped down on her. Just as she was, she was about to give up, a warm arm wrapped around her, and she felt her body pulled into a warm embrace as she was yanked back to the surface. She choked and found herself looking to Caspian's soaked but concerned face.

"I got you!" He cried. A cry of relief escaped her lips as she wrapped her arms tightly around his neck, burying her face into his shoulder and holding on to him tighter than she had held onto anything. A rope had been tied to Caspian's waist, and they were heaved back to the ship, through the tempest of dark waves. It took considerable effort for them to be hoisted to the deck. Despite Caspian's grip, Wynne felt as though she would slip through his grasp at any moment. So, she clung to him, relishing in his warmth and comfort.

Wynne frantically searched for the man with the trident, but he was nowhere to be seen. The serpent was above the surface again, lunging above them, grazing the ship's hull, and flinging Wynne and Caspian wildly out to the side, before slamming again the wood. Both grimaced, as shock splintered through their entire bodies. Wynne felt a cold hand grab her, yanking her up over the deck railing. She found herself staring up into the warriors, pale, bluish face. He studied her for a moment, then a small smile cracked over this hard features.

"Welcome home, halfling." He whispered, "Your journey has just begun." His grey eyes held her gaze.

"Journey with me to challengers end to find me in the looking glass." He quoted. Wynne felt her confusion just growing.

"I don't understand." She muttered.

He leaned forward and kissed her gently on the forehead, "You will little one, in time you will learn the truth and you will claim what's been lost." A black wave crashed on deck, covering him and an instant later he disappeared with the receding wave. Wynne felt hands on her arms, helping her to her feet. She glanced quickly to her side and saw Caspian looking at her with a mixture of fear and concern. Her legs were shaky, and she clung to him for support. Wynne quickly looked around but was shocked to find the serpent and seaweed warriors had vanished.

Sunlight pierced through the fog, sweeping over the ship and the crew like a wildfire. The delicate sun warmed Wynne's chilled body, kissing her damp calmy cheeks. Wynne wiped the tears from her cheeks and looked at Caspian who was wide-eyed, pale, and trembling slightly. But her moment of relief was short lived. A hand clamped down on her arm, spinning her around. Payne loomed before her with a bloody lip and cut shoulder. He apparently had a run in a seaweed warrior and had some injuries from the encounter. Wynne stiffened, recoiling from his touch.

"Did you enjoy your little swim?" he sneered, shoving her towards the rail, "welcome to the keep, Miss Hunt." She looked out across the blue waters and felt her heart stop. It was the island; the same one she had seen in her dreams.

Chapter 18

Orders had been given and the dinghy that would take them to shore was prepared. Payne's grip remained firm on her shoulder as they waited. Wynne, however, had fixed her attention on the horizon—on the island before them. It was smaller than she had imagined. But still looked large enough to hide something of value on. The water was a bright blue, lightening into a bright teal green closer to shore. The beaches were lined with bright white sand, that seemed to glisten in the sunlight. And the island was covered in bright green foliage, and no doubt teeming with tropical life.

Once the dinghy was lowered, Caspian threw the ladder over the side of the ship and climbed down the dinghy. Wynne internally still felt extremely shaky, she could barely keep herself upright. Had the black waters affected him in any way? Had the ghostly figures tried grabbing at him as well? He moved with ease and didn't appear to be shaken up in anyway. Though his face was slightly void of color, he acted as though nothing had even happened.

Wynne climbed down after him, followed by several other crew members and then Captain Payne. Wynne took her seat next to

Caspian, at the front of the dinghy, the rest of the members filed in, one by one, until Payne took up the rear. After a few moments of fumbling with the hooks and ropes Caspian managed to disconnect the dinghy without tipping them over. They were off moments later, the other crew members, rowing the boat for shore. Wynne heard shouts above, as the other crew members prepared the second landing party. There would be two landing parties, twelve people in total would be going to shore. She swallowed, she hoped, twelve would be returning.

Caspian's shoulder brushed against hers, bringing her focus back to the dinghy. *I'm the only friend you've got on this ship.* Caspian's words echoed in her mind, haunting her. Did he know she was thinking about those very words. Did he know how much hop she had placed on his shoulders? He was her lifeline. The warmth of his shoulder seeped into her own and butterflies rose in her stomach. She looked away, fixing her gaze on shore. Her nerves were getting the best of her. She glanced over her shoulder to see how far they'd done when she saw Payne eyeing her with narrowed eyes. Taking a deep breath, she turned back around, trying to ignore the eyes she knew felt on the back of her head.

Wynne's nerves grew, she felt antsy and stated to fidget. Clutching her palms, she felt the sweat start to build. Water splashed over the side, seeping into her skin, and tingling strangely. To combat her nerves, she started bouncing her knee with lightning speed. But her anxiety mounted. Fixing her eyes on the island, she tried convincing herself that everything was going to be alright. She would make it out at the end of this crazy nonsense. She would make it off this island.

A warm hand grabbed her knee, gently. She jumped, looking down at the hand, then to the owner. Caspian was staring at her strangely, his face revealed his concern; but there was something else there too. Was it worry, or was he trying to warn her? She looked away, but his hand lingered. His touch only made her more nervous.

Another wave lapped over the side of the dinghy, practically dousing her. Her senses instantly buzzed; sharpening with such clarity it startled her. Energy pulsed through her body, she gasped. Caspian eyed her again, sending more frenzied nerves throughout her body. Panicking, she started to bounce her leg again, trying to give her nerves an outlet.

"Keep us away from the rocks." Payne barked. The crew members at the oars, grunted in response. Wynne spotted the clump of rocks Payne was eyeing. They were black and jagged, dangerous to anyone or anything that dared to come too close. She winced at the thought of crashing into them. But maybe that was just the thing she needed.

A sudden tug in her gut made her gasp. She felt Caspian's eyes on her; but ignored him and wrapped an arm around her throbbing gut. It was not painful, but it was an unfamiliar sensation. What was wrong with her? As if in response, the dinghy moved for the rocks, despite the men frantically trying to steer them away. The tug in her gut tightened and the black rocks loomed before them. The dinghy was too close, there was no time to correct. Wynne braced herself and a second later the dinghy splintered on the monstrous pile of sharp rocks. The force flung Wynne into the sea, she vaguely heard shouts and yells around her before they all crashed into the sea.

The water was bone chilling, but strangely comforting. She felt like she had just been embraced in a loved one's arms. She felt the familiar hum of energy wrapping around her, wrapping around her, a tantalizing thrum at her fingertips. The water swept her away, and miraculously she missed all the sharp rocks, spitting her out on the other side. She choked, glancing around half expecting to see the other men, but she was all alone. A swell of relief swept over her. She spotted the shore, and started swimming, once she reached land she would decide where she needed to go.

As soon as her feet touched the sand, she ran. She dove into the jungle, pushing her way through the trees. She trembled in excitement, or was it fear? The only thing she knew was she needed to put as much distance as she could between her and Payne. Her mind went briefly to Caspian, but she quickly shook that thought away. She couldn't worry about him now, she needed to get away.

Wynne ran without any sense of direction; she figured it was better to be lost than to be a prisoner. Once she felt her chest fill with fire, she slowed her pace down to a walk, stumbling over vines and tree roots before stopping to take a breath and to assess which way she needed to go. The small of saltwater hit her, stronger than ever before, she was still close to the ocean. She walked a little ways further then came to the edge of the jungle. Cautiously, she glanced out onto the beach, when she was sure the beach was empty, she stepped out onto the sand and let herself relax for the first time in a long time.

Wynne walked along the beach until her feet started to ache. Part of her wanted to put more distance between her and Payne and part of her was convinced she had gone far enough. But still, she walked on. Finally, she dropped to the sand, completely exhausted. The waves lapped up onto her toes, the cool sensation filled her with a brief sense of relief. After sitting for a minute with her toes in the water, she decided to make camp along the tree line. If anything, the trees would help shield her in case anyone came to look for her. She sat with her back against a tree and watched the sun set.

Beautiful pink and purple hues, with navy undertones illuminated the sky. A soft gentle yellow, outlined the bright sun that slowly dipped under the horizon. It was breathtaking and for a few moments, time seemed to stop and enjoy the sunsets beauty. She smiled and thought about what she'd give to see a hundred more sunsets, just as beautiful as this one.

A hand clamped down on Wynne's mouth. Her eyes flew open and found grey blue eyes staring down at her, Caspian! Angry, she took him off and stood, brushing off the sand. She stared at him, warily, then glanced towards the beach looking for Payne and the rest of the crew. The beach was empty. She turned back towards him and noticed a gash above his eyebrow—a brow knit in anger.

"You're bleeding." She said softly, hoping to deter the wrath she saw in his eyes.

His eyes narrowed, "No thanks to you!" He growled.

"Me?" Wynne cried defensively.

"Yes, you!" He pointed, "You have a funny way of showing you trust me!" He cried, not hiding any emotions. Wynne's face flushed in indignation.

"What was I supposed to do?"

"You're supposed to trust me!" He snapped.

"I panicked!" Wynne cried, throwing her hands up.

"You panicked?" Caspian scoffed. Anger filled her entire body, she clutched her fist, stepping towards him, her anger propelling her forward. But Caspian was not deterred, he held his ground and stared right back at her.

"I've been tortured, beaten, dragged through a monster infested lagoon, thrown overboard, accosted by water demons and—and—" She thought back to the man she had met under water, the one that had touched his trident to her forehead and shuddered, "After all of that, you expect me to not run at the first chance I get?" Wynne cried as tears flooded her eyes and down her cheeks. Caspian stood there; arms folded completely relaxed.

"Are you done?" He asked. She clenched her jaw but nodded, wiping the tears from her cheeks, "You owe me an apology." He demanded slowly.

"For what?" She balked. She didn't owe him anything.

"You ran!" Caspian barked.

"Of course, I did!" Wynne retorted, folding her arms across her chest.

"Why?" He questioned with lethal calm.

"I already told you why!" Wynne shouted back.

"Why did you run?" Caspian demanded, his words slower and more forceful. Wynne clamped her lips shut. She couldn't quite bring herself to admit to the reason behind what she did.

He took a step towards her, "Do I need to repeat myself, again?" He questioned, eyes narrowing, voice lowering to a threatening tone.

"I had to!" She snapped.

"Why?"

"Because" she screamed, then stopped as something inside her cracked, she wrapped her arms around her waist as the tears trickled down her cheeks, "Something happened to me." She whispered, her eyes falling to the sand at her feet.

"What do you mean?" He questioned; his voice had suddenly softened.

"When I was tossed into the sea," she rambled, "something happened—I just—" she faltered, "I was scared." Silence fell between them as it was a minute before she could look back up at him. To her surprise, his face was filled with sorrow.

"Find my keeper; awaken me in the deep." He said slowly.

"What?" her voice trembled.

He met her eyes, "You have allure blood, Wynne, whatever powers you have from your mother were awoken when you entered that water."

Wynne shook other head, "That's not possible." She exclaimed, her arms tightening around her waist.

"That would explain the incident with the boat." Caspian remarked, rubbing his temple.

"What incident?"

"The boat," Caspian replied, harshly, "you manipulated the currents to push us into the rocks."

Wynne gaped, "I did not!" but there was a pin prick of doubt. The feeling she had felt on the boat, had been the same as the one she had felt when she had propelled herself out of the water and had fought off the water ghosts.

"Maybe not consciously, but" he sighed, meeting her eyes, "Wynne I felt the boat move."

Wynne held up her hands in defense, "This can't be real!"

"It's very real." He said firmly, "and now is not the time to—"

"Panic?" She asked, cutting him off.

He chuckled, "You said it, not me."

"Does Payne know you are here?" Wynne asked, suddenly aware that he was indeed here, and he was alone.

Caspian clenched his jaw, "He's the one that send me to find you."

Her face paled, "Does this mean you're going to take me back?"

He sighed, shaking his head, "No." the sincerity in his eyes startled her. "Wynne, listen to me," he started, "I meant what I said I am your only friend, I will get you out of this alive." He announced confidently.

"And how to you plan on doing that exactly." She demanded, folding her arms, and eyeing him closely.

"I knew your grandfather." He said quietly.

Her eyes widened, "Prove it."

"Your grandfathers name was Ferguson, and his ship was called the Charlocke."

Wynne shrugged, "Anyone could know that it was public information."

"Ah," Caspian remarked, "but what they don't know if that it's actually the name of your later grandmother, Charlotte Locke."

Wynne pursed her lips, "That still doesn't explain how you plan on getting us out of this, alive." Wynne remarked, skeptically.

"I was a cabin boy for you grandfather," he paused "I grew up on the Charlocke and when Payne attacked, well," he paused, rubbing the back of his neck, "it gets a bit complicated."

Wynne sucked in a quick breath, "You have a lot to explain." Caspian huffed, nodding slightly. Wynne looked at him slowly, his guards were down. His face seemed less stiff, and more lifelike. Emotions, now flowed easily across his face, as though his true self was shining through some exterior he had been wearing. The Caspian beneath the mask was someone who she wanted to get to know, wanted to know his story and how he had gotten here. This was a Caspian worth getting to know, the Caspian she could trust.

Chapter 19

Caspian and Wynne walked down the beach. Wynne was on pin and needles waiting to hear his explanation. When they finally found a shady place, he sat down and took a quick drink from his canteen, before handing it to her. She hesitated, but her parched throat won out.

"So, what's your story?" Wynne questioned, handing the canteen back.

He took a deep breath, "Like I said earlier, I grew up on the Charlocke. Your grandfather took me under his wing," He smiled slightly, "That's how I met your mother and father."

"You met them?" Wynne cried, surprised.

He nodded, "Once, it was before I joined Payne's crew." Wynne sucked a breath in. Of all the things she had expected him to tell her, this was not one of them.

"What does all of this have to do with my mother, Payne and some mystery chest?" She had to asked, even though her brain hurt with the idea that she might get an answer.

"Payne has been consumed with gaining power. The more control he has over the sea; the more power belongs to him." Caspian remarked and for the first time, Wynne thought what that had meant for her mother. Her mother, who had the ability to control the waters, the ability to control what lay beneath Payne's ship with just a flick of her fingertips. That, she thought, was power Payne would no doubt find appealing, a power that he coveted.

Caspian nodded, seeing her conclusion play over her face, "He wanted your mother's gift for his own and he sought a way to do it."

"So, what did he do?" Wynne whispered.

Caspian, however, just shook his head, "This is not my story to tell." Wynne frowned, who else was going to tell her?

"So, you're not going to tell me?"

He shook his head, "No, but we will rendezvous with someone who can." He stood quickly, holding his hand out for her. She took his hand, letting him haul her up to her feet.

"And who exactly will that be?" the demand in her voice loud and forceful.

Caspian swallowed, meeting her eyes, "Your father."

They had been walking sometime through the jungle, Caspian leading the way to some predetermined destination. Wynne following behind him, but her mind wandered, trying to put together the mess that sat before her. Her father's message whirled around among the thoughts, tying pieces together that she had not even realized. *Payne is coming. Meet you at the Keep.* It had been a warning to her, and a clue that he would not abandon her. But why, hadn't he told her any of these things before now? Why had he chosen to keep this all a secret from her. Wouldn't it have been better to tell her the truth, than let her stumble into the middle of this mess with no knowledge. At the idea that her father had done that, willingly and intentionally, made her anger burn.

Then, there was the little matter of Caspian. He was in on this madness, but she wasn't sure the exact extent of his involvement. He had grown up on her grandfather's ship, the Charlocke, had even met her mother and father once, but his story halted after he joined Payne's crew. Why had he left her grandfather's ship to join Payne's crew. Was he a traitor? If he was, did that mean he was now a double traitor? The more she thought about it all, the more questions she and the angrier she became.

"I can feel your anger." Caspian called over his shoulder.

Wynne scoffed, "You would be too if you were in my shoes."

"You're not wrong." He conceded with a gruff.

"I just want answers." She sighed, feeling some of her anger fizzle off.

Caspian sighed, "You'll get them, I promise." Wynne rolled her eyes, part of her wanted to believe him, but the other part of her thought getting all the answers to her questions was never going to come. But she kept her comments to herself and fell back into step with Caspian, following him in silence.

While they walked, her thoughts wandered to something less complicating. The Avanthian folk lore. Each patron deity belonged to a certain territory of Taeren. Her patron deity, Oaran, was god of the sea and it was why their territory was the leader in ship build-ing, seaside ports and all imports from other countries across the sea. Oaran's symbol was a trident. Wynne felt goosebumps raise all over her arms. Her mother's locket had a trident on the face of it and, she shivered, the man she had seen in the ocean had been carrying a trident. Had that been Oaran? She shook her head, no! There was absolutely no way, she had encountered her patron deity. But maybe it had been a servant of his. The fact that she was even contemplating the reality of all of this was utterly absurd, but it was the only expla-nation she could give herself at the moment.

"We're here." Caspian quietly announced, looking back at her with some care. Wynne looked past him, but only saw the jungle. Caspian pulled back the tree branches and Wynne caught a glimpse of a small fire on the beach. There were three figures sitting around the fire, but they were still too far away for her to distinguish which one of them was her father.

Carefully, she stepped past Caspian and out onto the beach, mak-ing her way slowly for the fire. She felt a mix of anxiety and relief flooding through her. As she got closer to the fire, she spotted her fa-ther's big burly frame, his attention was fixed on the flames before him.

"Who goes there?" One of her father's crew members shouted, spotting them approaching.

"It's Caspian and—" He didn't get a chance to finish.

"Winnie?" Her father's voice called, and she saw him stand up quickly.

"It's me, father." She called, her voice cracking as the tears suddenly started to well in her eyes. She watched as her father came around the fire and in two giant steps, she felt herself being wrapped up in his big strong arms. The tears were now streaming down her face, all the emotions she had worked so hard on keeping them at bay were finally released. Sobs wracked her body as she tucked her face into her father's shoulder. For the first time in a long time, she felt safe, protected.

"Shh, Winnie," He whispered into her hair, squeezing her tightly, "It's alright, I've got you." Hearing his voice just made her crumple even more. She hadn't heard his voice in months! This was not the reunion she had been expecting.

She pulled away from him, wiping the tears from her face, "You have a lot to explain." She chided. He smiled slightly, hanging his head and nodding.

"I know I do. I've been waiting for you. Hello, Caspian." He turned his attention from her to Caspian, who was standing beside them, watching them in silence.

Caspian shifted slightly, "Donovan." He nodded, much too formally for Wynne's liking, "We had a bit of a detour in getting here." He added, though deciding not to mention the incident with the dinghy and her desperate flee into the jungle.

"Thank you for bringing her." Caspian didn't respond, but merely nodded, moving towards the fire, and taking a seat.

"I will tell you everything." Her father said slowly, gesturing towards the fire. Wynne took her cue and made her way towards the fire, taking a seat next to Caspian. She felt his eyes watching her as she took a seat, he looked at her curiously, she just offered him up a small smile in response. Then turned her attention to her father. His black hair had more peppering than she remembered, and the creases around his eyes had grown. But there was something else that was there, he looked tired, worn in ways that she had not noticed before.

"I'm sure you have a lot of questions for me?" He started; did he sound nervous?

Wynne just nodded, "More than you know," she sighed, "why didn't you tell me mother was an allure?"

He winced, "She didn't want me to." Wynne felt a slight sting at his words.

"Why?" She demanded, pushing past the sting.

"She wanted to protect you."

Wynne felt her anger rising, "And this," She shouted, gesturing around her, "is protecting me?" The air around the fire grew silent, "No! Protecting me would have been telling me the truth, about everything!" The anger she had been feeling, bubbled out. But her father did not recoil, he did not seem angry at her statement. Instead, he leaned forward, held his hands together and looked her square in the eye. Not challenging her emotions but accepting them for what they were.

"It was the lesser of two evils." He replied. Wynne just stared at him, waiting for an explanation.

"If I had told you your mother's secret Payne would have found you much sooner. He couldn't know she had a child. He hunted your mother, relentlessly, and he would have done the same to you. I had to keep it secret, until the time was right." Wynne pressed her fingers to her brow; her head was starting to ache, but there was more to this story that needed to be unraveled.

"Why was Payne hunting her? Was it for her gifts?" She questioned. Payne, had been searching for power, Caspian had told her that much, but what exactly had her mother's role been in all of this?

He shook his head, then rubbed the back of his neck, "It's complicated."

"Well, I'm listening." Wynne's voice was harsher than she meant it to be, but for the moment a little bit of harshness was warranted.

"Allures do not age quite like humans," he began, "your mother met Payne when they were both quite young. He was her freedom; her adventure and she was his ticket to ultimate power. Who could stop him when he had a powerful allure by his side, at his every beck and call?" He sighed, it was not one of anger but sadness, "At first, their journeys were everything that she had hoped for, but Payne

125

was not content, he wanted more. So, he convinced your mother to steal Oaran's Orb."

"Oaran's orb? What is that?" Wynne interrupted, curiosity getting the best of her.

"Legend says the orb contains Oaran's power of the sea." He answered, patiently.

"And does it?" Wynne had her doubts but had to ask anyways.

He smiled slightly, "No. But at the time Payne did not know that. He believed the orb was his ticket to what he desired most and your mother," he sighed, this time his face was twisted in a deep sorrow, "she had been manipulated and deceived into believing Payne's goals, were also her goals. She had given him her heart, and Payne used that to his advantage." Wynne felt her chest ache for her mother. Payne had seen a young woman and had used her for his own gain.

"What happened?" Wynne asked, feeling some of her anger dissipate.

"The orb was not a source of power like the legends said, but rather a conduit of power. Your mother knew this, but she was desperate for Payne to return her love, so she stole the orb for him. But she didn't know the hell she'd unleashed in doing so."

"What do you mean?"

"Payne, when he learned that the orb could not give him the power he truly wanted because he himself did not have the ability to control the power. In order to possess the orb, he needed to be an allure. Angered, he unleashed his wrath upon your mother. But she stayed with him, vowing to help him find a way to get what he desired."

"And did she?"

He sighed, "Yes. But then she learned what he really wanted with the orb. The orb can be used to transfer an allures gift to someone else, essentially stripping them of their gift. Their power would become Payne's and the orb would be his to command and use as he wished."

"He was going to take her abilities??"

Nodding, he continued, "At first he had convinced her that they would find another allure to use, but it became clear that his only intention was to use her." Wynne felt a quick surge of anger, Payne had only ever seen her mother as a tool to use, to get what he wanted, and she wanted to make him pay. But her anger was softened, by a wave of sadness, for the realization that her mother, her emotions, had been manipulated and trampled on, with no regard for her wellbeing.

"How did she escape?"

"Your grandfather. At the time, had been a crew member on Payne's ship and had grown fond of your mother. She reminded him of the daughter he once lost." Wynne nodded, remembering her grandfather mentioning a few times that he had lost a daughter once. Growing up she had always assumed it was her mother's older sister but had never questioned him about her. Whenever he had had talked about either her grandmother or his lost daughter, the sorrow that flooded his eyes, over his entire soul, was unlike Wynne had ever seen before. It had scared her, so much so, that she had no desire to be the cause of such sorrow, even for curiosities sake.

"What about the orb?" Wynne questioned, drawing her attention back to her father's tale.

"Your mother and grandfather stole it back, right before they escaped and when she did, she sealed it in a chest. A chest that could only be unlocked with the proper key." His eyes locked onto the necklace hanging at her throat, "Your mother's locket." Wynne, involuntarily reached up and grabbed the locket, holding it tightly in her hand. Everything had been revolving around this locket, now she knew why. It was the very key Payne needed to unlock the chest to the thing he wanted most. She swallowed, and now since her mother was gone, the only one who had the power Payne so desperately craved, was her. Payne wanted to use the orb now on her!

"So now what?" Wynne demanded, "Payne is on this island too, he can't get the chest!"

"That is why we must get to the chest before he does." Her father replied firmly, his confidence beamed like a light in the dark. But it was not enough to keep the fear from filling her.

"Do you know where it is?" Her father rubbed the back of his neck, the look on his face told her, he didn't have a clue where to even start.

"Your mother was the only one that new. This island was Payne's treasure keep, there are coves everywhere. But the chest was hidden in one that only she knew about and had access to."

"So, what your saying is, we are shit out of luck?" Her father's eyes widened in shock, but she didn't care at this point. High society be damned, she was on an island, looking for a treasure that could potentially kill her. Caspian, who had been sitting beside her the entire time, letting the story unfold in complete silence, finally spoke.

"I stole his map." Caspian interjected softly. Holding out a folded map to Wynne

Wynne smiled, "The one from Payne's cabin?"

Caspian nodded, "The one and only."

"You stole it?" Harshaw asked, from behind her father's shoulder. Caspian eyes, flicked to the crew member, and Wynne saw the humorous gleam in his eyes fade.

"Can't steal something that belonged to you in the first place." Caspian declared; his tone somewhat defensive as he met Harshaw's gaze.

"Nerissa's map?" Donovan questioned, looking over Wynne's shoulder at the map in her hands.

Caspian nodded, "It was one of my bargaining chips." Her father nodded, understanding what he was implying. Wynne assumed it had been given to Caspian by her grandfather, to use when the time was right. But, since she had seen it in Payne's cabin, that mean he had used it to gain Payne's trust. And now, Wynne swallowed, it was with them, not with Payne.

"That was good thinking." Her father added, but his voice sounded wary. She looked and saw distrust written all over his face, Caspian saw it too. He shrugged his shoulders, nonchalantly, before fixing his gaze back on the fire.

"We will camp here." Her father's voice boomed, breaking the tension, "Harshaw, you will take first watch," He spoke to the man sitting at his right, "then Bradley, you will take the second." He said to the man at his left. Both men said nothing but nodded in response.

"We will leave at first light." Her father added, looking at her carefully. A small smile played on his lips, she could see the relief in his eyes, but it was shadowed by something less comforting, dread.

She didn't have the energy to even think about what tomorrow was going to mean for them all, so she smiled back, trying to put as much reassurance as she possibly could in her smile before laying down. Out of the corner of her eye, she saw Caspian lay down beside her, though he was careful to leave plenty of room between them.

Wynne's mind felt like sludge. She had finally been given the answers to so many of her questions, and yet she still felt dazed and confused. She was exhausted, worn down to the bare minimum and she dreaded closing her eyes. She wanted the night to last as long as possible and prayed that morning would not break. But there was a part of her, deep down inside that coaxed her into closing her eyes, convincing her that with sleep, her mind would clear. She closed her eyes, but restlessness settled over her, so she lay there, waiting, patiently for sleep to claim her.

Chapter 20

Wynne was still awake when Harshaw and Bradley switched watches. She heard Bradley take up his post, stoking the fire that was now just fervent embers. She heard him stretch slightly, before standing and walking slowly away from the camp. He no doubt would do a few rounds along the beach to wake himself up. Wynne was wired, she had been drifting aimlessly in and out of sleep all night long. She knew once daybreak came, the exhaustion she felt would only be compounded. Caspian lay still by her side, just an arm's length away. Slowly, she turned her head to look at him, he was laying on his back, his eyes were closed, but something told her he was just as wired as she was.

"How did you end up on Payne's ship?" She whispered.

Caspian took a deep breath in, slowly, "Payne had been hunting your mother for years, he believed she was still with Ferguson. Payne knew Ferguson had helped her." His deep voice, whispered across the distance between them.

"She was with my father?"

Caspian nodded, "After they were married, they snuck aboard another ship that took them to Whaeldrake, and they started their new life."

"So, what happened to you?"

Caspian blinked, "Your mother had already died at this point, you were young. Ferguson knew it would only be a matter of time before Payne found out she had died, found out she had a daughter." Caspian's head turned to look at her.

Wynne swallowed, "What happened to my grandfather?" Wynne whispered, almost afraid to hear the answer. She had been told he had died at sea, but the details had been blurred. He had died, five years after her mother had passed, she had been ten and his death had devastated her. Not long after that, her father dove headfirst into his shipping industry and it had taken off, like a wildfire. He started to travel more, and time and time again she was left alone, to sink into her own loneliness.

"Payne killed him." Caspian answered. Wynne had expected as much, but hearing the truth of Caspian's words, did not take away the sting of sadness that swept over her.

"And so, you just, joined his crew?"

Caspian sighed, "It was your grandfather's idea."

"I'm not following you." Wynne muttered, rolling over onto her side so she could face him.

"Your grandfather knew Payne would come after you. He wanted someone on the inside to protect you when the time came. When Payne finally caught up with us, Ferguson knew it was time."

"Time for what?" Wynne asked slowly.

"He asked me to betray him, to gain Payne's trust. I had information, information Ferguson knew Payne would want."

Wynne took a deep breath in, "What information?"

Caspian sighed again, "You." He whispered, "I knew you existed. Ferguson had kept your family's location to himself, so I didn't know where you were." Wynne felt a shiver run through her body.

"But you still told Payne about me?"

Caspian nodded, though his expression was filled with remorse, "It was part of the plan, I needed him to trust me."

"And did he?"

Caspian chuckled, "How do you think I became second in command?"

She smiled slightly, "How long have you been on his ship?"

"Eight years."

"Eight years!" Wynne hissed, before covering her mouth with fingers, hoping no one else had heard her, "It took you eight years to find me?"

Caspian smirked, "Your father kept you well hidden." Wynne's eyes moved from Caspian's to her father's sleeping form, across the embers. Admitting that her father's choices and actions were in her best interest grated on her nerves, but much to her dismay, she saw some logic and reason.

"That doesn't explain how you and my father became friends." Wynne whispered back.

Caspian rolled his eyes, "I wouldn't call us friends," he grumbled, "As soon as I had the chance, I sent word to your father of Ferguson's plan."

"That was a risky move." Her voice hushed, low above the sounds of slumber still surrounding their camp.

Caspian agreed, "But it worked. I helped Payne search for you, secretly keeping your father aware of his movements. And the day finally came when we stumbled on our big break, a desperate scholar in Whaeldrake, down on his luck, had heard of a pirate offering a handsome reward for information, and he delivered." Wynne felt her stomach turn sour, there were only two scholars she knew of in Whaeldrake that she had a direction connection to, Schmidt and Boswick and she had a sickening feeling who it had been.

"And what about the locket?" Caspian rolled onto his side, closing the gap between them, he was only inches away from her.

"Your father knew you would need it. Payne knew the locket was needed and your father thought it best for you to have it, it would be safer with you than anyone else." Her father had known Payne was coming for her, and the best thing he thought to do was write her a cryptic letter. Anger bubbled back to the surface, why hadn't he come himself? Yes, he was here now, but that had not kept her from the scars she now carried.

"Why didn't he tell me any of this?"

"Would it have made it easier?" It was a thought-provoking question, but it was one that just made her anger burn even more. No, it would not have made anything easier for her. Her innocence had been used against her though, and in the name of protection. But what had it done for her? It was a far cry from protection, it bordered down right deception and manipulation.

"I was—and still am, a pawn!" She hissed; her brows knit in frustration.

He hushed her, "You're a piece in a very elaborate puzzle." That somehow did not make her feel any better. She was a pawn, and everyone was out to control what she did. Her father hadn't trusted her enough to tell her the truth, so he decided on a plan that he thought would be best for her. Payne saw her as his ticket to the ultimate power her craved, just as he had seen her mother. He would stop at nothing to get what he wanted, even if it meant killing her. And Caspian, Caspian had kept the truth from her, to go along with her father's plan and choosing to value his loyalty to her grandfather than doing what was right.

"I was whipped, Caspian!" She felt herself shake, as her emotions suddenly exploded to the surface, she felt as though she could scream, "I have been scared!" She thought of the mark on her face, her hands, and her back. Tears flooded her eyes, and she could feel the sobs in her chest fight against her control, she wanted to let her tears flow freely and her sobs wrack her body, but she couldn't bring herself to wake up everyone else, especially her father.

"I'm sorry," Caspian whispered, she felt his hand cup her jaw gently, "I'm sorry I couldn't—" his voice faltered, not able to finish was he wanted to say.

"Couldn't what?" Wynne whispered, "Stop him from hurting me? No," her voice growled, "because that would have meant giving up your secret." Her words were laced with bitterness.

Caspian blinked, shocked by her words, "No," he argued, his voice louder than a whisper now, "because I was afraid, he'd hurt you!"

"No," Wynne shook her head vehemently, "you were afraid he'd hurt you." Tears filled her eyes, as the anger she felt poured out. She couldn't lay there another minute. She needed to move, and she needed to think. She stood quickly to her feet, Bradley jumped slightly at the sudden movement but didn't say anything to her as she passed, making her way towards the water. All the information she had learned from her father and Caspian tumbled in her mind, but her emotions raged within her, making it hard for her to decern true intentions.

Chapter 21

Wynne stood in the water, staring out at the ocean. The sun was just peaking over the horizon, greeting the new day with warm, fresh sunlight. The lagoon beyond her was alive with the sunlight, gold reflected off the water, back up to the arriving sun, almost looking like it was lit on fire. The sound of waves roaring onto the beach, echoed around her. It was a constant rhythm that reverberated deep in her soul, it grounded her, giving her some sort of peace even when her mind raged with her own chaos. She was trying to process it all, from the information she had been given, to the emotions she felt when digesting it all. Everything had been planned—but not by her, by those around her. But only one person, truly, lay at the center of everything that she now faced. Her very own mother. Tears pooled in her eyes, stinging as they rolled down her cheeks.

To be lied to, deceived by someone who was supposed to be your rock, the person you could always counted on, stung like nothing she had ever experienced before. Her mother had lied to her and even though she had died before even having a chance to explain everything to her, her own father had continued to uphold that lie.

Wynne had been a pawn and she was still a pawn in this whole mad adventure, just like her mother. Wynne shook her head, that thought brought little consolation, considering she now had scars down her back and face. Scars, that could have been avoided had she just been told the truth in the first place. How different would things have been, if she had been told the truth of who her mother really was? She folded her arms against her gut, trying to hold herself together. Yes, it would have made a huge difference. Her father and her, could have gone together, retrieved the orb themselves and hidden it! Or, better yet, they could have found a way to destroy it altogether! Payne would have been foiled and she wouldn't be in the position she was in now.

A splash of water behind her, brought her out of her thoughts. She stiffened, as somebody approached her, stepping up carefully beside her. Out of the corner of her eye, she saw Caspian, standing close beside her. He looked just as exhausted as she felt. Who knows, maybe she looked just as exhausted as he did. She huffed, she probably looked worse than he did.

"You were right." His deep voice broke the silence, then tension in the air seemed to lift, "I was afraid of what Payne would do to me if he found out. I didn't want to risk my position." His voice crackled slightly, "But I also didn't want him to retaliate on you. He would have if he had known the truth." Wynne nodded. Payne would have used Caspian's treachery to inflict more pain upon her, that she had no doubt of. The guilt for lashing out at him, seeped in, but what was said needed to be said.

Wynne felt a little bit of herself crumble at his words, "You were just as much of a pawn as I have been in this whole mess." It was the truth. Caspian had followed her grandfather's orders, joining Payne's crew, risking his life—all to protect her when the time came.

"Why did you do it?" She questioned. She wasn't sure if she had been in his shoes, he would have gone through with it. For the first time, she truly looked at the man standing beside her. He stood like a mountain beside her, still youthful and strong, despite the crinkles that had started to form around the corner of his eyes. A darkened beard filled his face, but his grey blue eyes were so soft and gentle, contrasting the deep, sternness of his voice. What had he lost when he agreed to this plan? Did he have a family? Wynne swallowed, was there someone who loved him, patiently waiting for him to return? A jealous streak surged through her, startling her somewhat. When he met her eyes, Wynne took a sudden step back, startled by the raw emotion found there. Deep gratitude, shown through his eyes, it was something she had not expected to find.

"Your grandfather gave me a home when I desperately needed one." He answered, quietly, "He was the family I needed. I would have done anything he asked me to." He added, his voice barely above a whisper. Wynne felt a burning sense of pride for her grandfather, and it made her smile. He had been the type of man who had a large and generous heart, despite his prickly past. He did not let that stop him from making a difference in the lives he met, and that included Caspian.

"Plus," Wynne added, "When your charged with protecting someone as beautiful as myself, it comes with its own benefits." A playful smirk played across her lips as she draped her hand dramatically over her chest, feeling the slight burn of embarrassment on her cheeks. But the comment had its desired effect. Caspian tipped his head back and laughed. It was deep and robust, like it had been waiting for a chance to announce itself. Wynne was astonished and pleased all at once. The laughter seemed so foreign and yet so natural coming from his lips. The sound of his laughter, played on her ears and she desperately wanted to hear it again.

His eyes narrowed as he returned the playful smirk, "And, of course, all said benefits must be explored." His response had its desired effect as well. Wynne felt her face flush completely and her toes curled in the sand beneath the waves still lapping at her feet. She could not maintain eye contact, and felt her gaze drop quickly to the sand. He chuckled, the deep sound reverberating in her bones, making butterflies in her stomach. What was the matter with her? She cleared her throat, still feeling the burn of embarrassment on her cheeks, as she looked back up at him. But before she could give her playful response, she felt a gasp escape her lips as she took in the beach at his back.

"What's wrong?" Caspian questioned, eyeing her with concern before glancing over his shoulder.

"I've seen this beach before." Wynne exclaimed, pushing past him, and making her way back onto the beach.

"What?" Caspian questioned, falling in step next to her. Wynne studied the beach; everything came flooding back to her. She had seen this exact beach in her dream!

"In my dream," she exclaimed, loudly, "my mother had shown me this exact beach!" The sound of her voice alerted her father and his crew men.

"What's going on here?" Her father demanded, coming up behind her.

"This beach," Wynne declared, facing her father, "I've seen it before, in one of my dreams." Her father's face showed no hint of excitement at this revelation and his crew members exchanged a brief look of doubt. But Wynne paid them no mind, she was sure of what she had seen, of what she was remembering now.

"Tell me about your dream." Her father commanded.

Wynne swallowed, her nerves were jumpy, "I was on this beach, with mother," she started, keeping all her attention focused on her father, "she showed me this beach, a gorge, a river and a lake." She decided to leave out the part of seeing other figures at each of these locations.

Donovan nodded, "They are way points."

"Waypoints?" Caspian interjected.

"Markers, left by Nerissa," he sighed, "clues for Winnie."

Wynne felt the burden rest back on her shoulders, "To find the looking glass?"

Her father nodded, "To where the chest is hidden." Silence fell among the group. This was the moment they all had been waiting for and dreading at the same time. Ignoring her fear, Wynne unfolded the map, taking a deep breath in as she realized the map had changed once again. Now that they were on the island, the map was filled completely. Wynne took a moment to study it carefully. The spot where they stood, contained a little dot and across the island, there were other little dots. But the one marking that caught her attention, was the little star on a lake. That was the looking glass, and it was the place they needed to go.

"You didn't happen to steal a compass while you were at it, did you?" She questioned, glancing up from her map she turned to Caspian, hoping he had a compass with him.

"I have one, here." It was Bradley that spoke, reaching down to his pocket quickly, pulling out a small compass.

Wynne smiled, "Thank you." She gingerly took the compass from him and fixed her attention back on the map. Her grandfather, years ago, had taught her how to read a map, using a compass. The memory brought a smile to her face, her grandfather had always made it a point to teach her something useful every time he had come for a visit. After he had died, it had meant one less person coming to visit her, it had made her feel even more isolated at the time.

"There." She said at last, pointing out to a spot in front of their group, "That is the way we need to go."

Her father looked at where she pointed, nodding, "Then that's the way we'll go." He waved his arm, "Harshaw and Bradley will bring up the rear, Winnie," He smiled, "You'll lead." She exhaled forcefully through her nose, and without hesitating stepped forward. Caspian fell into step behind her, followed by her father, and his two crew men at the rear. *Find me in the looking glass.* Those were the words haunting her mind as she dove into the jungle. She would find the looking glass, she would find the chest her mother had left for her to find, but what she was going to do with the chest once she found it, was still up in the air.

Chapter 22

I t took a total of ten steps into the jungle for Wynne to realize she preferred the beach and ocean to the dense jungle and vines that now surrounded her. The air surrounding them was hot, muggy, and entirely too dense for her to keep a deep breath. Every breath she took was nothing but hot sticky air, and never seemed to quench the heat that had built at the back of her neck. Not only was the air insufferable in the jungle, but everything around her seemed to move. Every couple steps she took, she felt herself flinch with every moving tree branch or bug that seemed pleased to invade her personal space. But despite the constant mugginess and threat of insects at every corner, the group trudged on, doing their best to follow the course Wynne followed.

Hours later, when Wynne's legs had started to burn, she signaled for them to stop. She was relieved that Harshaw and Bradley had brought fresh water with them. They passed around their canteens, letting everyone take a quick drink. The fresh water quenched the dryness that had formed in her mouth and throat but did little to quench the heat hanging in the air around her. She was convinced nothing would take away the mugginess surrounding her.

The group sat there for a little while, each collecting their breath and preparing themselves for the next stretch. Wynne knew they needed to make as much ground as possible this first day. Payne would be looking for her. Her only advantage was that the island was larger than she had anticipated, and they had the map. There was a chance Payne still might find them, but she hoped when they did it would be too late for him to stop them. But, she winced, there was also a possibility that he would find them before they could get to the chest and then there would be hell to pay.

"Ready?" She cried, standing quickly to her feet with newfound motivation. She glanced around at the men surrounding her, and though they did not complain, she could see it in their eyes, they were tired. She checked her map, verifying that they were still on course, then dove headfirst into the jungle, with the men behind her in tow.

The journey through the jungle was slow. The foliage was thick, beautiful to look at, but impossible to move through. Vines covered almost every surface and were stronger than they appeared. At one point Wynne glanced up, hoping to see blue skies, but was surprised when all she found was green staring back down at her. How the sun even managed to poke through was a mystery. But soon, the jungle started to grow darker and darker. Before she knew it, they were stopping once more, this time, for the night. As Bradley and Harshaw started to work on a fire, Caspian decided to look for some food. Wynne sat awkwardly beside her father, wondering if she needed to say anything, or just let the silence between them grow. She decided on the later. Not, that she didn't want to engage with her father, but so many things had happened since she had last seen him and strange as it may be, she felt like an entirely different person. She wasn't entirely sure her father would recognize the woman she was becoming. So, the silence, for once was welcome.

Just as Harshaw and Bradley got the fire lit and going, Caspian ducked into view, with an armful of fruit. He took a seat next to hear and started to pass out the green and red skinned fruit. It was soft to the touch and looked decent enough. She took a cautious bite, not entirely sure what to expect. It was juicier than it looked, sweeter, with a soft delicate, fruity flavor. The explosion in her mouth was tantalizing and made her return for a second bite, before she knew it the entire fruit was gone, leaving her with nothing but a strange looking pit in its place.

"What will Payne do now?" She directed her question to Caspian. It had been weighing heavily on her mind all day now and she need-ed to break the silence that had fallen among the group.

Caspian swallowed, "Probably try to follow us." He threw his fruit pit over his shoulder.

"That doesn't bother you?"

He shook his head, "Should it?" Wynne bit her lip, it bothered her.

"He'll follow us until he knows he can get the upper hand." Her father spoke up. Caspian nodded in agreement.

"And when will that be?"

Her father shrugged, "There is no telling."

"When we get to the looking glass." Caspian remarked, firmly. Wynne's eyes drifted off to the jungle, she had a million questions still flitting around in her mind.

"What are we supposed to do when we get there?"

"We find the chest." Her father remarked.

Wynne rolled her eyes, "Yes, but after that, what do we do with the chest then?" Up until this point, there was no plan beyond that.

"Easy, you destroy it." It was Harshaw who spoke, though Wynne felt as though he had no opinion in what they decided to do. Her fa-ther must have seen the thought play out in the expression on her face, because he cleared his throat, giving her a pointed look.

"If we destroy it, Payne will not be able to use it." Harshaw con-tinued. The group nodded in agreement, but something tugged at Wynne's gut, why was she doubting the plan to destroy it? It didn't make any sense, but she couldn't bring herself to voice the doubts in her head.

The men decided on the schedule for keeping watch. They con-veniently left Wynne out of the rotation. She felt snubbed that they did not want her in the rotation, but she was also relived that there was a better chance of her getting some well-deserved sleep.

Wynne hadn't realized until they had stopped the second time, how tired she was. She had been running on empty fumes for a while, and her body was slowly shutting down. She lay down, as close to the fire as she could and closed her eyes, letting the sounds of the jungle lull her to sleep. The jungle sounds, however, were unfamiliar and strange to her. It was loud, and there were constant sounds of beings moving in the darkness, though they never came close to their camp. Despite being exhausted, her mind stayed alert with every rustle, snap, or crack. But, after some time past, her exhaustion won over and soon she had lost herself to sleep. But even though she had found sleep, she had opened the door for her dreams to begin.

Wynne was standing, alone, in a cave. She looked around her and found her mother standing at her side. Just beyond her mother, her father stood, eyes wide, watching her mother. Neither her father nor her mother seemed to even notice her standing there. And even stranger still, her father was holding a little girl's hand. Wynne frowned, trying to get a closer look at the little girl. Wynne gasped as she realized that the little girl's hand that he was holding, was her! She had to have been five years old or so, about the age she was when her mother had died. Wynne felt a shiver run down her spine, as her younger self stared back at her. It was a bizarre enough event to make her skin crawl.

"There has to be another way to do this, Nerissa!" Her father shouted; his voice echoed along the cave walls.

"Don," her mother sighed, "we've talked about this—I cannot undo it."

"But this is our daughter's life, Nerissa!" Her father cried, the agony in his voice made Wynne's heart ache. Her mother just winced, slightly.

"Don't you think I know that!" She snapped; her face flashed in anger. Wynne's younger self shrunk away from her mother, hiding slightly behind her father's leg. Was this a memory?

"Then what do we do?" He asked, looking down at the little girl who now had tears growing in her eyes, "How do we protect her?"

"By giving her the only thing, I can give her." She whispered.

But her father just frowned, "Do you know what that could do to her?"

Her mother nodded, tears now streamed down her face, "It's the only way Don." Her mother then turned suddenly, looking straight at her. Wynne felt her mother's hands, grasp her face. But Wynne couldn't stand to look at her, and she stepped away, her mother's hands falling reluctantly from her face.

"I've been beaten!" It was her five-year-old self that shouted. Her voice childlike as she shouted and started to cry in anguish. But her scream had been enough to cause her mother's shoulders to sag.

"You don't understand," she whispered through her tears, "but you will." She grabbed Wynne's hand and together they started to walk through the jungle. They crossed a bridge, then came to a river. When they crossed, a face leered up at her, but vanished just as quickly as it had appeared. Wynne had a nagging feeling she had seen him before.

They followed the river until they came to a lake. It was beautiful, a deep dark blue that was still as glass. Her mother pulled her to the edge and then stepped out on top, like the water was completely solid. Wynne glanced up at her mother and saw her hand outstretched, waiting for her to take it.

"Don't be afraid." She whispered and Wynne took her hand, stepping out onto the glass. She looked down in amazement and saw her wide-eyed face starting back at her. She felt a drop and looked up, but the sky was clear. But even so, she felt another and another, yet, she wasn't wet. She looked up at her mother, who smiled sadly then lifted her hand and Wynne dissolved into the glass.

Chapter 23

"Wynne!" Caspian shouted, shaking her awake. She jerked up, feeling a momentary rush of panic, but she was not in her cell, she was in a jungle, lying on the ground. Wet ground. Thunder rumbled above while lightning illuminated the jungle around them, casting haunting shadows all around them.

"We need to find shelter." He called. She nodded, looking across the doused fire to where her father had been. He was standing on his feet, waving an arm at them.

"Caspian! Winnie!" His voice sounded loud over the rain. Caspian helped her to her feet, gently pushing her in the direction her father was motioning. But they did not move as quickly as they should have.

Rain descended upon them in a torrent of heavy drops. The group stumbled through the rain, soaking everyone in a matter of minutes. Caspian stayed close to her side, picking her up when she stumbled or slipped. Harshaw shouted up ahead, Wynne squinted through the rain to see what he had found. Her eyes slowly adjusted and saw a giant rock wall. How was this going to help them? If anything, this was the opposite of what they needed. But as they got closer, Wynne saw what had attracted Harshaw to the spot. All along the rock wall there were little coves that one could tuck themselves into and would keep most of the rain from soaking them to the bone.

Caspian pushed her forward, and she dove into the first little cove she saw, Caspian following behind her. She saw her father dive into a little cove next to them and Harshaw and Bradley, she was assuming had found their own little shelter. Caspian settled in next to her, but only after did she realize how close they were. She felt her cheeks flush, as she was suddenly aware of her body pressed against his chest.

"Nothing like a nice rain shower to wake you up out of a dead sleep." Caspian remarked. Wynne, however, couldn't look him in the face, not when she was this close, so she just nodded, hoping it was still too dark for him to see the blush that burned her cheeks. But her lack of response just resulted in him chuckling. The sound of his chuckled vibrated in her chest.

"What?" She questioned, forcing herself to look up at him.

"Just enjoying one of my benefits." His voice was low, and she could almost see the mischievous grin that she could hear in his tone. It did not help the blush on her face to go away either.

"How long do you think it will last?" She questioned, changing the topic altogether.

"Hard to say." His reply had a hint of amusement to it, as if he knew she had changed the topic on purpose, but mercifully, he let the matter go entirely.

The rain thundered around them. Wynne was surprised at how much water was coming down from the sky at one time. But, as the light in the jungle began to lighten, the rain fall started to slow. Then, just as quickly as the storm had appeared, it had vanished altogether, leaving the jungle and all its inhabitants, completely soaked. Wynne thought the rain would have chased away from of the mugginess from the jungle, but it only managed to make the air even thicker and stickier.

"We should get going." Caspian stood quickly to his feet, stretching his limbs out as he did so.

"Everyone alright?" Her father's voice called.

"We're good!" Wynne shouted, as Caspian helped pull her to her feet. Stretching out her limbs just like a cat. The group gathered back together, and everyone looked miserable. Wynne hoped that as the sun got higher, they would dry off, and would find some sort of comfort after their evening.

"The rain was in our favor. It washed away our tracks." Harshaw stated, glancing around them at the jungle.

"A little rain won't deter Payne." Caspian mumbled.

"Then we must get going, the more ground we make today, the more distance is between us and them, if they are following us." Her father stated quickly, giving Wynne's shoulder an assuring squeeze. She quickly consulted her map and checked their course with her compass. Once she was sure of the direction they needed to go, she dove headfirst into the jungle, and the group followed close behind.

They trudged through the jungle at a rather slow pace. The ground beneath their feet was soggy and unpredictable, and the rain from the shower lingered, not evaporating even as the jungle around them got hotter. But Wynne was struck with just how beautiful the jungle was. The green hues that permeated all the leaves and plants, were all different and seemed to glow with a vibrancy that she had never seen anywhere else.

After they had been walking for a while, Wynne signaled for them to stop. Her legs were burning, she was hot, and her throat was parched. She took a quick glance at everyone in their group, everyone's faces were flushed a bright red, and sweat trickled down their faces.

"Let's rest here for a bit." Her father called, taking a quick seat before wiping the sweat off his face.

"Tired?" Wynne asked Caspian, stepping up next to him.

He huffed, "How can you tell?"

She shrugged, "The bright red on your cheeks and the flow of sweat is a pretty good clue." He laughed, wiping the sweat off his brow.

"What's in it for you?" Wynne questioned, taking a swig from the canteen.

"What do you mean?"

Wynne gestured to the jungle around them, "At the end of all of this, what is in it for you?" He had given up so much of his own life, was there anything at the end of it for him?

He glanced at her, "A ship." His face beamed, "Your grandfather left it to me." Wynne felt a smile grow on her face. She was not surprised her grandfather had done that for him. Quite frankly, he deserved it.

She raised a brow, "A ship? Just a ship?"

He chuckled, "And a crew."

"Well, you have to have that." Wynne replied smiling.

"The sea if the only life I've ever known." He stated curtly, "what else would I do?" She thought for a moment but didn't have any spectacular alternative. She didn't know him well enough to suggest anything else.

"What about your family?" She asked, but Caspian did not answer right away. His attention seemed fixated on the ground beneath his feet. Had she crossed some line? Maybe talking about his family was a sensitive subject.

"What was my mother like?" She questioned, deciding it was best to change the topic all together.

"She was lovely," he replied, a faint smile on his lips, "I met her a year before she died." He stopped and offered her another fruit. She graciously accepted, suddenly aware of the gnawing sensation in her gut. "I met you too," he added with a grin, "you were little though."

"What?" She laughed.

He nodded, "You were really little.".

Wynne blushed, "I'm so sorry, I don't remember meeting you."

"You were about," Caspian reached low, barely a foot above the ground, "this tall, give or take." Wynne laughed again, shaking her head. She couldn't believe he remembered that. But she didn't exactly doubt his story either. She had distant memories of visiting her grandfather with her mother, but the details were fuzzy, and she did not remember meeting Caspian either.

"You look like her, you know." He said quietly, "Except for your eyes." He added looking over his shoulder at her.

Wynne smiled, looking at her father sitting a few feet away, "I have my father's eyes." Her mother's eyes had been a deep navy blue, like the churning deep ocean waters. Wynne on the other hand had her father's light blue eyes, like the light currents that washed up over the sand. Wynne grabbed the compass, unfolded her map, and decided to check their course once again.

"Everybody ready?" Wynne called, folding the map back up and returning it to her pocket. Without much argument, they resumed their trek through the jungle. They dove further into the jungle, but this time Caspian stayed by her side. There was silence between them, but it did not feel awkward or strained. She thought back to when she had been young, if her mother had not died, would she have gotten to know Caspian? Would they have grown up to become friends? It was a thought worth pondering, but she couldn't determine a satisfying answer.

They trudged through the jungle in silence, trying to cover as much ground as they could. Every now and then, they would stop for a momentary break and Wynne could check her compass and map. The exercise was draining, Wynne was no resigned to the idea that she would be forever wet and sticky. But still she managed to keep their pace steady, with Caspian sticking close to her side.

"What will you name her?" She asked, huffing slightly.

"Excuse me?" Caspian exclaimed.

"Your ship?" She smiled, "You'll have to christen her, so" she glanced out of the corner of her eye, "what will you name her?" He thought for a moment.

"I haven't thought that far." He shrugged, "What do you think I should name her?" Wynne pursed her lips, trying to think of something clever.

"Oh, what about the Pathfinder?" She smiled, nodding slightly, but he was unimpressed, "Np? Alright," she hummed, "How about something more mysterious, the Storm?" He cracked a slight smile.

She shook her head, "No—that's a horrible name, oh!" she cried, "How about something a little more classical?" she glanced at him and saw the look of hesitation, "The Hesperus!" She exclaimed. Caspian leaned his head back and laughed. The action, still unfamiliar to her, startled her. Her cheeks flushed, she liked his laugh, it made her feel warm inside.

"I'll consider them." He remarked, the laugh left the remnants of a smile of his face. She pushed aside a branch and stopped, gasping. There stretched out before them was the gorge, just like the one she had seen in her dream.

Chapter 24

The gorge was massive with sheer cliffs that plummeted to a river below. Together they stepped forward, a breeze caressed her cheeks as she peered cautiously over the side. The river was far below them; she felt her hand and feet go numb.

"This is the place I saw in my dreams," she looked beside her at her companions, "but there should be a bridge, somewhere." She scanned the expanse and found what she was looking for. The bridge was just a few feet away and swayed ominously in the wind. It was dilapidated and Wynne wondered if it would even hold them.

"Looks promising." Bradley grumbled, Harshaw grunted in agreement.

"There is no other way across." Wynne declared. She felt her father step up beside her, whistling slightly as he peered down into the gorge.

"It looks much further than I thought." Wynne whispered, glancing to the opposite side.

Her father nodded, "But it looks sturdy." Thankfully, the bridge did appear to be in good shape. Another breeze, brushed by her, though something about this breeze felt different. Wynne heard a gentle laugh in the freeze. She frowned, straining her ears to see if she could hear the sound once more, but all she head was the breeze whispering past her and into the jungle.

"You alright?" Caspian whispered beside her.

She nodded, "I thought I heard something."

"Harshaw, Bradley!" Her father's voice boomed as he flicked his head to the bridge. The two men didn't hesitate to step forward. They would be the ones to test the integrity of the bridge. Together they stepped out onto the bridge, slowly making their way over the wooden planks. The bridge dipped and creaked with the new weight, but it held fast. When they made it a little over halfway, her father stepped out onto the bridge, following them. His steps were not as cautious, but still he appeared to tread as delicately as possible across the bridge. Once he had made it over, he turned back around and with a big beaming smile, motioning for them to come over.

"Ladies first." Caspian eloquently drawled, gesturing to the bridge.

Wynne frowned, "How chivalrous of you." She grumbled, stepping forward and taking a cautious step onto the bridge. She gripped the rope railing as she took tentative steps out onto the wood panels. They continued to hold firm. But the bridge began to sway in the wind, and it dipped slightly under the addition of weight. Carefully, she inhaled a deep breath, forcing herself to continue shuffling forward. Everything about this bridge, screamed at her to retreat, but she knew it was the only way forward. She swallowed her nerves, gripped the roper tighter and moved her feet, slowly picking up the pace.

Caspian stepped onto the bridge behind her, immediately making the bridge dip even further. The nerves in her chest fluttered as the bridge now groaned in protest. Together, they shuffled, slowly towards the center of the bridge, the closer they got the more the bridge rocked. A breeze sent a shiver down her spine and filled her nose with a sweet earthen scent and the faintest hint of the sea. Wynne gripped the rope tighter as they descended to the lowest dip, the center of the bridge.

The wood beneath her creaked as a gust of wind rose, rocking the bridge even more. Had it been this windy for her father, Harshaw and Bradley? A shiver of fear ran down her spine. The breeze trickled past but this time, she heard a gentle whisper. She stopped, straining her ears once more to hear the sound.

"Everything alright?" Caspian called behind her, clearly not too pleased that she had stopped, but she ignored him. Everything inside of her was telling her something was not right; she had the same tingling sensation she had had when they had sailed through the ghost invested waters. She shuddered; she would do everything she could possibly do to avoid what had happened after feeling that tingly sensation. She continued forward, all her senses were on high alert as she took step after step.

"Wynne." This time the whispering voice said her name. She froze, where had that come from? Movement caught in the corner of her eye as the breeze rippled past her.

"Wynne?" Caspian's voice made her jump.

"There's something out there." She called over her shoulder, to her relief he did not question her, "Keep moving." She called again, quickening her pace. Just then a gust of wind came ripping down the gorge, slamming into the bridge, pitching it dangerously back and forth. Wynne gripped onto the rope railing, feeling the coarse strands rip into her skin, as she was pitched to the side. She felt her stomach fly into her throat. Wynne's head whirled to the side, as a figure appeared, flitting in the wind. When Wynne met the woman's gaze, her eyes narrowed and her face turned into a sneer, another laugh escaped her lips. The woman, made of swirling air and what looked like clouds and wind circled around them, Wynne following her with her eyes, as she stopped, hovering above the bridge.

"Caspian." Wynne gestured behind him. He frowned, but turned to look, she could not see the reaction on his face, but she hoped beyond all hopes, that he was seeing what she was seeing. His shoulders tensed, part of her was relieved, but the nerves she felt washed away all her relief. The woman stared them both down, still wearing the smirk on her face while her laughter flitted past them in the wind. Ever so carefully she lowered herself towards the bridge, and just as her foot touched the wood, it exploded, sending a shock wave through the entire bridge.

"Wynne," Caspian yelled turning quickly towards her, urgency filling his eyes, "run!" He commanded; she did not hesitate. Turning, she dug her heels into the wooden planks and started to run.

"Winnie!" Her father's voice called, from somewhere above her. His voice was panicked, which meant he could also see the woman behind them. Wynne felt Caspian at her back, his sturdy hand pressed to her lower back, pushing her forward, faster, and faster. Wynne glanced over her shoulder, the woman behind them continued to advance and every step she took, the wood splintered beneath her. Every wood plank that shattered to her touch, sent a shock wave through the bridge, causing Wynne's stomach to fly into her throat with the sensation of dropping.

"What is she?" Wynne screamed, pushing herself to move faster.

"An Etheri!" Caspian yelled back. It made sense, an Etheri was a child of Estris, goddess of the sky. Wynne swallowed; they were just like Allure's, but their gifts pertained to power related to Estris. Hence, Wynne grumbled, the exploding wooden planks from a woman made entirely of swirling air and clouds! Wynne looked, once again, over her shoulder, but stumbled in shock. The woman had now moved from the wooden blanks to hover over the rope railing. It was the only thing keeping the bridge from collapsing completely.

"Caspian!" Wynne shouted, fearing etching itself into her very tone, but he did not look.

He pushed her forward, "Keep going!" he yelled, "We're almost there."

Wynne met the woman's eyes, "This is the point of no return, there is no going back." The woman whispered, her haunting voice melted into the wind, surrounding them, sending shivers down her spine. The woman touched her foot to the rope, which severed immediately, causing the bridge to twist. Wynne screamed as the rope she clutched so tightly in her hand, fell to her side. She turned her focus to the land, just within her grasp, on her father, who stood with an outstretched hand, waiting for her to be close enough for him to grab. The bridge shuttered once more, and Wynne felt the other side railing fall away from her grasp. She screamed again as she fell forward, grasping tightly at the wooden planks beneath her.

The rope snapped behind her, sounding like a gunshot. The ground beneath her feet fell away. Instinctively she dove for the wooden planks, grabbing on tightly as she felt the bridge drop beneath her, taking her and Caspian with it. She held in her breath as they were sent plummeting to the cliff side. The impact of crashing into the cliff was too much. The sudden jolt made her grip falter on the planks, and to her horror her fingers slipped off the wood. She screamed, closing her eyes shut, as started to fall, sheer panic filled her mind and soul. This was it; this is how she was going to die, careening down a gorge in the middle of some unknow island. But just when she thought her life was over, a hand grasped her arm, it was solid and sure, holding onto her with a vice like grip. Her eyes popped open to see Caspian holding onto her, his face straining as he held her in one hand and held onto a single wooden plank. He was holding them both up, how he was doing it, she did not know.

"Climb!" Caspian ground out, the strain in his voice matching the lines on his face. Frantic, her eyes searched for a way to do just that. The adrenaline, pumping through her veins held to clear her focus. She saw the wooden plank, just above her grasp. She looked at Caspian, and nodded, trying to let him know she saw what he was talking about. Bracing herself, she took a deep breath and pulled herself up, just barely far enough for her hand to grab onto the wooden plank. Caspian yelled under the strain, but she kept her grip on his arm. She hung there, for just a moment, trying to collect herself, trying to settle the nerves that wracked her chest. Then, after a single breath in, she quickly moved her second hand from Caspian's arm to the wooden plank.

"You good?" Caspian called from above.

She nodded, "Yeah!" She confirmed, looking up to make sure he himself had grabbed the wooden plank. To her relief he was already moving up the remainder of the bridge, clearing a way for her to follow. Wynne wasted no time in climbing up after him. It took every effort within her, to keep her arms from shaking, and her legs from giving out on her. Instead, she focused on the solid ground above her, where her father stood, wearing a worried look as he watched them helplessly climb up what was left of the bridge.

Caspian made it to the top first, Harshaw and Bradley helped him up over the ledge. Wynne was not far behind him her arms and legs burning, her chest fluttering with the remaining adrenaline. Her father was waiting for her with an outstretched hand and as soon as she was in reach, he grabbed onto her tightly and heaved her the rest of the way up. Solid footing had never felt better. As soon as her feet hit the dirt, she sunk to her knees, the quivering she had been keeping at bay for so long, finally took over. Warm, sturdy arms wrapped around her; her father buried her into his chest.

"Are you alright?" He asked, the worry in his voice was undeniable. His eyes scanning her from top to bottom looking for any sign of injury.

Wynne nodded, but her body shook, "Just a little shaken." She managed, surprised at how unstable her voice sounded. Her eyes moved past her father to where Caspian sat. His face was pale, and he too seemed shaken. Seeing him like this, suddenly reminded her that he was human. Up until this point, he had always been the strong one, had never shown her much emotion. But this, this was the human side of him and maybe it was the side he didn't want her to see, but it was the side of him she appreciated the most.

Together, the group sat there for a few moments in silence. Wynne was grateful for the chance to still her racing heart and settle the nerves that bounced recklessly through every limb in her body. She stared at the gorge they had just crossed, searching for the woman in the wind, but she was gone. In fact, there was not even a trace of the wind to begin with. Just as quickly as she had appeared, she had come, wreaked havoc and disappeared without a trace. But the message she had come to give, had not been lost. Any doubts that Wynne had about returning to the beach, had been silence when the bridge had been destroyed. There was only one way off this island, and it was to continue forward. She shivered; she wasn't entirely sure what the outcome would be when they did reach their destination.

Carefully, she dug the map and compass out from her pocket. It was a miracle that they were still in there. Slowly, she opened the map, scowling slightly at her fingers that continued to shake like leaves. She popped open the map and studied it carefully. They had made it, barely, over the gorge, and the trail on the map led next to a river. In a moment, a memory from her dream flashed before her, she and her mother had crossed a river. Each time though, Wynne had seen a man's face. She shook her head, hopefully that did not mean we would try to drown them when they got there.

"Where to next?" Bradley asked, handing her the canteen for a quick drink of water. She was grateful to have something cool to wash away the dryness in her throat. She had not realized until then how thirsty she was. Apparently almost falling to your death means you also become dehydrated.

"To a river." She said simply.

"Are there going to be any surprises there as well?" Harshaw asked, with much more of a sneer than Wynne had the ability to handle.

"I didn't know that was going to happen to the bridge!" She snapped, lunging to her feet, much faster than either she or Harshaw expected. Harshaw jumped back slightly, tipping back off his heels. Wynne felt a hand on her shoulder, reigning her back in, she glanced to the side and spotted the owner of the hand, her father. She half expected a warning gaze to be directed at her, but instead he was looking as Harshaw.

"This island is not like others. We can't expect this journey to be easy." His voice held a bit of anger and a majority of rebuke. Harshaw simply nodded, it would be the only apology she would get.

"Nerissa wouldn't have made this journey easy for anyone." Caspian added softly. Her father froze at the sound of her mother's name, but after a minute, nodded in agreement. Wynne saw the flash of pain fill his face, and she wished she could reach out and ease the pain. But she knew that would be a foolish attempt. What her mother had done, it had affected both her and her father, more than she had ever realized.

"We should get going," Bradley spoke up, breaking the tension that had suddenly grown among them, "before we lose any more daylight." He added, much more softly. Wynne nodded, shoving the map and compass back into her pocket, before diving into the woods. She didn't care if they followed her or not, her adrenaline was far from gone, but she needed to move. The crash would come later, moving as much as possible now was in everyone best interest. Caspian fell into step next to her. His face was still pale, but he appeared to be much more stable than just a few minutes ago. She was grateful he was walking beside her and not behind her.

"Are you still as shaky as I am?" She questioned, just loud enough for him to hear.

He nodded, "But I need to move." Then he felt the same antsy feeling she did too. She shouldn't have been surprised. They had both been so close to falling off that bridge.

"You saved me," She whispered, "again." She added with a twinge of sarcasm, hoping to get the color to return to his face.

He smiled slightly, "You'd never forgive me, if I hadn't." It was her turn to laugh. She couldn't remember the last time she had laughed, and it felt good. It was as if some of the darkness that she had been feeling for some time had been lifted.

"True, so it's a good thing you caught me." She smiled, pushing deeper into the woods, but her smile quickly fell.

"What's wrong?" Caspian questioned, glancing at her sidelong.

"I have a feeling there is someone waiting for us—for me—at the river." She said slowly, barely above a whisper. She wasn't sure why, but she didn't want her father of his crew men to know, at least not yet.

"Why do you say that?" Caspian asked, keeping his voice equally as low.

"Because there's been a man in my dreams, every time my mother and I cross." His haunting face still leered back at her from her memories.

"And you think he's going to do something?" Caspian's voice was low, as he glanced back at their companions. Wynne glanced too, though she did not think any of them could hear their conversation.

"I don't know," she confessed, "it's just a feeling." She added. The feeling of impending danger lingered, no matter how hard she tried to shake the feeling, it would not go away. Every time she had crossed the river with her mother in her dream, she had seen a man's face, usually staring up at her in the water. But did that warrant the unease she felt?

"We'll be alright." Caspian reassured, smiling slightly, "We've made it this far." He added, a little lighter heartedly.

She chuckled, "We aren't even close to the end of this."

He studied her for a moment, "We'll make it to the end." He playfully jabbed his elbow into her arm, pushing her slightly to the side.

"I hope you're right." She sighed, smiling slightly before returning her focus on the ground before her. They still needed to cover as much ground as they could. Though, with the destruction of the bridge, she wondered if Payne would even manage to catch them at all. But again, that sinking feeling in her gut returned. He was still out there, and she had a feeling that her journey with him was not yet finished.

Chapter 25

The group tarried on for several more hours, before Caspian finally suggested they stop to find some shelter for the night. Wynne couldn't have agreed anymore with his suggestion. Her body demanded rest, her legs felt heavy, like bricks. Thunder rumbled above them. Wynne glanced up at the sky through the jungle branches, grey clouds were rolling in, and ever so slowly, the jungle darkened around them. But, to her relief, they found a little nook in the side of a hill, almost hidden from view. Just as they settled in, and gathered some wood for a fire, the rain started to drizzle.

Wynne watched in awe as the jungle was swept away in a wall of water. The ability for so much rain to fall at one time was unbelievable! The sound alone was incredible. No longer did it have the gentle pitter-patter she loved, but now it roared through the trees. It splattered violently against the jungle leaves, drenching the earth beneath them, consuming the entire jungle. Thankfully, the nook they had stumbled on kept them relatively dry. The space, however, was small for the five of them, she ended up squeezed in between Bradley and Caspian. The group sat in silence, watching, and listening to the rain and thunder rumble around them.

Her father took charge in delegating the watches for the evening, though Wynne wondered if the watches were even necessary at all. Caspian, volunteered for the first watch. She almost protested, thinking that he, out of all the men, needed the most rest. Wynne bit her tongue, knowing that he wouldn't appreciate the objection, and it would bring attention on her from her father, that she wasn't entirely sure she wanted right now. So, she kept her mouth shut and watched everyone else settle down, and after minutes all three were fast asleep. The pitter-patter of rain above them, helped to lull them to sleep. But she could not sleep, her mind was wandering aimlessly, evading sleep.

"This reminds me of when I was a child." Caspian whispered. Wynne turned slightly, curious to hear his story, "I was born in a northern seaside town."

"Of Gallanmar?"

He nodded, "It rained like this every now and then and every time it did, I loved every second of it."

"What was your childhood like?" She asked.

"Broken," he sighed, "My father left when I was eight. He broke my mother's heart." He started, "I was ten when I left to be a cabin boy on your grandfather's ship." Thunder rumbled, loudly above them, but the rest of their group still slumbered on.

"Is your name really Caspian?" She asked. He chuckled, the rumbling sound filled her chest with warmth and put a smile on her face.

"I was named after my father."

She started, "Your father's name was Caspian?" It wasn't unheard of, naming your son after their father, but Caspian's name was such an unusual one, she found it hard to believe there was more than one Caspian in this world.

"No," he shook his head, "I changed it after he left."

"So," she mused, raising a brow, "what is your real name?" She questioned.

He shook his head, "That's my secret." He replied, a mischievous gleam filled his eyes.

Wynne folded her arms, "Is there anyone here who doesn't have secrets?" She frowned, "I will find out!" She remarked, matching his mischievous gleam, "I have my ways, you'll see."

He shook his head, "Your resilience is admirable."

"Thank you." She purred.

"Annoying" he added, "but admirable." He replied smugly.

Wynne ignored him, "Do you have any siblings?"

"Two brothers and a sister." Wynne tried to picture him as a brother, wondered if he had had good relationships with them before he had left.

"And your mother, what was her name?"

He smiled, "Rosalie or Rosie for short." His smiled faded, "I haven't seen or heard from them in years."

"Will you find them once this is all over?"

He shrugged, "I'm not sure, we didn't exactly part on good terms. I was supposed to be an apprentice at a shipbuilder's warehouse, and I left without telling any of them that I was leaving."

"Ten-year-old boys are not known for their outstanding decision-making skills." Wynne stated, "and mothers have a way of loving their children, against all odds." She remarked, nudging him slightly with her shoulder, "I have a feeling she'll be delighted to see her little Charles, all grown up!"

"Charles?" He laughed, "That is not my name." He smirked in a whisper, shaking his head, his smile still lingered.

"You're right," Wynne grimaced, "Charles is such a snooty name." She thought for a moment longer, "What are your siblings names?"

"William, Gregory and Eleanor."

"Well, I can cross those names off my list of potential names then," She smiled "Which is a shame really," smirking, she taunted him, "because you look so much like an Eleanor."

Caspian rolled his eyes, "Funny."

Her smile grew, "In all seriousness though, I think they'd be excited to see you. Excited to know that you're alive and well."

He shrugged, "They might not even remember me—they were all so young when I left." His voice was wistful and almost got lost in the roar of thunder and rain around them.

167

"Maybe not, but you won't know until you try." She pulled her knees to her chest, "At least you have a family." The words were out before she had a chance to hold them back.

He studied her for a moment, "You do have a family." His expression was soft and gentle.

"Not really," She whispered, shaking her head as her eyes drifted across the fire to where her father lay, "My father is the only family I have and he's always away on business—so, it's usually just me and my servants."

"What would you like to do?" Caspian's voice cut through the rain and the silence that had settled between them. The question had startled her, she'd never really thought about it before, nor had anyone asked her.

"Travel." She said dreamily, "I'd like to see the other territories, experience their culture and see their history."

"Your grandfather should have left you a ship and a crew." he remarked, making her chuckle.

"That would have been a delightful surprise."

"What would you have named your fine vessel?"

She pursed her lips, "It would have to be something elegant and fierce," she mulled for a minute, "the Tempest!"

Caspian chuckled, but shook his head, "Too serious."

"Well, then what do you think a good name would be then?" Wynne questioned with a pointed look.

"The Calypso."

Wynne smiled, "I would name it anything, if it meant a chance for me to travel."

He nudged her shoulder, "Maybe, one day you will."

She sighed and learned her head back, "Maybe." It was a good thought, and maybe someday after their endured this mess, she would do just that. Caspian looked out at the continuing down pour of rain.

"I don't think the rain is going to stop." He muttered.

"Well, this," she looked up at the shelter surrounding them, "isn't too bad." She snuggled down beside Caspian, his warmth seeped steadily into her own body, keeping away the chills from the rain.

"Are you going to be alright?" She questioned, feeling her eyelids becoming heavy.

He nodded, "I'll be fine." He whispered, "Just get some sleep." She nodded, her eyes were already closed, sleep waiting to embrace her completely.

Wynne stood in a river, holding someone's hand. She looked up, she was holding Caspian's hand. Her cheeks flushed, but she didn't pull away. Something shifted beneath her, she looked down and saw the water moving. A shadow loomed above her. Wynne glanced over her shoulder to see a man made entirely of water standing before her. At his side, was a sword, that was drawn, but he made no move to attack them.

Wynne tightened her hand around Caspian's, but her hand was empty. Whirling around, only to find herself all alone. Panic seized her as she forced herself to turn back around and face the man standing before her.

"What do you want?" Wynne cried.

"To prove your worth." He purred, leaning towards her, "To prepare you for what you must do—for what you must claim as your own." He peered down at her; his face held a mix of curiosity and sadness. Wynne glanced at the sword dangling from his hand.

"Are you going to hurt me?"

He shook his head, the sadness in his face grew, "I will challenge you, but only for proof."

"Proof of what?"

"Your worth!" He shouted, his voice bellowing all around her. Then, all was quiet and she was left standing on water that looked just like glass.

"You are the only one worthy." Her mother's voice sounded behind her. She spun and found her mother standing before her.

"What do I have to do?"

"Find me in the looking glass."

Wynne's eyes popped open. The rain had stopped, and sunlight had started seeping through the jungle. She frowned; her head was resting on something soft, warm. Her eyes widened as she sat up quickly, glancing at Caspian, whose shoulder she had just been using as a pillow. His head was resting on the wall and ever so slightly she saw his lips curl into a small lazy smile as he opened one eye.

"Did you sleep alright?" She asked quickly, feeling the flush in her cheeks grow.

"I did," He sat up slowly, "until someone decided my shoulder would make a great pillow." He purred, "How did you sleep?" He gave her a knowing smile. Her face just flushed even more; it took her a minute of fidgeting to still her nerves.

"I had the weirdest dream." She replied, rubbing the kink from the back of her neck, "We were at the river and then," she frowned, glancing around their shelter, Bradley was awake, but her father and Harshaw were still lying still, "I was at the looking glass with my mother."

"You had a dream about him?" Bradley spoke, a grin plastered on his face as he glanced at her over his shoulder.

Caspian smirked, "I do have that effect on the ladies."

"Not with my daughter." Her father's voice grumbled.

Wynne laughed nervously before giving Caspian a pointed look, "Don't get too excited," she remarked, "You disappeared as soon as a man with a sword disappeared." Caspian chuckled, standing quickly to his feet before stretching his limbs out like a cat. By now, Harshaw was also awake with all the exciting chatter, though the expression he worse was sour at best.

"You've been having dreams?" Her father questioned, coming close to her side. His voice was tender but there was also remorse in his blue eyes.

She nodded, "Just of mother and this island," she gestured, "nothing completely earth shattering." She added pointedly.

He winced, "I know we haven't really had a chance to talk, a chance for me to explain."

She held up her hand, "I am not sure you could explain any further than you already have, what's done is done. No amount of explaining is going to change anything." His shoulders fell slightly at her words, the guilt must have been weighing heavily on his mind.

"Mother made choices and now we are the ones left to deal with those choices, whether her intentions were good or bad." Wynne spoke quickly, trying to convey as much comfort as she possibly could into her words. She did not blame her father for what was happening, even though she desperately wanted to point a finger at someone, she couldn't. She had been wrestling with all her emotions and anger ever since she saw her father sitting by the fire on that beach. But where had that gotten her, nowhere. She was still on this island, and she was still searching for the looking glass, no amount of blame was going to change that.

"Once this is over though," Wynne remarked, "I want to sit down, have a nice cup of tea and talk."

Her father smiled, "I promise, we will do that as soon as we get off this blasted island."

"Let's head towards this river you keep dreaming about." Harshaw drawled, rubbing the back of his neck. Wynne scowled but bit back her retort. Instead, she pulled out her map and compass, determining their course quite quickly. The sooner they got on their way, the sooner they made it to the looking glass the sooner this would all be over.

Chapter 26

Wynne dove into the jungle, with her course set, and fresh new determination. Caspian fell into step behind her, followed by her father, Harshaw and Bradley. Everyone was silent as they trudged through the jungle. The journey had slowed some due to the rain the night before. The ground beneath them was soggy, making their footsteps labored and unsure. But they managed to set a decent pace, regardless, covering ground quicker than Wynne could have hoped. The stopped a few times for water and to eat the occasional fruit. Despite the juicy sweetness of the fruit, Wynne was growing tired of eating nothing but fruit. She longed for something salty and savory, anything but sweet.

The group continued to trudge along through the jungle, with each step bringing them closer to the river they would need to cross. In the back of Wynne's mind, she thought back to her dream, to the man made of water. He had told her that he was going to prove her worth, because she was the only one worthy. Worthy of what though? The man holding the trident had told her to claim her birthright, was that was she needed to prove she was worthy of doing? And what exactly would that mean when she claimed it?

Though many of her questions had been answered, more questions centering around her mother remained and she wasn't sure if she'd ever truly know all the answers to them. The only person that could give any credence was long gone. Had her mother even been alive at this very moment, would she have been honest with her? Would her mother have told her the truth, or would she have chosen to keep the truth hidden for as long as possible? There was no real point in asking the question either, she would never get an answer.

"Do you hear that?" Caspian questioned stepped up beside her, drawing her from her thoughts. She strained her ears for a moment, listening carefully to the jungle around her. The chatter of birds filled the majority the jungle sounds, but there was a rushing sound in the distance. Almost like wind, blowing through the tops of the trees, but there was no wind.

"The river?" She questioned, recognizing the familiar sound.

Caspian nodded, "We are close."

They continued, pushing forward through large green leaves and mossy covered vines. The humidity in the air clung to them, sticky, and stifling. The thought of running water was tantalizing. Maybe, if she was lucky, she could wash away the stickiness that seemed to permanently cover her skin and wash the salt water that still clung to her lifeless hair. The more steps they took, the louder the rushing noise because, sounding more like a roar. When the roar became loud enough to be the only sound filling the air around them, she knew they were there. She pushed through the treed and was greeted by a very large, rushing river.

"We made it." Wynne cried, stepping out onto a slight shore. The river was much larger than she had realized. In her dreams, it had seemed too small and insignificant. The water, rushing past, called to her. She could feel the tingle of anticipation, flooding through her veins. It excited her and terrified her all at the same time.

"We need to look for the narrowest point to cross." Her father remarked, stepping out from the jungle. Everyone in their group looked relieved that they had made it to the destination, they were one step closer to the end.

Wynne let her father and his crew men decided what point would be the safest to cross. She watched them carefully but chose to say anything to them about the man from her dream. Would it make any difference even if she did? She felt eyes, watching her and she knew they belonged to Caspian. He was the only one that knew what waited for them in this river, and mercifully, he too kept silent.

"Here!" Her father called, "We will cross here!" He pointed to a spot, that seemed narrower than any other part of the river.

"Are you sure about this?" Caspian whispered, as they made their way to the spot her father had chosen.

"No," she admitted, "but in my dreams, we always cross." She heard him sigh beside her, but he did not question or challenge her decision.

"I'll go first." Wynne declared, coming up to the group. Her father studied her for a moment, she thought he would protest, but he said quiet. Harshaw and Bradley weren't going to protest either, in fact they looked relieved that she had volunteered to go first.

Wynne turned to face the river, taking a deep breath in before stepping into the water. The water was cool, but nowhere near the coolness she craved. All her sense were alive, alert, waiting for any shift in the water. The water swirled around her, greeting her like a long-lost friend, filling her with a warmth and comfort, that calmed her soul. But just as she made it knee deep, a cold piercing sensation ripped through her entire body, causing her to double over. The water swirled beneath her, gathering in the center of the river.

"Winnie?" Her father called, she heard splashing behind her, and felt the water rage beneath her.

She held up her hand, stopping him in his track, "Stay there!" She screamed, clutching at her chest with her free hand. As her father stopped, the rage subsided beneath her. The swirling water in the center of the river continued, building, steadily and steadily before her. Slowly, the swirling water billowed upward, taking shape. Wynne swallowed, as she watched a man's figure form before her. And true to her dreams, it was the same man she had seen before.

"Hello halfling." He greeted. "I am Rhymus." Wynne bristled; he had also called her halfling. She made a quick mental note of the sword he held at his side. She wanted to keep her eye on that sword.

"What do you want?" Her father demanded from the shore. The man turned to him; his anger visible on his watery face.

"Do not interfere, humans." Rhymus spat, "This journey is not your own." His voice rumbled through the air.

"What do you want?" Wynne reiterated. Rhymus's face softened at the sound of her voice, as he turned back to face her.

"To prove your worth." He answered simply. Wynne felt her face drain of color. It was what he had told her in her dream.

"And how will you do that?" Wynne whispered.

"Step forward." Rhymus gestured to where he stood, "You will learn to control what lies within." She nodded, taking a step forward, but stopped suddenly when she felt a hand grasping at her own.

"Wynne," Caspian's voice sounded frantic, "You don't have to do this!" The water that made Rhymus's form began to swirl in a frenzy, he was angry that Caspian had interfered. Rhymus rose taller, looming above them, drawing his sword, he started angrily at Caspian.

"She must!" Rhymus yelled.

"Caspian, please." Wynne whispered, taking his hand off her own.

"Wynne—"

"I warned you," Rhymus hissed, raising his sword at Caspian, "do not interfere." He growled, and Wynne knew he would not hesitate to unleash hell on any of them if they dared interfere.

"It will be alright." Wynne said softly, looking deep into Caspian's eyes, "I promise." She added, as tenderly as she possibly could. Caspian studied her for a moment, then took a few steps back, leaving her alone in the water.

"Let us begin." Rhymus declared, lowering his sword before her. Wynne faced him confidently, but there was a twinge of fear trickling beneath her skin. She tried to focus, feeling the water before her. She could feel his presence in the water, along with the threads of power that flowed past her. His presence was powerful, radiating a strength she could not even fathom.

"You can control and manipulate the water to your will." He bellowed. He raised his hand and as if answering him, the water stood before her, a great wall. It was not solid but continued to flow. Before she could really process what, she was watching him do, he hurled the water right towards her. Closing her eyes, she raised her arms, bracing herself for impact. She felt a sudden tug in the pit of her stomach, like a string had been pulled taught, tethering her to the water surrounding her. But it felt so weak, if she even breathed funny, the connection would be lost. The blow never came, carefully, she opened her eyes and gasped. She had formed a wall of water surrounding her.

"You do not feel, it does not run through your very soul." Rhymus yelled. Her wall of water, disintegrated, the string she had had been tethered to, split, severing her connection. Rhymus saw his opportunity, either by seeing it on her face, or feeling her lost connection. He lunged for her, like a viper. He thrust his sword towards her, Wynne saw a flash of silver shooting towards her. But she was too slow, she stumbled, trying to move out of the way, but she was now waist deep and moving quickly was not an easy task. Rhymus's sword slammed into her, cold metal spliced through her shoulder. She screamed in agony as she fell back, instantly swallowed by the water. Slowly, she picked herself up, her shoulder throbbing, and aching in fiery pain. Rhymus squared up to her, holding his sword back out in front of him, his face was filled with consternation. He was angry that she had allowed him to hit her with his sword.

"You have to feel it!" He yelled, "It must flow through you!" He shouted again, as she tried to stand to her feet. Everything was fuzzy, she was disoriented and suddenly exhausted beyond anything she had experienced so far. Another wave slammed into her, sending her back down into the water.

"You are not even trying!" Rhymus growled, lunging at her again and again. Wynne felt her anger kindle in the pit of her stomach, she gritted her teeth and glared up at him.

"It's not a tether," he spat, "It's a cord that runs through you, binds you—makes you who you truly are!" He shouted. Wynne clamped her fists right, reaching for the cord. She could feel it in her chest, connecting her to the water around her. It was powerful and strong, she focused and grabbed for it. All at once, she felt the cord settle into her chest, she was connected and the power she had felt surging past her in the water, now belonged to her. It was unpredictable, it was chaos, and it now flowed through her, like her very own blood.

She held onto the force as she stood on top of the water, flinging out a torrent of water towards him. He melted into the water beneath him, missing the blow completely before reappearing unscathed a few feet away. Amusement danced on his face, but Wynne was left more frustrated than ever. How had he avoided her that easily?

"Is that the best you can do, halfling?" He questioned, shaking his head, "It is not enough!"

"Don't call me that!" Wynne grumbled.

"Why?" He sneered, with some measure of amusement, "It's what you are." Anger bubbled within as she reached for the cord within her. The air was suddenly sucked from her lungs as water shot towards him at lightning speed. But her frustration only grew as she watched him step easily to the side.

Wynne screamed, holding onto the cord tight as she summoned a stream of water to rise. It was paltry compared to the water he had summoned, but she flung it at him anyways. He didn't move though, instead he held up a hand and the water parted around him. The movement reminded her, she had seen that movement before, but where? In her moment of thought, he pounced. A cold wall of water blasted into her, knocking her straight onto her back.

"You are still grasping for it, like you can call upon it at your leisure." He said slowly, disapprovingly.

"What do you want from me!" Wynne shouted, spitting water from her mouth. He leaned down, his face mere inches from her. Her breath caught in her throat.

"I want you to free it." He whispered, "Let it consume every fiber of your soul." Wynne suddenly realized that he was not angry with her, but he was pleading with her. The realization made her cheeks burn. He didn't want her to fail. *You are worthy*—those had been her mother's words to her in her dream. Then, it dawned on her, she had seen her mother control him—just by raising her hand.

"I don't know how." She muttered. The look in his eyes was not one of anger but of deep sorrow. Slowly, he reached out and touched her chest.

"It's in here. It always has been." Then he rose to his full height, his face clouded in sternness, "Now, stand," he commanded, "and claim it!" She did as he asked, feeling a slight shake in her knees. She reached inside herself and grabbed the cord and held on fast, wrapping it around her, every part of her, tightly, so it wouldn't break loose. She took a deep breath in and felt her nerves clang around in her like a bell. She heard a rush of water and opened her eyes as the Rhymus stood before her, holding a wave of water behind him. His face was grave, as he studied her. Then, he attacked.

But the panic never came. Wynne felt the cord, now bound to her soul, light up, setting her body on fire. It was no longer a cord she felt around her, it was an everlasting cord, one that bound her to the water, filling her entire soul. The power pulsed through her veins and into her fingertips. She was the water, and the water was her. Just before Rhymus could plunge her into the water, she raised her hand, and he vanished into a cold mist.

Wynne stood alone in the middle of the river—as though nothing had happened. But the power she had bound to her was still there, pulsing through her. It was there to stay, she realized. The water beneath her was silent. Rhymus has really and truly vanished, she couldn't even feel a lingering of his presence.

"Wynne?" Caspian's voice was like a boon, it grounded her, back to the task at hand. She turned and saw him standing knee deep in the river watching her, "Your shoulder." He cried; his eyes fixated on her spliced shoulder. She glanced down carefully and saw blood spilling down her arm, but she couldn't feel the pain.

"It's fine." She whispered. Rhymus had been so precise in his attack, the sword had grazed her shoulder, opening her enough, but not enough to make the blow a deadly one. His attacks had been devised to get her to act, and he had not been afraid to harm her in the process.

Behind him, stood her father and his men, watching her. The look on her father's face was one of sorrow, while the looks on Harshaw and Bradley's faces conveyed their overall shock. She shouldn't have been surprised, but she was. Her attention returned to Caspian, who was slowly wading out to her, his hand outstretched for hers. He was pale and his eyes were wide, frightened. Seeing him starting at her in fear, made her panic. The tingling in her fingers disappeared, but the cord remained firm, beating within her chest. There was no going back now, what she had done, was permanent.

Stealing her courage, she reached out to his hand and grasped it firmly, smiling as she did. Caspian looked from her to her hand, there was some hesitation in his gaze. She willed the water away, and on command, it receded from their feet until they were standing on a solid riverbed. She looked up at him, he was studying her carefully.

"Your eyes," he whispered, "they're brighter." She blushed, looking away from him, but relief swept through her. She had thought he might turn away from her, once he knew she had become different—something unfamiliar. She felt him squeeze her hand tightly, the reassurance that squeeze gave her was more than she could have ever asked for.

"I believe we have a looking glass to find?" She declared, looking from Caspian to her father and his men, standing still on shore. Her father gave her a small smile, before he and his men joined them.

"Are you alright?" The concern in her father's voice made her smile, slightly.

She nodded, "Better, than alright." He studied her a moment longer, before nodding his approval. His eyes fell onto her wounded shoulder, but he did not say anything. He merely ripped off a portion of his shirt and wrapped it around her shoulder, sinching it tight. After, he met her eyes and gave her the smallest smile. Wynne could see the guilt shining through, so she forced a bright smile in return. She hoped it would be enough to ease some of the guilt that was ransacking his soul.

The group continued through the river, on solid ground as Wynne pushed the water out and away from them. This newfound ability was handy, she thought. Once they stepped up onto the opposite shore, Wynne released her hold on the water, and the water retreated, covering the path they had just crossed, burying any evidence that they had even been there.

"From here," Wynne's voice was quiet, "we follow the river." She looked between Caspian, her father and his men and saw no questioning looks or concerns. Wynne nodded, and dove into the jungle, making sure to keep the river to her left. The river would lead them to the looking glass, she was sure of that. She moved along slowly, keeping her hand still locked in Caspian's.

180

Chapter 27

*W*ynne whirled around, searching the jungle for something, anything that looked familiar, but everything was different. Panic welled in her throat, she felt like screaming. Why was she alone? Where was Caspian? He was nowhere in sight. Wynne breathed in deeply, but the confusion clouded her mind and her judgement, making the panic more real. Suddenly, a voice whispered among the trees. Quickly, she turned and frowned, the jungle was empty. But the voice continued to whisper, all around her and nearer this time. Her head swiveled around, searching for the source of the whisper, but the jungle still was empty. The voice whispered behind her; she could feel the breath tickle against her neck. She flinched, jumping to the side.

"Who's there?" She screamed. Her voice echoed among the trees. But no one answered her. She stood there, holding her breath, waiting for a response. A soft whisper drifted through the trees, sending a shiver down her spine.

"Wynne." The voice called. She stumbled back. The voice—she knew that voice. She pushed through the jungle through the mist that had now gathered. The voice continued calling her name, luring into the darkness. She finally pushed back some branches and froze. It was the lake; she was at the looking glass.

It was beautiful, filling her with a sense of calm and ironically, dread. A figure stood in the middle of the lake. Wynne took a few more steps, before the figure turned towards her. It was her mother. Her mother smiled at her, opening her arms, beckoning her to come out to her. But Wynne stood, frozen on the shore as the base of her neck began to pound, a dull achy pain Though her mother smiled, her face was stained with tears.

"Find me!" She screamed and the pain in Wynne's head exploded.

Wynne gasped, sitting up, her heart pounding in her chest and her neck throbbing in pain. Where was she? She looked around, she was still in the jungle, laying by the fire in the little camp they had made for the night. Her father lay asleep across the fire, along with Harshaw. Bradley must be on watch. She looked to her side, Caspian was there, just a fingers length away from her, sound asleep.

"Wynne?" she jumped as a hand touched her arm gently. Caspian had rolled over and was now staring at her. She must have woken him when she sat up.

"Are you alright?" He whispered.

"Yes," she croaked, "I'm fine, just a bad dream." She added, rubbing the goosebumps from her arms.

"About what?" Caspian questioned, sleepily.

"The looking glass," She shivered, "and my mother." She laid back down, propping her head up on her arm, looking at Caspian.

"It's beautiful," she muttered.

"The looking glass?" Caspian questioned.

She nodded, "My mother was screaming at me to find her," she sighed, shaking her head.

"Is she standing in the middle of a lake?" He asked.

Wynne frowned, "How did you know that?"

"You're not the only one who's been having dreams lately." He muttered, rubbing his eyes.

"Why haven't you said anything?" Wynne demanded. Caspian held a finger up to his lips. She carefully looked past him, Harshaw and her father were still fast asleep.

"You should have told me!" Wynne snapped, slightly annoyed.

"You have enough to worry about, you don't need to be worrying about me." He answered, with some sternness. Wynne frowned, but she wasn't sure she could argue with him.

"Then you've seen the lake?"

He shook his head no, "Just your mother."

"Does she say anything to you."

He nodded, "Nothing that makes any sense though."

"What does she say?" But Caspian just laid there, letting the silence grow between them, "Caspian!" Wynne hissed, poking him on the shoulder. His eyes popped back open, and a mischievous grin spread across his lips.

"Do you have any patience?" he hissed at her.

She stuck out her tongue, "Only when it suits me." He sighed, rolling over onto his back, but he still did not answer right away.

Suddenly, he let out an exasperated sigh, "She wants you to open the chest."

"What?" Wynne cried. Caspian held up a finger to his mouth again, giving her the look that said she needed to be quiet or else.

"Why does she want me to open it?"

"I don't know," Caspian sighed, "that's all she ever says." Wynne shifted uncomfortably, the ground beneath her suddenly becoming harder than a rock.

"Do think that is wise?" She questioned. If she opened the chest, who knows what it would do to her? Payne wanted to use it to gain an allure's abilities, her abilities, but what would happen if the chest was merely opened?

"It's up to you." Caspian replied softly.

Wynne groaned, "You're no help." She mumbled.

"I'm not going to tell you what to do, Wynne." He chided.

"I wish you would," Wynne snapped, "it would be so much easier that way."

Caspian chuckled, "The decision must be yours, Wynne, no one else." Wynne sighed. He really wasn't going to tell her what she should or shouldn't do. She wasn't sure if she should be angry at him, or grateful. She readjusted, trying to get as comfortable as possible, slipping her arm back under her head. The uncertainty of what lay ahead, for her, lay heavily on her heart. Caspian made it seem like the decision was hers, but was it really? Nothing about this entire journey had been her decision, and she had a feeling nothing that would happen soon would be her decision either. Her decision had been made, long ago, before she had ever gotten to this point.

Wynne was lost in her own thoughts. Caspian's dreams hadn't really helped to shed light on anything but had successfully managed to confuse her and raise even more questions. If her mother had wanted her to open the chest, why hadn't she been telling her that in her own dreams? If she did go through with what her mother was telling Caspian she should do, what would that do to her?

Caspian shifted beside her; his warmth gently seeped into her body. It was reassuring and comforting to have him so close. Wynne closed her eyes, vaguely aware of a hopeful feeling settling into her soul. A feeling that promised, they may get out of this in one piece. But there was another feeling too, the familiar feeling of slumber, knocking at her door, and promising her the escape to another dream. A dream, she thought, that might contain some answers.

Wynne stood on the lake shore. She was not surprised to be here. It was quiet, so much so that she was afraid to move and disrupt the stillness. But something dropped into the lake. A rippled shattered the glass, causing the beautiful picture to fracture. Standing in the middle of the lake was a figure, dressed in white, which glowed in the moon light above. Her eyes were closed, her head cast down towards the fractured water. Just as the first ripple splashed against her foot, her eyes opened, glowing in the night. She straightened upright and fixed her eyes on Wynne.

"I've been waiting." The figure grumbled. Wynne knew from the voice that it was her mother.

"I'm sorry?" Wynne offered, slightly confused.

"Do you know what you must do?" She asked, sternly.

Wynne nodded, "You want me to open the chest?"

Her mother frowned, "It will not be easy, and it will cause you great pain." Wynne shivered. At this point, she was no stranger to pain. But she had been hoping to avoid anymore. Everything blurred around her before clearing to reveal a dark, damp cave. The cave was filled with treasure beyond her imagination. But only one item, caught her eye. A small golden chest, sparkled in the darkness. Wynne reached for it tentatively, grasping it in her hands. Something familiar radiated from within. She was suddenly overcome with the desire to open it and see what lie inside.

"Winnie," a voice called to her from the damp darkness, it was her father, "if you open the chest—your life, it will never be the same again." His voice was sad as he spoke, as if he knew what lay ahead of her.

"Father?" She gasped, feeling a flood of emotions, sweep through her. He smiled gently, and stroked her cheek, tenderly.

"If you open it—our lives will change, forever."

"They've already changed, father." She whispered, feeling the truth radiate through her words. Her father smiled sadly, as though he could already feel the truth himself. Everything had changed, there would be no going back.

"Open it." Caspian spoke softly, standing close beside her, his chest pressing into her back. His eyes were bright, with an intensity she had never seen before. His grey blue eyes glowed, churned, like a storm brewing in the ocean.

"What about the pain?" she whispered. He smiled, grabbing her face, gently in his hands. His thumb rubbed her cheek, softly.

"We will endure it, together." Wynne felt her chest ache with his words. He leaned hir forehead against her, his breath mingling with her own.

"Will it be worth it?" She asked, peering up into this handsome eyes. The warmth from his fingertips seeped into her cheeks. But his response, never came.

"That is for you to decide!" Payne's voice shattered the calm, sliced through the darkness like a dagger. Caspian, no longer stood before her. The trace of his warm fingertips still on her face. Payne stood two feet away from her, his sword was drawn, the metal pressed dangerously to her throat.

"Give the chest or perish!" He demanded. The blade of his sword, cut into her throat. But she refused to answer.

Payne shrugged, "Very well then!" and he thrust his sword through her throat.

Chapter 28

Wynne woke up screaming, clutching frantically at her throat, searching for the blade the knew was there. She expected to feel blood, but her hand came away clean. She leapt to her feet, hands trembling at her heart raced in her chest. Everything had been so real, so vivid. She had felt the sword pierce her neck. Her scream had woken everyone else up. She now had four set of eyes, watching her, searching her for the cause of her duress. They waited patiently for her to explain her scream.

"Winnie?" Her father called. But Wynne ignored him, pacing back and forth. Her eyes suddenly noticed a familiarity in the jungle around her. In desperation, she plunged into the jungle, pushing through the vines and giant leaves, ignoring the shouts of concern from behind her. She recognized everything from her dream. Caspian called after her, but she didn't stop. Dim light poured through the jungle; morning would be here soon enough. Just as she pushed the last few branches away, she stopped dead in her tracks. There, right in front of her was the lake, just as beautiful as it was in her dream. Caspian came up beside her, huffing, her father was not far behind.

"How did you know it was here?" Caspian questioned, breathlessly.

"In my dream." Wynne recalled, "She led me to it."

"Your mother?" Her father asked, looking at the lake before him with awe. She just merely nodded; her eyes fixed on the lake before her. The water was perfectly still and looked just like glass. Seeing it was altogether eerie and comforting.

"So, where's the chest?" Caspian whispered.

Wynne frowned, "I think its inside the lake."

"In a cave maybe?" Her father suggested. Wynne nodded in confirmation, it was the cave she had seen in her dreams, she was sure of that.

"How do we get down there?" Caspian questioned, looking at the lake with a calculating look.

"Not we," Wynne replied, shaking her head, "just me."

"No!" The answer came from both her father and Caspian.

"You can't go alone." Caspian added, his face full of concern.

"He's right," her father added, though he seemed pained to admit it, "it's too dangerous for you to go alone." His voice was firm as he spoke, "I will go back and get Harshaw and Bradley and when we come back, we will figure out a solution." Wynne nodded. Her father studied her for a moment longer, trying to decide if she would heed his command. He turned slowly to head back into the jungle, but stood quickly, resting a firm hand on Caspian's shoulder.

"Watch her." He said quietly. Caspian nodded once, then turned to fix his gaze on Wynne. Wynne watched her father disappear into the jungle, then counted to thirty. Once she hit her mark, she turned quickly, stepping for the water. A hand, however, halted her from continuing any further.

"What are you doing?" Caspian demanded.

"There is only one way to get that chest, and no amount of discussing will lead to a different option." Wynne snapped.

"You're not going alone." He sighed, pinching the bridge of his nose.

Wynne stood there, staring at him, "You're going to come with me?"

"Is that even a question?" He smiled, slightly, "So where is this cave?"

Wynne swallowed, pointing to the center of the lake, "In my dreams, I'm always at the center of the lake."

"So," Caspian started, "we swim out there and boom, a cave?"

She laughed, "We aren't swimming anywhere. We're going to walk."

"What?" The confusion his face was priceless. Wynne chuckled again, gently taking his hand in hers and pulling him towards the water.

"Don't worry," She winked, "I won't let you drown." He rolled his eyes, but did not resist, as she led them to the water.

Just at the edge, they stopped. Wynne glanced over her shoulder at him, he gave her a nervous smile and squeezed her hand. Wynne stepped out onto the water; the water hummed beneath her. It was solid, just like stepped onto glass. Caspian gripped her hand and stepped up beside her. Something pulsed beneath her, faint. Slowly, they walked forward, Wynne could feel Caspian's tense steps next to her own. But she turned her focus on the pulse she felt beneath her feet. With every step it became steadily stronger. Wynne frowned, it reminded her of a beat, she swallowed, like a heartbeat. The water beneath them, was dark and void of any movement, unlike the waters of lagoon or river, which had been teaming with life and energy. This water was different, it was quiet and much too still for Wynne's comfort.

Wynne spotted a faint glimmer beneath her feet. The pulse now radiated through her in a strong steady beat. Wynne looked up to see how far they had come, and they had made it to the center.

"This is it!" She announced, gripping Caspian's hand tighter.

"From here we swim?" Caspian questioned, thought Wynne detected some nervousness in his voice.

"Just follow me." Wynne responded as confidently as she could. He nodded, and without giving him much time to contemplate, she moved the water around them, to swallow them completely. Wynne swam towards the pulse, pushing herself deeper into the water and towards the glow. As she got closer, she was able to depict a hole. She stopped, the water became darker and colder that she had expected. She glanced over her shoulder at Caspian and pointed to the hole. He nodded, quickly, this was it—they were so close! The drumming heartbeat was even stronger in the hole. Wynne trembled, gripped her hands into fists and she plunged herself deeper into the hole.

The water bit at her skin and pressed down on her, somewhat stifling her. She fought to keep the rising panic—forcing herself to remain calm. Now was not the time to panic, Caspian was counting on her. Wynne groped her way through, using the rocks to guide her. The tunnel went deeper and deeper until, she ran right into a wall. Panic seized her, it couldn't be a dead end! Relief swept through her as her hand felt an opening above her head. She turned and pushed herself up, seconds later, she broken through the surface. Another moment and Caspian followed, gasping for air. They had made it!

Wynne looked up at the ceiling and gasped. Above them there was a dome covered in a display of beautiful golden lights, that almost looked like stars. The golden sparkles showered the cave with a warm light, but also cast dark shadows. They swam towards the shore, both eager to get out of the black water. Wynne heaved herself up onto the shore, startled by the black sand beneath her fingers. As she stood, she frowned, there was nothing there! How could this be? It didn't make any sense; she could feel the pulse reverberating in her very bones and yet the entire cave was empty!

Caspian heaved himself up onto the shore beside her, lying face down in the black sand, taking deep, gasping breaths. He mumbled something, but Wynne couldn't heart him. She suppressed the urge to giggle.

"Caspian, are you alright?" She inquired. He just groaned in response, flipping over onto his back, and staring up at the ceiling. Black sand covered his face and lips, Wynne laughed. His gaze flicked up to hers and the look he gave her was completely void of any amusement.

"Let's not do that again." He muttered.

Wynne chuckled, "Hate to break it to you, but that's our way out." She remarked, pointing at the water.

"This cave is pretty homey." He remarked, gesturing to the sparkling ceiling above them.

"Come on Leopold!" She laughed, extending her hand to him, "You can't give up that easily."

He took her hand, "Leopold?" He stood, sighing as he stretched himself to his full height.

"Too snooty?" Wynne guessed. He nodded, some amusement flickered on his face as he brushed his face free of the black sand, surveying the cave around them.

"It's empty." He drawled.

Wynne frowned, "It doesn't make any sense. I can feel it, it's here!" She declared, the beat in her chest growing stronger and stronger.

"Well, there has to be some explanation." Caspian mused, starting to walk around the room. Wynne watched him, quietly search the cave. He walked carefully along the water, eyes focused and intent on looking for anything to explain the lack of gold in this cave! His hand, moved slowly across the cave walls. He stopped suddenly, his hand disappearing into darkness.

"Wynne," he called, "over here." She did hesitate to join him where he stood. Gently, he grabbed her hand and directed it towards the wall, but instead of feeling a wall, she felt empty space.

"A tunnel?" She asked.

He nodded, "A tunnel." He grabbed her hand in his, and stepped into the darkness, pulling her with him. Wynne felt her breath catch in her throat, as the darkness became absolute. But thankfully, the tunnel was not long and, in a moment, they were stepping out into a separate chamber.

Wynne felt her breath escape her lungs. Gold, sparkling and glittering, was scattered along the entire chamber. Some stacks were close to reaching the ceiling. Lanterns that were lit, lined the walls, causing twinkles of starlight to cover the black cave walls. How was this possible? Caspian whistled, slightly, utterly amazed at what lay before them.

"Wow." He uttered; his eyes wide as he stared at the sparkling room. The room was not large, but any means, but the hoard of treasure inside was vast.

"What does the chest look like?" Caspian questioned.

"Aren't you supposed to know that?" She retorted.

He shook his head, "Not at all."

Wynne frowned, biting her lip, "It has to be small." She pursed her lips, "And I think it is gold." She had a vague feeling of seeing it before, but she couldn't be sure, "Look for anything with a trident on it!" She cried, holding out her locket for Caspian to see, "Like this one." Caspian made a quick mental note and the two of them moved carefully through the trove, stopping at any chests they found. They worked together, sifting through gold and jewels. All the while, Wynne could

191

feel the pulse beating, echoing all around her. Her head started to pound, along with the steady beat she could feel, pulsing around her.

The first two chests held nothing but jewels and more gold. The third chest Caspian smashed open only revealed silver cubes. Wynne grabbed another chest when a glint caught her eye. She moved towards the mount and spotted a small gold chest, poking out from a stack of gold coins.

"I think I found it!" She cried.

"Really?" Caspian exclaimed coming up beside her. Wynne fell to her knees pulling the chest from a stack of gold coins that covered it. Gold pieces tumbled down around her, clanking loudly, echoing throughout the dark cavern. Wynne held her breath as she caught a glimpse of the top the chest. It was a similar design to the one that was on her locket, but what really caught her attention was the gold trident at the center. It matched the one that was on her locket, this was the chest.

"It's heavy." She muttered, cradling it in her arms.

"And small!" Caspian muttered, "This is supposed to hold Oaran's orb?" Wynne shrugged, it looked small, but felt like it weighed a ton.

"It's beautiful." She whispered, fingers running along the golden filagree. The box hummed in response to her touch. Coins dropped behind them, they both turned quickly, but found nothing there. A cloud of concern darkened Caspian's face and he slowly stood, drawing the dagger from his belt.

"Stay here." He whispered. Wynne watched him prowl away from her and towards the noise. He moved like a cat, lethally hunting for whatever it was that had disturbed the coins. Caspian gave her one more quick glance before disappearing behind a tall mound of gold. Wynne held her breath, clutching the chest to her heart, hoping that it had just been a fluke. They had encountered someone at every way point, would there also be someone here, waiting for her? She shuddered at the thought, hoping beyond hopes that she was wrong. But the minutes that clicked by with no return from Caspian, made her wonder and her worry began to grow,

Suddenly, she heard a grunt as something fell to the ground. Coins and golden trinkets scattered on the floor, echoing along the cavern walls. Wynne was moving before she could even think.

"Caspian!" She called, but her echo was the only response she got. She turned the corner and stopped. There, on a pile of gold, lay Caspian, unconscious and towering above him stood a woman clad in darkness. She turned to Wynne and smiled over her shoulder.

"Hello halfling." The woman purred.

Wynne gritted her teeth, "What did you do to him?" She demanded. But the woman waved her hand in silent dismissal. She turned all the way around the face her, a smile played on her lips. The woman was dressed in a gown made of smoke, black smoke that curled and flitted in a hidden breeze, swirling around her body, not like a normal dress should. Her skin was like a pearl, white and almost translucent, accentuated by long black locks that framed black eyes. Wynne felt a shiver run down her spine as the woman fixed her black eyes on her, there was nothing natural about this woman.

"I see you found what you've been looking for." The woman gestured to the chest in Wynne's arms. Her voice was sultry but laced with poison. Instinctively, Wynne took a careful step back, trying to put as much distance between her and the woman as possible.

"Who are you?" Wynne asked shakily.

"I am Orphia, daughter of Asta," the woman smiled, "goddess of death." Wynne felt her blood run cold as the temperature suddenly dropped in the cave.

"What did you do to him?" Wynne demanded, forcing her voice to remain calm.

Orphia sniffed, "He will live." She fixed her eyes once again on Wynne, "My business is with you, not with him."

"Are you here to kill me?" Orphia laughed, the sound was like a cat screeching, making Wynne's ear burn in pain.

"I have no desire to kill you," her smokey dress flitting in the air around her as she glided effortlessly towards her, "I am here to deliver the truth, as promised." Her voice turned somewhat sad with her words, but the momentary lapse in emotions, quickly faded.

"What truth?"

"Not what truth," she sighed, "but who's truth." Her eyes fell to the chest in Wynne's hand, "Do you know what lies in that chest you're clutching so tightly to your heart?" The chest hummed against her skin as if whatever was inside it was alive.

She nodded, "It's Oaran's orb."

Orphia smirked, "Only a mere human would be naive enough to think it was Oaran's orb." She mocked; Wynne felt her cheeks burn.

"If it's not his orb, then what's inside?" Wynne demanded, feeling her courage returning slightly.

"It's your birthright." Orphia stated, simply, as though she should have known that to begin with.

"What?" Wynne stumbled, "I don't understand?" Wynne questioned, the confusion starting to cloud everything everyone had told her before. Orphia's eyes narrowed as she studied her and, in an instant, she was standing before Wynne, only a fingers length away.

"Why do you think I am here, halfling?" She whispered, her voice sending shivers down Wynne's spine. The air around her, turn cold as ice as Orphia stood mere inches away from her. Her breath fogged as she breathed, her fingertips ached for the warmth of another human's touch.

"I have the ability to manipulate sleep, dreams and memories," she whispered, "close your eyes halfling, and I will clear away the clouds in your mind, I will reveal what your mother kept from you for so long." Wynne took a deep breath and did as she was told. Orphia gently grasped her head in her hands and rested her forehead against her own. Surprisingly, her touch was warm and comforting. Suddenly, there was bright flash—and everything went black.

Chapter 29

Wynne was at the bottom of the ocean, floating in the darkness. The smell of salt and seaweed permeated her senses. She blinked a couple times, trying to clear her vision to see what lay ahead. Something beyond her sparkled in the distance. She willed the ocean currents to float her towards the light. As she got closer, she could make out a castle of sorts, looming before her. It was made entirely of ocean rock and shells, bigger than any she had ever seen on shore. She floated closer and closer to the gate of the underwater palace. The gate was lined with pearls, sparkling bright and shining as a beacon to all that could see. She floated past the gate, and felt herself being pulled to a specific spot, she did not resist.

Wynne floated into a great hall, the pillars were iridescent, like the inside of a clam's shell, leading up to a giant throne. Wynne spotted a man, sitting on top of the throne, a crown of coral sat upon his brow and at his side, he held a giant golden trident. Wynne recognized the trident immediately as the one from her locket, but she had a nagging feeling she had seen it somewhere else as well. The man was not a huge man, but his presence commanded power and strength. His hair was dark and swirled about in the water around him, but he didn't seem to mind the constant ebb and flow.

As Wynne floated closer, she saw six women standing before him. Each one was more beautiful than the next, but there was one that stood out to Wynne. It was her mother, standing at the head of the line, wearing a dress made of seafoam. Her blonde hair billowed around her, floating in the ocean currents drifting past them. Her porcelain face and rosy cheeks was stunning in the ocean light. There was a twinkle in her green eyes, making them glow through the dim light.

"Six daughters of Oaran," Orphia's voice echoed through the deep, Wynne turned and saw her, floating beside her. Her smokey dress still wafted around her, seemingly out of place in the ocean view before her, "Goddesses of the sea, each with their own abilities to control what Oaran gave them." Wynne returned her gaze to her mother, so was she an Allure, or something more?

"Not an allure," Orphia answered, as if reading her very mind, "But flesh and blood of the god himself." Wynne stared; her mother had been a goddess? But everyone had told her she had been an allure! Did Payne know that she was more than just an allure? But Orphia, if she could indeed sense the questions, did not care to answer them.

The picture before them swirled, turning into something new. A different time, a different memory. Wynne felt her vision blur, as her eyes tried to focus on the newest scene Orphia was now showing her. The six daughters were still standing before Oaran, but her mother stood, alone in front of Oaran's throne, kneeling as he draped a necklace around her throat. Wynne held her breath as she realized it was her mother's the necklace, the very one that hung from her own throat. Then, from the center of Oaran's chest came a bright orb. Was this the orb in the chest?

"Once a daughter, now the heir to the godly throne. Oaran had gifted her, a birthright as his eldest and most precious daughter." Orphia's voice declared, as though she herself was declaring the words that had been spoken that day. But Wynne focused her attention on her mother, studying her face as she took the orb in her hand. She had a difficult time reading the expression on her mother's face, was it one of fear or dread? Did she not want her birthright as the daughter of Oaran? Would that have meant she would have taken Oaran's place?

Orphia chuckled, "Each deity can choose to declare an heir, whether it be a daughter, son, or child. And if they choose, a deity can move on to Iteala leaving their chosen heir to rule anew." Iteala, the name given to the land where all souls reside after death. Wynne vaguely remembered reading of it in the Avanthian history book Mr. Schmidt had given her, but at the time, hadn't thought, reading of Avanthian mythology was pertinent to issue at hand.

"Few deities have ever chosen to let their heir reign anew, and those that have, their names have been lost to time, replaced by the one they chose to continue on." Orphia continued, "But Oaran was and is not like other patron deities, he chose to give his throne, to Nerissa, daughter of sea and chaos. But she did not want her birthright, at least not right away." Wynne detected a note of sadness to Orphia's voice, but her face betrayed nothing.

The scene shifted again, colors and beams of light swirled around her, and Orphia and Wynne were transported to another time, a different memory. Suddenly, the picture became clear, and Wynne spotted her mother standing on shore, her toes barely in the water. Standing before her, trident in hand and sparkling in the golden sunlight, stood Oaran, his face tender and loving as he beheld his daughter.

"Oaran loved his daughter," Orphia's voice made the picture clear even more, Wynne could see the tears in his dark blue eyes, "But he would not keep her where she was not happy, so he let her go, to find her own path. But warned her to keep her true self hidden, because desperate men will go to great lengths to get the power, they crave the most." Orphia's words were pointed, as though she was foreshadowing the arrival of Payne. Oaran's warning would prove true, but had her mother told Payne of her true self?

Wynne watched as her mother turned and left Oaran standing in the water, not once did she look back. Wynne felt a pang of sadness for her patron deity, but also some measure of pride, that he had not forced her mother to take what he had given her freely. He let her leave, even if it meant watching his favorite daughter leave.

The scene shifted in an instant, Orphia and Wynne were now standing aboard a ship. The sunlight poured down onto golden beams, the ship was new and sparkled in the sunlight. Crew men scurried about, hurry to get their appropriate tasks finished. It was a mess, but Wynne saw order in it all. But that is when she saw her mother, sitting on a barrel, laughing with a young man. Wynne squinted, the man's get black hair, flowed to his shoulders, big broad shoulders. He was tanned from time spent in the sun, and his hand were rough, from handling tackle and line, far more than any other.

Wynne felt her breath catch in her throat; it was Payne! Granted, he was much younger and not nearly as grisly as she would describe him now. His eyes were not yet blackened with greed and his face was absent his renowned scar. He seemed human, still capable of feeling emotions, and acting appropriately on those emotions. He was not tainted by greed—not yet.

"Captain Atherol Payne," Orphia's voice spat, the smoke of her dress billowed as her anger seemed to rise at the sight of Payne, "He stole your mother's heart, charming her to help him get what he truly desired, power." Wynne watched as the gleam in Payne's eyes turned sinister, but her mother remained unchanged in her regard for him.

"But Payne never learned of her true self, she let him believe she was an allure, though she was deceived by him, she had enough foresight to keep that part of her hidden." Wynne watched as the ship whirled past them, traveling around the world, seeing sights only Wynne has ever dreamed of seeing. She watched her mother wield a sword, just as well as any other crew member around her, and she watched her mother control the sea. It was an extension of herself, like a second arm, but it was different than the connect Wynne had. This connection was deeper, stronger and with a far greater reach than Wynne had or could ever hope to have.

"Even though Payne had your mother, had her heart, he desired more, and he sought out a way to make himself just as powerful, if not more than her." Orphia's voice darkened, and the scene before her shifted into darkness, cold seeped into Wynne's arms. A shiver ran down her spine as the light before her brightened, revealing Payne speaking to a hooded figure. The figure was shroud in darkness and filled Wynne with dread. Wynne watched as the two spoke, fervently, Payne's face was lit in excitement.

"Even the most guarded secrets can be revealed for the right price." Orphia's voice whispered. Wynne swallowed; the realization of what secret dawned on her as she saw Payne's countenance shift. The sinister look in his eye grew, and what was left of the little humanity he possessed was swallowed whole. The man standing before her, that was the Payne she knew. The Payne who only saw the world and the people in it for his own use, his own gain. He knew her mother's secret, he knew who she was.

"He wanted her birthright for his own." Orphia's words sent a chill down Wynne's spine. It was the power he craved most; the power that had been promised to her mother. The scene shifted again before her. Wynne was standing in the corner of a darkened room, the details of the room murky, blurred from view. But the figure standing in the middle of the room were crystal clear. Her mother was there, tears pouring down her face as Payne stood before her hands gently resting on her shoulders. He was speaking to her quickly and passionately. But Wynne saw past the passion and saw the snake he truly was. She knew he was crafting his words, spewing poison onto her mother's soul. Did she not see his true intentions? How could her mother let him manipulate her like this?

"Because she loved him." Hearing Orphia say the words, however true they might have been, angered Wynne. She thought of her father, she couldn't accept that her mother could have loved someone else, loved anyone but her father.

Wynne found herself standing back underwater, in Oaran's palace, it was empty, except for her mother. Like a thief in the night, she swept into the palace, no one knew she was there. Wynne watched in horror and sadness as her mother stole the chest, containing her birthright. Out of the corner of Wynne's eyes, she spotted a flicker of light. Wynne squinted, there was a figure watching her mother in the shadows. Her mother did not see, she was too focused on the task at hand to notice. Wynne gasped, as she floated closer to the figure lurking in the shadows, it was Oaran. He stood by in silence, watching her steal her birthright, but why? And her mother had never even known he'd been there, watching her.

Wynne returned to the ship, searching for her mother. As her mother stepped foot onto the ship, it was not Payne that greeted her—it was Ferguson, her grandfather. Wynne felt a pang in her chest at the sight of her grandfather, a little less wrinkled with a spark of life gleaming in his big eyes.

"He spoke the words your mother refused to speak herself, that Payne only loved her for the power she promised him. He gave her a way out, an escape from the only world she had experienced since leaving her father's realm." Orphia whispered.

Wynne watched her mother's composure break, anguish flooded her beautiful face, and then was quickly replaced with rage. Ferguson stood there, giving her the space to feel the emotions that must have torn through her. But then a bell sounded on the ship, and men started to swarm. Wynne watched in horror as men descended upon her mother and grandfather, swords drawn. Payne strutted on deck; his eyes fixed on the chest in her mother's arms.

Her mother screamed his name, but Payne did not register her voice. That was Wynne saw the light flicker in her mother's eye, the realization that what her grandfather had told her, was true. As Payne reached for the chest, her mother whipped out her dagger, faster than any could comprehend and lashed out at Payne. She gouged him from temple to chin. He grabbed his face in anguish and blood poured from his fingers. It was the distraction they needed to get away. And no one, not even Payne's crew could keep her mother aboard ship.

"But your mother was not finished," the scene shifted with Orphia's words, scenes of her mother's life passing quickly before her, "Payne would continue to hunt her." Wynne saw her mother meeting with a woman, dressed in black. Wynne blinked, the woman she was staring at was Orphia!

"Your mother had come to me for help," Orphia answered, "she needed a curse, one that would keep Payne from ever possessing her birthright." Wynne watched as her mother pleaded with Orphia, the desperation on her face was visible and it pained Wynne to watch.

Orphia nodded, "I agreed, but" She paused, "all curses come with a price." Wynne saw the color drain on her mother's face as Orphia delivered the payment, "To protect a godly birthright, her godly powers would be forfeit. But the curse must be sealed, and it must be sealed by the one who returns the birthright." The realization of Orphia's words hit her mother, and Wynne watched as her mother's face contorted in concentration, weighing the gravity of Orphia's words.

After just a minute of deliberating, her mother nodded her head, once, firmly. Orphia's eyes squeezed close while a hand rested on her mother's forehead. A flash of light exploded from her hand. Wynne squinted, shielding her eyes from the sudden explosion of light. Everything that was her mother was being removed from her. Wynne watched as a light was suddenly extinguished from her mother's eyes, she was alive yes, but it was as if a part of her had died. Wynne watched as Orphia contained the light within the chest, closing it tight.

"You must guard this with your life." Orphia commanded her mother, "Payne will do everything in his power to find this chest." Her mother nodded; her entire countenance drooped in sadness. Her mother clutched the chest to her heart, holding it tenderly. Wynne felt a pang of sadness well in her heart. Though her mother had not been honest with her, her reasoning, now, had

been justified. Her mother turned, just then and looked Wynne dead in the eye. Wynne felt a shiver run down her spine.

"Find me in the looking glass." Her mother whispered, "Return me to the sea and claim my promise." Suddenly a bright light flashed before Wynne's eyes. Wynne jerked away, trying to shield her eyes from the sudden peel of light. But the intensity only grew, searing into her. Then, just as quickly as the light came, it was replaced with utter darkness, an inky black that Wynne felt she could almost swim in. Then, she felt her body tip and she was falling, through the darkness. She opened her mouth to scream, but was only swallowed whole, in the inky black.

Chapter 30

Wynne sat upright, gasping for breath. Panic surged through her body, as the world around her suddenly came back into focus. Her eyes struggled to focus, but every so slowly, the darkened cavern came into view. Orphia was still clutching her face in her hands, her black eyes peering into her own. Wynne suddenly remembered where she was, and what she had just been shown, and shivers ran down her spine.

"Why didn't she seal the curse?" Wynne questioned, quickly.

Orphia sighed, "To enact the curse, she forfeited her powers, she had no way of returning to Thalatia and no way of returning her birthright."

"She sacrificed herself for nothing?" Her anger bubbled; her fists clenched at her sides.

"No, not for nothing—for you." Orphia's ice-cold words, sliced into her. Wynne staggered back, "You are the one who must return the birthright. You," Orphia pointed, "are the one that will seal Payne's curse. You are the one that will make her sacrifice worth all the pain and sorrow! You will gain what was once lost." Orphia shouted, "You." her words reverberated off the black cavern walls and echoed deep into Wynne's soul.

Wynne shook slightly, "Payne wants the chest, he will do anything to get what's inside." Her voice quivered, her mind was reeling to the unlikely, "What if he opens it?"

Orphia's eyed widened, "He must not open the chest!"

"But what if he does?" Wynne questioned, the fear of the possibility of him even finding her, was causing her mind to overthink.

"Your mother's essence is bound to the chest, if opened, her essence can be absorbed," Orphia's eyes were wide with an intensity that scared Wynne, "and her birthright can then be claimed." Wynne swallowed, then Payne could potentially get what he truly desired, and that realization scared Wynne even more.

Wynne looked tentatively to the chest, laying by her feet. Her choices were limited. Take the chest and return it to Oaran, enacting the curse upon Payne or, she took a shaky breath, leave the chest here and find another way off the island and live the rest of her life in constant fear of being hunted. She shuddered, Payne would hunt her, with a bloodlust that would outrun her willingness to survive.

Orphia was studying her carefully; her dark eyes watched her like a hawk would its prey. She no doubt could probably read the thoughts running through Wynne's mind, but she kept silent, allowing Wynne the space needed to process what she needed to do.

"Where do I take the chest from here?"

Orphia smiled slightly, "When you get the ocean, press the trident to your lips and say 'Oaran, your child awaits you.'"

Wynne eyed Wynne carefully, somewhat skeptical of the cryptic call, "And he'll come to me?"

Orphia chuckled, "My dear halfling, he's been watching you since the day you were born. If you call him, he will come." Wynne considered her words for a moment, before retrieving the chest. The chest felt heavier than before, the weight of her responsibility settling in on her shoulders. There was also a sense a dread, settling in the pit of her stomach. That had evaded Payne this long, but that didn't mean she'd managed to avoid him altogether. Caspian was still unconscious, breathing, but not even close to waking.

"What did you do to him?" Wynne questioned, quickly checking on him.

Orphia scoffed, "Merely put him into a deep sleep." She waved her hand nonchalantly, as though putting him into a deep sleep was beneficial for everyone present. Wynne envied him, she half wished Orphia had put her into a deep sleep and had handed the all the responsibility to Caspian instead, he was more than capable!

"Can you also wake him?" Wynne ground out, the annoyance she felt was suddenly making an appearance, although Orphia didn't seem to notice or mind. Orphia simply snapped her fingers and Caspian jolted upright, gasping for air. Wynne jumped back, startled at how quickly he had woken up.

"Wynne!" He shouted, grabbing her arms tightly in his hands, "There is someone here!" His eyes searched wildly around the cavern, looking for the intruder. Wynne suddenly remembered that they had been disturbed by a sound and he had gone to look for it. The sound was undoubtedly caused by Orphia.

"It's fine, Caspian," Wynne chuckled, "it's just—" Wynne turned to point to Orphia, but she was nowhere to be found, "she's gone." Wynne whispered, frowning, and looking quickly around the cavern to make sure she was not going crazy.

"Who's gone?" Caspian questioned quickly, the panic in his voice was at an all-time high.

"Orphia." Wynne replied simply, double checking that she wasn't just hiding behind a stack of gold coins.

"Who's that?" Caspian demanded.

Wynne smirked, "I believe she's called a Necros."

His eyes widened, "A child of Asta?"

Wynne nodded, "The goddess of death."

"What did she do to me?" Caspian's face paled.

Wynne laughed, "Put you into a deep sleep," Wynne stood quickly, extending her hand, "Lucky for you." Caspian grasped it tightly and she helped heave him up onto his feet.

"Dare I even ask what she did to you?" His eyes narrowed and searched her from head to toe for any signs of injury.

"She showed me my mother's memories, what really happened, and" she gestured to the chest, "what's really inside." Caspian looked at the chest, it wasn't really anything extraordinary to look at, but what was contained inside, Wynne shook, she would never let Payne open it.

"It's not Oaran's orb?"

Wynne shook her head, "Not even close." She started back towards the tunnel, "It's my mother's birthright."

Caspian frowned, "Well what good is a birthright to Payne?"

Wynne held her breath, "Absolutely nothing," she led the way through the tunnel, "But my mother's essence is inside and that is what Payne wants. He needs that to gain the birthright." Wynne remarked.

"Why does he want your mother's birthright?"

Wynne bit her tongue, "She was not an allure." Wynne whispered, turning to face Caspian, "My mother was a daughter of Oaran, a goddess."

Caspian whistled, "That's a bit different than just an allure." The shock on Caspian's faced mirrored the shock still rippling through her own mind, "But what does that have to do with the birthright?"

"Payne wants to absorb my mother's essence so he can then use her birthright." Caspian frowned, the reality of Payne's plan not yet dawning on him.

"With her birthright, Payne would have access to the Oaran's throne." Wynne clarified. The shock on Caspian's face just deepened. Silence slowly descended between them, as both processed the situation, they realized they were in the middle of.

"What's your plan?" Caspian prodded carefully after a few quiet moments.

"Return the chest to Oaran. Orphia said it was the only way to seal Payne's curse, forever." She looked over her shoulder, "And then, we get you home to your new ship." She smiled, but Caspian did not smile back. For a split-second Wynne was worried Caspian would protest her decision. But she quickly shoved those feelings aside. This was nothing something Caspian truly had a say in. This was the only way to resolve the chaos that had enveloped her life, and she would do what she needed to do for some resemblance of normality to return.

They stopped at the water's edge, both staring down at the water black water. Wynne was hesitant to go—here in this cavern she was safe from anyone else. But the weight of the chest in her hands reminded her that she couldn't stay here forever, no matter how much she wanted to.

"You ready?" She turned quickly to Caspian, searching his face for any kind of response.

He nodded, avoiding her gaze, "As ready as I'll ever be." He sighed. Something about him was off, maybe it was the deep sleep Orphia had put him in? Or maybe he was still working out all the nuances with the chest and what needed to be done. Wynne couldn't know for sure, and she wasn't sure she wanted to prod the answers out of him either.

Wynne took a deep breath, before stooping down and lowering herself into the water. The coldness seeped into her, chilling her core instantly. Caspian was in the water beside her in an instant. She studied his face for a moment, he looked up at her slowly, and gave her the smallest hint of a smile. That was enough to satisfy the anxiety coursing through her. She nodded to Caspian, who took a deep breath, before they both plunged beneath the surface.

Wynne felt her body sink, immediately, the chest weighing her down. Clutching it closely to her chest, she let the weight carry her down to the hole, she knew was directly beneath them. Using her free hand, she stuck it out in front of her, hoping it would be enough to stop her from colliding into any rocks. With the weight of the chest, she felt like she was moving slower, but knew she needed to move fast. Caspian could only hold his breath for so long. So, she kicked her legs, harder and used the water around them to help propel them forward.

Wynne suddenly felt the tunnel give way above her, and her hand felt open water. Excitement swelled within her as she pushed herself up. The water outside of the tunnel was not nearly as black, she glanced below her and saw Caspian's dim form swimming up out of the tunnel. Smiling, she pulled the current around them both and in rush of bubbles, they both surged to the surface. Wynne smiled, as she felt a slight sticky breeze brush her cheeks and heard Caspian gasp for breath beside her. They had made it! The sky above them was slowly growing dim, Wynne frowned. How long had they been down in that cave?

"Your father is not going to be happy." Caspian muttered beside her; his eyes focused on the sky above.

"Were we down there all day?" Wynne felt the panic rise in her throat. It hadn't felt that long at all! How could they have been down in that cavern for almost an entire day?

"Looks like it." Caspian huffed. Wynne altered the water around them, pushing them up to the surface. Caspian eyed her quickly, impressed by the handy new skill.

Wynne blushed, "Why swim, when we can just walk."

"Work smarter, not harder." He grinned.

"It's going to take me a minute to adjust to," she paused, her blush deepening, "this." She gestured to the solid water beneath their feet.

Caspian smiled as he reached out and brush a wet strand of hair from her face, "It suits you."

"You think so?" Wynne shrugged, feeling her cheek tingle from where her fingers had touched her.

Caspian nodded, "It's like a missing piece of you has been returned." His grey blue eyes studied her carefully, "You're the person you were meant to be."

Wynne smirked, "Careful," she chided, "if you keep talking like that, I might fall for you." She teased but felt her heartbeat pound nervously in her throat.

Caspian chuckled, leaning towards her slowly, "Might?" he purred, "I thought you already were." Wynne felt her face grow hot; her eyes instantly dropped to the water. Caspian's chuckle turned into a hearty laugh.

"We better head back to shore." The replied, quickly, and somewhat breathlessly. This, this flirting game was dangerous, and she did not feel skilled enough to keep up with his quick wit.

"Don't want to anger your father any more than we already have?" Caspian asked, his voice still low and she could still feel his eyes on her, waiting for her to lift hers to his. But, she swallowed, she couldn't, her cheeks still burned.

"Exactly." She said quickly, moving towards shore. Caspian didn't tease any further, but followed her, matching her steps. Together they made it back to shore. But when they stepped out onto solid ground, Wynne was met with another wave of panic. The shoreline was empty and there was no sign that either her father or his men had ever been there. Wynne glanced quickly around, double checking that there was indeed no sign of them. But how could that be? Her father had left to go get Harshaw and Bradley, had they not made it back? Had something happened to them?

"We'll find them." Caspian said quickly, seeing the rise of panic on her face.

"Why aren't they here?" She muttered. She had expected her father to be waiting for her return on the shore, with arms folded and barely contained rage on his face, but he was nowhere to be seen.

"You stay here," Caspian placed a hand on her shoulder, "I will scout the area and see if I can find them."

He turned to leave, but Wynne grabbed his arm, "Don't leave." She whispered, the panic slowly turning to fear. He halted in his step, turning to face her he gently brushed a thumb across her cheek.

"You'll be safer here, closer to the water." He gestured to the lake at her back.

She nodded, "You promise?"

He chuckled, drawing her in close, "You're more capable than you believe." He gently, pressed a kiss to her forehead, meeting her eyes, "I promise." He whispered. Wynne felt the breath catch in her throat, as he turned quickly, disappearing into the jungle, her forehead hot with a tingling sensation from his lips. She stood there for a moment, listening for his footsteps, until they faded completely, and she was left all alone on the beach. She quickly found a spot to sit and wait for him to return, praying that he returned with her father and his men in tow.

Wynne sat as still as possible, holding her knees tightly to her chest, letting the noise of the jungle cover her in some sort of security. She listened carefully to the sounds filling the space around her, waiting for anything that sounded out of place or different. But the only sounds she could make out were insects buzzing throughout the jungle branches with the occasional chatter from birds and other animals hidden deep within the jungle.

Wynne waited and waited, but no one came out onto the beach. Slowly, she uncurled herself, stretching out her legs before her, she allowed herself to relax slightly. Her gaze turned towards the chest, resting in her lap. She took the time to examine the chest, the intricate filagree that covered the surface of the chest and the blue jem stones peeking out at her. It was intricate and delicate, but also bold and commanding. The trident in the center was large and sparkling, taking up most of the lid, telling all who gazed upon it who this chest belonged to. Wynne looked from the chest to the locket. The locket was designed the same, it was intricately designed and the trident's matched.

As Wynne sat there, her mind began to wander. She was an allure, her mother—Wynne swallowed—had been a goddess. She shivered, pulling her knees back up to her chest. A daughter of Oaran, his chosen daughter at that; but she had given it all up. Her life had been forfeited the moment she decided to go through with Payne's curse, her mother's death was a result of Payne. Had her mother done things differently, though, Wynne might not have ever been born.

For the first time, in a long time, Wynne wished that her mother was sitting with her. She had questions she wanted to ask her yes, but mostly, she wanted to just talk to her mother. She had been so young when her mother had died, she never had a chance to really experience a deep relationship with her mother, at least not as an adult woman. The fragment of memories she did have of her mother, were tender ones, but very few and fleeting. The more time went by the fainter the memories became. Had it not been for the dreams she had been having of her mother, Wynne wasn't sure she could even remember her mother's face.

A branch snapped in the distance, Wynne glanced up quickly, holding her breath as she waited. The rustle in the jungle became louder, heavy footsteps echoed across the shoreline. Wynne shrunk back into the shadows, as a figure stepped out onto the shore. The sky had dimmed tremendously, and all sunlight was almost gone. She held her breath as the figure waited for a moment, searching the shoreline, before walking slowly towards her. Wynne waited until the figure came closer and her view less obscured. A sigh escaped her lips, Caspian had returned, but the worried look on his face, did nothing to soothe her nerves.

"No sign of them?" She questioned quickly as he approached.

He shook his head, "I found a path leading back towards the beach."

Wynne frowned, "Towards the beach?" Why on earth would her father gone to the beach without them?

"My guess is your father thought it would be the safer option." Caspian met her gaze, "That was always the rendezvous point after we made it here." He added. Wynne nodded, it just seemed odd that her father, of all people had chosen to leave her. But if it was indeed the rendezvous point, there was no sense in questioning his actions.

"His ship is waiting for us." Caspian added, as though he could read the doubt still lingering on her face. She reached for the map that still lay folded in her pocket, but was distraught when she pulled out a solid, still damp, wad of paper.

"Damn it!" She cried, trying to delicately unfold the map, but watched in horror as it just ripped to shreds. Caspian chuckled, his laugh adding more frustration to Wynne's detriment.

"Why are you laughing?" She snapped, still trying to salvage what she could of the soggy map.

"You," he chuckled, "swearing."

Wynne smiled, "I am so glad you are enjoying this."

"We don't need the map." He added smugly.

Wynne folded her eyes, "And how exactly do you plan on making it back to the beach without a map?"

Caspian's brow raised, "See that spot over there?" He pointed across the shoreline to a particular spot, Wynne followed the gesture, nodding, "That is an overlook that looks out to the beach." Wynne's eyes narrowed, she didn't particularly like the sound of an overlook, she wished the map was still intact, so she could see it on paper.

"We can climb down the cliff, and we will be much closer to the beach than if we go back the way we came." He prodded, "It will be faster too, like a short cut." He added, his voice light, his attempt to reassure her.

"You call climbing down a cliff a short cut?" Wynne's eyes narrowed, folding her arms across her chest. She felt a prick of indignation that there could possibly be a faster route back to the beach when they had just spent days getting her to start with!

He smiled, "If it means getting to the beach quicker, it's worth it." Wynne groaned, how was she going to argue with him? Besides, she felt anxious, ready to be safe and not constantly looking over her shoulder. The quicker they got to the beach, the quicker she could return the chest and seal the curse, forever.

She nodded, "We will take your short cut first thing in the morning." Caspian nodded, he looked somewhat relieved that she had agreed to his plan. He was just as anxious as she was to get back to the beach, to have this whole thing resolved and over with.

Together they decided to set up camp along the shoreline. The evening was warm and there was no need to assemble a fire. Though, Wynne had a pretty good idea that the only reason Caspian had suggested no fire, was because he didn't want to be the one to get the firewood. Wynne chuckled to herself; she couldn't say she blamed him. His face mirrored the exhaustion she felt throughout her entire body. So, Wynne settled down, laying on her back with her elbow propped behind her head, her gaze fixed on the sky above them and the slow twinkle of the stars that were starting to come out for the evening.

"Tomorrow," She whispered up to the sky, "I will end this." She felt Caspian settle in beside her. He was close, his shoulder brushed up against her own. She felt her heartbeat flutter into her throat, and her stomach turned in knots. She felt his hand brush up against hers, everything froze inside of her, as his fingers touched hers. Instinctively, she folded her hand into his, letting his fingers thread through hers and squeeze her hand tight. The warmth from his hand fluttered into her, matching the flutter of her heartbeat. She turned her head smiling at him through the darkness. Even through the light was almost gone, there was still enough for her to see him return her smile.

Peace and calm swept through her soul. It was the first moment, she had felt such calm in a long, long time. She never, in all her years, would have thought her life would have looked like this. Nor would she have thought she'd be here, holding the hand of the one person she thought she'd never trust. She smiled to herself, things had changed, and for once, she was completely content with this change.

Chapter 31

Morning light came sooner than Wynne had wanted. Slowly, the sunlight crept over the top of the trees, spreading across her cheeks, gently waking her. She fidgeted, feeling something heavy draped over her. Frowning, she opened her eyes and saw Caspian's arm gently resting over her. She felt her face flush, as her eyes adjusted, and her awareness of her surroundings awakened. Caspian was at her back; his breath tickled her neck. As carefully as she could, she turned her head, Caspian's eyes fluttered open, and a lazy smile spread across his face.

"Morning already?" He questioned, his voice low and groggy.

Wynne nodded, sitting up quickly, his arm falling away from her, "We have a beach to get to." She declared, her blush still lingering on her face.

"Mmhmm," Caspian drawled, rubbing his eyes, "and a ship to get to."

"Exactly." She stood quickly, stretching herself upright. Caspian groaned, but stood up beside her, stretching himself like a cat. The groggy look still lingered on his face.

"Let's return that chest." He remarked, waving a hand for her to follow him. Together they made their way across the shore to the spot Caspian had pointed out to her the night before. They dove into the jungle, Wynne took one last look over her shoulder at the lake, she would most likely never see this place again. It was for the best; it would mean she succeeded. She let the jungle swallow her whole, sealing her off from the looking glass forever.

They walked a short distance before Caspian halted. Wynne peered over his shoulder and saw that they were standing at the edge of a cliff. Just as Caspian had said, there was the overlook and beyond them, through the trees, she saw the glisten of the ocean water. Wynne held her breath and stepped around him, peering over the side. The cliff was nothing but volcanic rock, that led down to the jungle below and then off in the distance, Wynne could see the faint outline of creamy sand and the water beyond. They were much closer to the beach than she thought, which brought a fresh wave of hope. But, the path to the beach was probably the most treacherous path they would endure.

"A short cut huh?" Wynne exclaimed.

"It's a better than going back the way we came." He replied with such confidence, but his confidence was not enough to keep the fear from flooding through her, making her knees buckle beneath her.

"How is this better?" She asked, swallowing, the shake in her knees growing.

"This is faster, if we go back the other way it will be days," he argued, "Plus, the bridge is no longer there, remember?"

Wynne nodded, feeling her stomach drop slightly, "I remember." She muttered, closing her eyes as she willed away the memory of the bridge snapping and the sensation of falling to her death.

"Look," he pointed, "There are little ledges all the way down," Wynne followed his finger, and saw a ledge not the far below them, "It will be easy." She pursed her lips, not entirely sure "easy" and "climbing down a cliff" belonged in the same sentence. Carefully, Caspian lowered himself down to the nearest ledge. He made it easily before turning to help Wynne. Gripping the chest in one arm, she lowered herself to the ground inching her way to the edge of the ledge. Caspian grabbed her waist and lowered her easily over the ledge, setting her down carefully beside him. Wynne took a deep breath, trying to soothe the nerves that thundered through her.

Caspian met her eyes and smiled, "Piece of cake."

"One ledge down," Wynne sighed, "a hundred more to go." She muttered. They started climbing, slowly and steadily with Caspian leading the way. Any precarious spots they came to, Caspian made sure to help her. But despite the slow and steady pace, it wasn't long before Wynne and Caspian's hands were shredded to pieces. Stopping a few ledges down, Caspian ripped strips from the bottom of his shirt, handing two to Wynne for her hands before ripping two for himself. She chuckled at the sudden shortness of his shirt. The ripped strips had now made his shirt, considerably shorter, exposing his skin below.

"Do you find something amusing?" He purred, holding his hands out to Wynne.

"I love the new look!" She cried, gesturing to the shortened shirt, as she began to wrap his hands.

"It's not too revealing is it?" He teased.

Wynne laughed, "Anymore and I'd say you'd be ready for a burlesque show."

"Don't pretend like you wouldn't want to see it." Caspian grinned. Wynne felt her face flush, and the laughter flew from her mouth.

"You're right, I would like to see it!" Wynne teased, as Caspian started to wrap her hands. He merely chuckled in response, she was half expecting him to come back with a flirtatious remark, but he didn't, he just stood there smirking. After a minute, he grabbed the last couple strips and gestured for her hands. She held them out slowly towards him, suddenly aware of the throbbing from the cuts covering her palms. Wynne watched as he carefully placed the stirp of cloth over her hands, careful to wrap them tightly, but not too tight.

"You ready?" Caspian asked, tying the last strip tightly to her hand. She nodded, and watched him climb down to the next ledge, before looking back up at her. They continued the grueling climb down the cliff face. The cloth strips provided some protection to their hands, but the sharp volcanic rocks still scratched away at their hands.

As she continued the climb down the cliff, her mind wandered. They had not seen Payne this entire journey. Yes, that had meant less worry for Wynne, but now that they were towards the end, her nerves were jumpy. Payne had been so adamant to get the chest, to possess her mother essence, and yet he had remained in the shadows. Wynne was grateful they had made it to the looking glass without any problems, but the feeling that there was something waiting for her, made her stomach twist in uncomfortable knots.

"Caspian?" She called, "Do you have a funny feeling?"

"About what?" He asked, lowering himself to the next ledge.

Wynne readjusted the chest in her arms, "This has been way too easy."

"What's been easy?" He cried, looking up at her quickly.

"This!" She gestured to the jungle around them, "Payne's been wanting this chest for years!" She cried, lowering herself carefully to the ledge beside Caspian, "And yet, we haven't seen him, at all!"

Caspian frowned, "Were you hoping we would?"

"No," She shook her head, pursing her lips, "but—I can't explain it," She bit her lip, "I just have a funny feeling." Wynne peered up at Caspian, but he wasn't looking at her. His face was twisted in a frown deep in concentration. She was somewhat curious to know what his thoughts were, but she held her tongue. Tightening her grip around the chest, she moved to lower herself to the next ledge.

They continued in silence. The jungle below them was getting closer and closer as they made their way down. Both were breathing heavily, and Wynne felt trickles of sweat dripping from her forehead and running down the ridge of her back. The climb was strenuous, and she was anxious to be done climbing. Her throat was dried out and her mouth felt like she had eaten a whole container of chalk. They couldn't stop now though, not when they were so close to the end of their climb. She had a restless feeling building in her limbs, prodding her to move quicker. The quicker they could get to the beach, the quicker they could leave and maybe—just maybe the uneasiness she felt would lessen.

They came to the last section and Wynne could finally see the ground beneath them. She smiled, feeling a wave of relief sweep through her. Caspian jumped the last section, landing gracefully on his feet. But as quickly as he landed, he was turning to help Wynne scurry down the last little section. Wynne had no inclination of throwing herself off the last little bit but was grateful for the assistance. Both of their hands, despite their crude bandages, had been ripped to shreds from the unforgiving rocks.

"We could have just scaled that cliff instead of following the map." Wynne sighed, looking back up the cliff they had just climbed down.

"There was a reason we had to go that way." Caspian chided.

Wynne frowned wiping the sweat from her brow, "Other than absolute torture?" she smirked.

He laughed, "Yes." He fixed her with a pointed look, "All of that torture," he emphasized, "was for your benefit." She rolled her eyes, but knew, deep down he was right. That path leading to the looking glass had been specifically crafted for her and her alone.

"Well," Wynne breathed in deeply, "shall we continue on to the beach?" She brushed past him, leading the way while ignoring the smug smile that was plastered onto his face. The journey had been to test her, she knew that, and in the end, she glanced down at the chest in her arms, she had made it through. But she had had some help, she glanced back at Caspian over her shoulder, and smiled slightly. Had it not been for him, she may not have made it this far.

They walked through the jungle at a slow steady pace. Neither one spoke, both had a fervent desire to get to the beach as quickly as possible, which held to spur them forward. But, despite the renewed energy, weariness tugged at the back of Wynne's body. It was a lingering feeling in her bones that threatened to pounce on her if she let her guard down. She was afraid that if she stopped now, she would not be able to continue. So, she kept charging forward through the large deep green leaves, past the ensnaring vines that reached out to her, trying to hold her back.

The further they walked and the closer they got to the ocean, the stronger the scent of salt became. Wynne breathed deeply and felt herself smile; they were getting close. Excitement pulsed through her veins. A few more paces and she could hear the faint roar of waves crashing onto the shore. The thought of digging her toes into the sand and feeling the water splash on her legs her quicken her pace even more. She pushed back the final branches and smiled, the joy she felt pulsed through her. She was standing on the tree line, looking out onto the beach, blue waters lapping up onto creamy white sand. It was beautiful, the best site she had seen in days.

Slowly, she stepped out onto the sand, there was something in the water though not too far away. Her eyes squinted and she noticed it was a dinghy! Well, that was a relief, but how had it gotten there. For the moment, the question flew from her mind with the excitement of finally being back on the beach and out of the jungle.

"We made it!" She cried over her shoulder, stepping out onto the beach smiling brighter, "Caspian, we made it!" She cried again, louder this time and spinning lightly on her toes. But Caspian was nowhere to be seen. Frowning, she stepped back into the jungle, had she really been walking that fast? Had she lost him?

"Caspian?" She called. Wynne stopped, listening for any movement, but there was nothing. Panic set in, had she lost him? She took a few steps back the way they had come, searching for any signs of him.

"Caspian!" She called again, trying not let the panic set in. She paused, holding her breath. Movement flickered in the corner of her eyes. She turned but was too late. There was a flash of pain on her temple and then everything went black.

Chapter 32

Wynne's head throbbed; her jaw ached. Her eyes slowly fluttered open, her cheek was pressed against the sand, the scent of dry salt filled her nose. She shifted slightly and then realized her hands were empty. Panic flooded through her, the chest! Gasping, her eyes popped open, and she sat up quickly. A fresh wave of pain surged through her body and throbbed painfully in her temple. A shadow fell over her face. Slowly, she looked up and felt her breath catch in her throat. Payne stood above her, holding the chest in his hands, grinning from ear to ear.

"Hello, Miss Hunt!" He greeted with sinister delight.

"How?" She gasped, her eyes filling with tears.

He smiled, "The only way I knew how," he purred with every bit of satisfaction on his face, "Manipulation at its finest." He laughed, "and the deceit involved," he shook his head, his smile growing, "made it so much more enjoyable to watch."

Wynne frowned, "What are you talking about?" She blinked, trying to get some of the throbbing to subside.

Payne's smile grew even wider, "Why don't I let you explain," his gaze flicker to a spot behind her head. Wynne frowned, glancing behind her slowly, and felt her heart stop in her chest.

Caspian stood there before her.

His face was made of stone as he stood rigid in the sand, watching her. Everything inside her grew limp. Confusion gnawed at her; her chest ached. She frowned, trying to comprehend, she had been lied to—deceived. But how—he—Wynne hung her head as the tears clouded her vision. A hand grabbed her chin, forcing her head up to look at Caspian. She didn't try to pull away, as the emotions swept over her, and the tears flowed freely. Wynne blinked, as the tears continued to trickle down her face. Payne leaned down, inches away from her own.

"I knew you would do everything in your power to resist my plan—would try to keep me from getting what I wanted." He spat, then chuckled, "So Caspian devised a plan." Wynne's eyes flitted from Payne's to Caspian's. Caspian was not looking at her but stood behind Payne. His face was pale, making him look sick. As if sensing her stare, Caspian looked up and met her gaze. But she saw nothing there.

"He fed you the story you wanted to hear, gained your trust— all to bring me my beloved treasure." He laughed, cradling the chest closer to him, "You will die a valiant death though," he sneered, "I will see to that." Wynne pursed her lips and looked back at Payne. Anger flared in her chest, she had been used, manipulated, and betrayed!

Wynne spat into Payne's face and swung a fist, connecting with his jaw. Payne reeled back, groaning as his hand flew to his jaw. Wynne didn't stay to enjoy her triumph. She jumped to her feet and ran, diving quickly into the jungle, pushing branches aside she tore through the jungle foliage, not looking back. But, just like every other time she had run, she didn't get very far. A hand grabbed her arm and pinned her to a tree. Caspian's grey blue eyes met hers. She fought against him, but he held her firm.

"Let me go!" She screamed, fighting against him, feeling the sting of tears burn her eyes.

"Wynne." He cried, trying to hold her back. But she managed to free a hand and slapped him as hard as she could. He let go of her and started to run again. But she didn't get very far before he caught her again, only this time he tackled her to the ground. She fought him tooth and nail before Caspian successfully pinned her arms down and sat on top of her.

"What was that for?" He barked.

"You lied to me!" She screamed, her eyes filling with tears, "You tricked me!" She gasped, her lower lip trembled, "I never," her voice faltered, "I never should have trusted you!" Caspian stared down at her, his face was filled with so many emotions. He closed his eyes, sighed, then looked at her again. His storm grey eyes locked onto her with such intensity it made her shake.

"What I told you, was the truth." He whispered.

Wynne frowned, "Even you believe your lies!" she hissed.

Caspian groaned, his face flashing with anger, "I told Payne what he wanted to know!"

"Yeah," she cried, tears streaming down her cheeks, "Just like you told me what I wanted to hear!" She screamed, letting the anger fill her words.

"Dammit Wynne!" He shouted right back at her. "I had no choice." Wynne saw her frustration mirrored in his face.

"You said you'd get me out of here alive, not stab me in the back" She cried hiccupping once, "What kind of monster are you?" He looked her in the eyes, his face flushed white before coloring pink. There was a quick flash of anger, but then it was replaced by something hard, determination.

"I keep my promises, whether you believe me or not." He pulled her to her feet and dragged her back to the shore where Payne was waiting patiently. Payne's face twisted into a smug smile. The dread settled deep in her gut, she felt like crying, the despair was overwhelming. She was going to die on this island—her mother's sacrifice—would be all in vain.

"It is no use Miss Hunt," Payne chided, "Running will get you nowhere." Her lower lip trembled as Caspian pinned her to his chest with one arm while the other pressed a blade to her throat.

"Give me your hands." Payne commanded. Wynne frowned, gripping her hands tightly at her sides, the defiance rippling through her.

"Why do you need my hands?" She demanded.

Payne's dark eyes narrowed, the smirk on his lips grew, "Only an Allure's blood can open this chest." He fixed her with a pointed gaze and Wynne felt the dread settle in the pit of her stomach. She held her fists by her side, refusing to cooperate. She would not yield easily, and she would put up as much fight as possible.

Payne eyed her gripped fists, sighing loudly, "Caspian, assist Miss Hunt." He drawled, not at all amused by her defiant spirit. Caspian pressed the blade into her throat. But instead of feeling the blade bite into her skin, she only felt a dull pressure along her throat. Why did he had the dull side pressed to her throat? No, she, he had betrayed her, whatever he was doing was still a ploy, blunt side or not. She refused to budge. When she made no move to open and extend her hand, Caspian pressed the blade harder into her throat. And although it did not break her skin, the pressure was enough to choke her. Squealing, she pressed herself back into Caspian's chest, trying to relieve some of the pressure from her neck and instinctively extended her hands. As soon as her hands were out, the pressure on her neck ceased.

"Excellent." Payne hissed, snatching her hands, removing the tattered cloth bandages, revealing already damaged hands beneath. Carefully, he ran his dagger across her palms. She winced as a thin line sliced through her delicate skin. She helplessly watched as dark, crimson blood pooled into her palms.

"Please don't do this." She whimpered, seeing Payne's black eyes widen with blood lust, as he watched the blood gathering.

His eyes snapped up to hers, "Your mother's birthright shall be mine." He cried setting one of her hands on top of the golden lid, "Any last words, Miss Hunt? I am afraid you will not live to see my final triumph." He purred. Panic surged through her, but she managed to keep it from taking over her body. Caspian, ever so slightly, squeezed her. It was just enough to offset the panic she felt, but it did not stop the confusion that now swept over her. Was he trying to comfort her, give her some sort of reassurance before Payne killed her? Or was this his way of showing her that he was going to keep his promise? She couldn't rely on Caspian, not when he had managed to gain her trust, she swallowed, gained her heart, and then trampled it faster than she could even blink! No, she would end this—some way—and she would do it herself.

"Do you have any last words, Captain?" She asked with a sudden surge of boldness.

Payne laughed, "I hope you die slowly, and painfully." He sliced open his palm and then grabbed her other hand. Caspian's arms fell away from her as she collapsed to her knees. Pain, that was all she could feel. It started in the hand that held the chest, and flowed through her, shattering her very soul. Wynne gritted her teeth, resisting the blackness that tugged and ripped at the very fiber of her being. She cried out as the cord that she had bound to her soul began to unravel. Everything inside of her was being ripped apart. She wasn't sure how much more pain she could endure.

Suddenly, an ear-splitting crack spliced through the air, and she felt herself falling, uncontrollably. Time had stopped around her, she felt herself slowly falling, then colliding painfully with the hot sand beneath her. There was a moan, maybe it had come from her own lips, but she wasn't sure.

Darkness covered her face, someone was standing above her, was it Payne? This was it, he was going to finish her now. She had failed her mother, her essence was gone, consumed by the monster that had hunted her. She felt tears stream down her face, stinging her eyes. There was a shout above her, but the words were warbled, like her head was trapped under water. Maybe, just maybe, Payne wasn't going to kill her, although the dull pulsating feeling throughout her body told her otherwise. Her eyes widened, trying to catch a glimpse at the scene before her, but the images refused to stop moving. Everything was warped, moving extremely slow. She felt like she was trying to stay afloat in a feverish dream.

Wynne turned her head, ever so slowly, her vision cleared. Payne was on his knees, clutching his chest, the moan was coming from his lips. There was blood pouring through his fingers. Had he been shot? Wynne frowned, trying to make sense of what she was seeing. Payne was enraged, shouting between his moans, but why?

"What have you done!" He screamed. Wynne felt herself suddenly lifted into a warm, sturdy arms. Why was she so cold? A hand brushed against her cheek, she winced. The hand felt like fire against her skin. She turned her head slowly and saw grey blue eyes staring down at her. She felt her breath hitch in her throat, Caspian. Etched over the hard lines of his face, was concern, tender and gentle. His eyes, were wide in shock, glistening in the sunlight.

"I made a promise." He whispered.

"No Caspian!" Payne shouted, "You can't!" he bellowed from somewhere behind them. But Caspian ignored him, his attention fixed completely on her.

"I'm so cold." Wynne muttered, her voice barely above a whisper.

"Stay with me." He pleaded, holding her tighter against him. She couldn't keep her eyes focused—he kept coming in and out of focus. Ever so slowly, she felt the numbing cold start to freeze over, starting in her fingertips and working its way up her body. Something warm trailed down her cheek, it was a tear. She was dying, she could feel the darkness creeping in on her.

Something warm and fuzzy brushed against her fingertips. Then, a loud crack shattered above her, she felt herself falling from Caspian's arms into the sand. Someone shouted above her and someone moaned, again, loudly. She felt a vague sense of panic amid the darkness that was slowly closing in on her. But there was still some resilience left in her. She forced herself to focus, calling on whatever light she still had in her, and turned her head to the blurred figures next to her.

Wynne's eyes widened and her vision became clear. Caspian and Payne were rolling in the sand, Payne was screaming unintelligibly, as Caspian struggled to throw him off. Wynne squinted, trying to clear away the fog that lines her eyes. Caspian managed to throw Payne off, but his arm hung, limp by his side. His sleeve was tinged with crimson. Wynne tried calling to him, but no words came from her mouth.

Something inside her, fractured, tingled. She knew that feeling, but what was it? She turned her head slowly and saw the chest lying beside her, glowing in the sand. Her mother's essence, it was still there, she could feel it! Carefully, she reached for it, it was just out of reach. Clamping her eyes closed, she stretched herself, her whole body pro-testing with the movement. Just when she thought she could stretch no further, her fingers settled on the lid. A jolt of energy, pure and sweet, surged through her. Someone was screaming, it was a minute before she realized that she was the one screaming. Wynne gritted her teeth as energy, more powerful than anything she had ever felt, coursed through her body, filling every part of her. In a heart rendering moment, she went from being consumed by darkness and cold to being consumed by radiating light and fire. A deafening roar filled her ears, and she could taste iron on her tongue. The heat behind her eyes made her clamp her eyelids shut, hoping the burning sensation would cease altogether.

Wynne gritted her teeth and looked up from where she sat, burning. Maybe Caspian could through her in the water, cool off the fire that burned through her. Caspian, though was on the ground, scurrying back from Payne who hovered above him, a dagger in his hand. Wynne felt herself yell, but neither one of them looked her way. She was helpless as she watched Payne thrust his dagger into Caspian. Wynn watched, in horror, as Caspian fell back, lifeless into the sand. Payne ripped the dagger from Caspian and turned to face her, he was covered in blood and his face was twisted in rage.

Time stopped. The roar in her ears ceased and the fire stopped, replaced by a cool rush of calm. An energy, new but strangely familiar, pulsed through her. She stood, clutching her fists to her side as tears gathered in her eyes as she looked from Caspian to Payne. She could feel the swell of the waves at her back, calling to her. There was something different about the power that flowed through her. It was familiar, but stronger, different than before. She felt something similar, oozing out of Payne. Wynne scowled, stolen power, that was what he had. Payne laughed; blood dribbled down his mouth.

"You think you can win?" Payne shouted, taunting her as blood spewed from his mouth.

"Do you think you can stop me?" Wynne called; her voice unfamiliar to her. Payne's face turned pale as his eyes found the empty chest at her feet. Anger flashed through his face, he charged at her, brandishing a blood-soaked dagger. Despite the rage that filled her entire being, there was an underlying calm that soothed her. Wynne reached out for the humming she could feel residing in Payne, grasping it with a vengeance. Payne halted before her—no, she realized—

he was not halting, she was holding him back. What flowed through her, flowed through him, though much fainter and weaker. She smiled, she was in control of that strength, not him. His eyes widened in fear as he came to the same conclusion.

"Do you think you can do it?" Payne yelled, "Your mother couldn't, she was weak!" He spat, as he pushed against her hold. She could feel his resistance growing, she had to quench the ember altogether.

"I am not my mother!" Wynne whispered. Movement beyond Payne caught her eye before a crack split through the air. Payne's eyes bulged as more blood dripped from his mouth and onto his chin. Wynne could feel the life slipping from him, the power he contained becoming faint beneath her grasp. Payne gasped and just like that, the power he contained extinguished before her. His eyes rolled back into his head, and he fell back into the sand. Wynne looked beyond Payne's lifeless form to Caspian, who was propped up on one arm and a pistol in the other.

Chapter 33

Wynne fell to her knees, suddenly flooded with aches and pain she didn't know she had. Exhaustion poured through her, she felt drained. The strength that had filled her, evaporated, leaving her feeling battered and beaten. But the energy she had gained, remained. With the little strength she had left, she crawled across the sand, dragging her weary limbs towards the spot where Caspian lay. She could see his chest rising and falling, blood still oozing from his wound.

"You're alive!" She cried, choking back her tears as she crawled up beside him, "What happened?" Wynne cried, seeing for the first time, a bullet wound in his shoulder, accompanying his stab wound.

"I told you," Caspian winced, gasping, "I keep my promises." He grunted.

"You tricked Payne." She whispered. Tears clouded her eyes as she looked from his ashen face to his wounds. The bleeding needed to be stopped, he couldn't die just yet, she was still mad at him. They had come so far; she couldn't lose him now. She started to tear the bottom of her tunic, when Caspian's hand grabbed hers, stopping her.

"What are you doing?" He hissed.

Wynne shoved his hand aside, continuing to rip her tunic, "I have to stop the bleeding, or you will die." She cried, the urgency in her tone was quite clear.

"Leave me, Wynne." He sighed, "You have to get to the ship." He added through clenched teeth.

Wynne clamped her eyes shut and shook her head, "Shut up!" She snapped, pointing a finger in his face, "You have plenty of explaining to do and I am not letting you die yet!" Caspian groaned, though she wasn't sure if it was from his wounds or from her stubbornness. He clutched his belly wound and his breaths came in short painful gasps. His face was pale, and his lips quivered. Wynne quickly ripped several more strips, hoping they would be enough. Gently, she grabbed his fingers, trying to carefully pry his hand away from his wound. His whole body jerked and groaned in protest.

"Don't!" He hissed.

Wynne bit her lip, "Caspian," she pleaded, "I have to stop the bleeding." He took a shaky breath as she pried his fingers away. She bit her lip, inhaling a quick, deep breath, taking in the sight of his wound.

"That bad, huh?" He asked breathlessly.

She forced a smile, "You're going to be fine." She offered, replacing his fingers quickly with the cloth and pressing firmly down on the wound. He jerked again, hissing at her, but she pressed the cloth down firmly. He would thank her later.

"You're not going to die on me, Caspian." She whispered. Caspian met her eyes; she could see the faint outline of a smile on his lips.

"Even after all I have done?" He muttered.

She scowled, "Especially after all you've done!" She bit her lip as she watched the cloth filled with blood, not at all stopping it. Frantic, she grabbed for another cloth, pressing it on top of the other soaked strip. He sucked a breath in, his face turning up into a painful wince.

"Sorry." Wynne whispered, grabbing the final bandage, placing it on top of the others. But, just like the others, it did nothing to stop the flow of blood. Trying to keep the tears from springing to her eyes, she quickly looked away. The water lapped at the shore behind them, as peaceful as ever. Beyond them though, her eyes caught site of a ship. Was it her father's ship? It was still too far away to tell. If she could get Caspian to the dinghy, she could get them to the ship.

"We need to get to that ship." She cried, the idea flooding her without any further thought.

"No!" Caspian cried through gritted teeth.

"If you think, for one second, I am leaving you here on this beach to die," she cried, grabbing his hand, and pressing it firmly to his wound, "You have another thing coming! Keep pressure on that." Wynne ordered, tearing off the rest of the bottom of her tunic. She used a portion of it to wrap the bullet wound in his shoulder and used the rest on his gut.

"Stay here." She commanded, leaving him no room to argue.

He chuckled, "I'll think about it." She glared at him, not at all amused with his sudden burst of humor. Trotting back to the water, she studied the ship sailing towards them, hoping to catch a glimpse of her colors. She held her breath, squinting her eyes against the sun. Her heartbeat thundered in her chest, as she saw the crimson and gold flag flutter in the wind. A smile spread across her ship; those were the colors she knew best. It was her father's ship; she hoped the ship's arrival meant he had made it back to the ship. Wynne ran back to where Caspian was, fresh determination flowing through her.

"Are you ready?" Wynne asked, stooping beside him.

He frowned, "No." he growled.

She ignored him, grabbing his hand in hers, "This is going to hurt." She tugged him upward, gritting her teeth as his body weight pulled against her.

"You're going to have to help me!" She struggled. Caspian frowned but nodded his head. Moving quickly, she came around him, bending low, she put his arm up over her shoulders and wrapped her arm around his back hooking tightly onto his waist. Ever so closely, she braced herself and stood, groaning as his weight settled over her shoulders. Her body strained, and Caspian groaned with the movement, but by some miracle, they were able to stand. Clutching his hand to his side, he cried out in pain as his balance gave way. Wynne dug her heels in and tightened her arm around him, holding him fast. His weight pressed down on her, she bit her lips, worried that she would not be able to carry him. Gritting her teeth, she forced herself to take a step forward. There was no way, she was leaving him,

They hobbled forward, slowly. Every step Caspian took, Wynne felt him tense, the pain etching deep lines across his pale face. He kept his eyes closed shut, taking each step slowly and carefully. Thankfully the dinghy was not far away but getting Caspian in was a whole different battle. He had to lean on her as she stepped over the side, his weight threatened to squash her, but she held firm. Once he stepped over the side, she helped was Caspian gently down to the floor of the dinghy. He slumped down and groaned, then sighed slightly, relief flooded his face. Wynne took a deep breath, before checking his wounds. His shoulder wound had stopped bleeding, and his side wound was bleeding still, probably from moving. She bit her lip, she had no more bandages to put on it. Turning her focused on the next challenge—getting the boat into the water.

Wynne wedged the dinghy against her shoulder, took a deep breath and dug her feet into the sand, throwing every single ounce of her weight into the dinghy. The dinghy though, remained in the sand. Wynne groaned, taking another deep breath before throwing her weight, again, into the boat. She put everything she had into moving the boat. The wood dug painfully into her shoulder. But, to her relief, it inched forward. But she didn't stop; she poured all her strength into her legs, keeping the momentum moving forward. She pushed until she felt the weight of the boat settle on top of the water. A wave crashed against the boat, knocking her over. But the water felt good against her skin, giving her a fresh wave of energy. She picked herself up and threw her shoulder against the dinghy. The water swirled around her, welcoming her presence. The current responded to her command, helping her to push the boat further and further away from the beach. When the water came up to her waist, she heaved herself up into the dinghy, falling in next to Caspian. He hadn't moved.

Wynne turned, slightly, looking at his pale face. He was still breathing, but it was faint. Wynne felt alarm ripple through her, it was as if she was watching his life drain out, right before her very eyes. She grabbed his arm carefully and readjusted herself beside him, pressing her body to his. His eyes opened, and slowly, he turned his head to look at her. His grey blue eyes met her, the spark that usually was there was fading. Wynne could feel the water currents beneath her, humming around them. She willed them to move faster, carrying their dinghy out to sea, to the ship that was heading their way.

"Stay with me." She whispered, recalling the same intensity with which he had spoken those words to her, had looked at her, when she had felt her life draining from her. Wynne thought about losing him, after all they had been through and felt her throat constrict.

"I know what you should call your ship." She whispered, forcing herself to swallow her tears, "the New Dawn." He blinked slowly, she thought she could see a faint smile flicker on his lips.

"It's going to be a beautiful ship." She said, wistfully, "You will travel the world and won't have to worry about anyone trying to kill you." She smiled, squeezing his arm, "It'll be a grand new adventure, full of new beginnings." He blinked heavily, sighing, and wincing slightly. But he held her gaze, studying her face carefully.

The currents swelled beneath her. A sea breeze flitted across the dinghy, carrying with it shouts. Wynne perked up, sitting up quickly, searching for the source. Relief swept through her as she saw the ship, looming before them. Crew men were lined along the railing, peering at them from over the side of the ship. But Wynne's eyes searched for only one face. When her eyes settled on her father's face, tears sprung to her eyes. He was standing on the edge, his eyes fixed on her, watching her carefully.

The dinghy came to rest beside the ship, Wynne forced the water to hold the dinghy in place, while the crew members above threw ladders over the side of the ship. Two men with hooks scurried down to the dinghy, they didn't say anything as they fastened the hooks to the dinghy and shouted to the men above. The dingy jerked, throwing her forward. Slowly, the men above began to lift the dinghy up out of the water and towards the main deck. Wynne looked down at Caspian and saw his eye fluttering, barely able to stay conscious.

"Stay with me Caspian." She cried, gently caressing his cheek in her hand. Her touch seemed to bring him out of the fog that was starting to gather, but it was just for a moment.

The next few moments were agonizing for Wynne. The dinghy was lifted and over the railing before coming to rest on the main deck.

Shouts from every direction swarmed her. Men from every direction were asking her if she was alright, if she was hurt. When she assured them she was alright, their attention immediately turned towards Caspian and getting him out of the dinghy and to the doctor. Wynne felt her heart swell with relief at the mention of the doctors presence on board, even more so when she realized it was Doctor Simmons. He often accompanied her father, caring for the men on board while able to travel and learn of other countries medicinal practices. It was an arrangement that served both her father and the doctor quite well.

Several men gathered around Caspian, slipping hands under him to lift him from the dinghy. But, in their rush to get him out, they jarred him. He was still conscious and moaned loudly. The sound ripped Wynne's heart in two.

"Careful!" Wynne barked, but her voice was drowned out by all the other shouts of care that came from the other men. Wynne looked around, bewildered, did these men know Caspian? Carefully, they removed him from the dinghy and retreated to Dr. Simmons quarters, closing the door behind them. Wynne wanted to follow but stopped when the crowd parted and she saw her father standing before her.

"Winnie!" Her father's voice shouted above all the rest. Wynne slowly raised her eyes to her father's face and everything inside her melted. She took a step towards him, but before she could continue forward, he closed the distance and swooped her up into his arms. Tears spilled down her face as she buried her head into his shoulder. She was so relieved that he had made it and was not still trapped on the island. Her father set her down and wiped the tears from her cheeks. His blue eyes, so like her own, were red with tears.

"I was so worried about you!" He choked; tears spilled down his face.

"I was worried about you!" Wynne protested, "Where did you guys go?" She demanded.

"When I returned with Harshaw and Bradley and you were not on the beach," He shook his head, "I knew you had gone on without me."

Wynne blushed, "I'm sorry, father."

He shushed her, "There is no need to apologize, this journey was for you—not for me." He gripped her shoulders in his hands, "I just wanted you to be safe." He smiled slowly, "Harshaw, Bradley and I decided it would be best to return to the ship, to make sure there was a ship for you to return to."

"Caspian said you would rendezvous at the ship." Wynne whispered.

Her father nodded, "I knew you would be safe with him." He said softly.

Wynne frowned, "You trusted him?"

Her father nodded, "I've trusted him for many, many years. I knew he would do what was necessary to ensure your safety." Guilt, deeper than she had ever know, filled her heart, weighing her soul down. She glanced quickly to the doctor's door, tears springing to her eyes.

"Is he going to be, ok?" She whispered, trying to choke back the tears. Her father slipped his arm tenderly around her shoulders, pulling her in tight.

"Dr. Simmons is very capable." He stated with confidence, though made no other efforts to give her any kind of reassurance, "Why don't you go to my quarters. You can freshen up there, and you can rest. We still must get out of this lagoon and clear the pillars." Wynne nodded, looking out across the lagoon to the black pillars. They were the ones they had sailed into upon arriving at the island. Wynne took one more glance over her shoulder at the island behind her. She hoped she would never see its shores again.

Chapter 34

Wynne slipped into her father's quarters and locked the doors behind her. The next few house of solitude was invaluable to her. Her mind replayed the events of her adventure since day one. Her father's ship was the only one that she knew that had a working tub. She smiled, he had met an extravagant engineer on one of his journey's and had commissioned him to make some unique upgrades to his ship. That had included a tub in his quarters and Wynne was pleased he had arranged the upgrade. Wynne filled the tub, sinking down into the water. It was cold, bone chilling, but the coldness cleared her mind and eased the tension in her shoulders.

Wynne sighed, relaxing in the water until she felt all the tension in her shoulders loosen. Then, she grabbed the soap, slowly lathering her arms and body. Once she rinsed the soap from her arms, she moved to her hair. Her blonde locks were stringy with salts, days—weeks—without washing her hair had taken a toll on her precious lockets. Gently, she worked the soap into her hair, tenderly washing the salt from her curls. Then, taking a deep breath, she dunked her head under the water, washing away all the suds from her hair.

When she emerged, she felt like a whole new woman. Grabbing her towel, she climbed out and carefully dried herself off. Blood slowly returned to her limbs, and an alertness she had not felt in some time, slowly filled her. She gazed at her reflection in the mirror and frowned. Her body had been reduced to nothing but bones and was covered in scars. She winced; the most gruesome ones though were on her back. She studied them over her shoulder, they would never go away, she would have them forever—a constant reminder of what she had been through.

Lying on the cot was a fresh set of clothes. Wynne picked up the first garment and smiled, it was a simple, light linen dress. She never imagined she'd be able to wear a dress again. She had gotten so used to the trousers and tunic that slipping into the dress felt strange. Her bony frame drowned in all the excessive fabric, but the linen was smooth, light, and airy on her skin. Even though she was being swallowed by folds and folds of fabric, she was glad to be in something clean. A knock sounded at the door.

"Come in." She called, eyes moving for the door. Her father stepped in quickly, followed by Dr. Simmons. Wynne was instantly alert, studying the doctor's face for any signs of bad news. Her heartbeat quickened as she noticed the worried expression, but as soon as he saw here standing there, seemingly unharmed a small smile spread across his lips.

"How is he?" Wynne questioned quickly, not waiting for either men to settle down comfortably in their respective chairs.

The doctor's smile grew, "He's fine, he's lucky actually." He corrected, "But for now, I am actually here to see you." Wynne frowned, glancing from the doctor to her father.

"I'm fine." She snapped.

"Ah," he snapped back, "save me the speech." He quipped, eyeing her carefully, "You've lost a lot of weight." He observed. Wynne blushed, wrapping her arms around her tiny frame, suddenly very aware of how boney her arms felt.

"And" The doctor added, standing quickly from his chair, "your father informed me of an injury to your shoulder?" Wynne's eyes moved from the doctor back to her father. Her father met her gaze with unflinching resolution. Sighing, she slipped the sleeve from her shoulder, revealing the wound she had received from Rhymus. Simmons examined the wound carefully before setting to work. Opening his bag, he mumbled to himself, hunting for the perfect concoction. When he found what he was looking for, he applied a generous amount of a white cream onto her shoulder. Once that was finished, he took out a long strip of pure white cloth, much cleaner and nicer than the scraps she had been using from her very own shirt. He wrapped the wound tight, before smiling proudly.

"That should do it!" He cried, "Any other injuries I should be aware of?" He eyed her carefully. Wynne shifted uncomfortably under her stare before she extended her hands out to him, revealing the myriad of cuts and scrapes. The most prominent ones, however, were the slices down both of her hands.

"How did you get these?" The doctor demanded, quickly examining her hands.

"Climbing down some rocks." Wynne replied.

The doctor's gaze flicked up quickly to hers, "Rock's do not slice one's hands in a perfectly straight line."

Wynne swallowed, "It was from a knife." She admitted. Her father shifted slowly in his chair, frowning. But Wynne did not want to explain, now when the doctor was here. Thankfully, he had accepted her explanation and did not question her anymore. Silently and quickly, he applied more ointment to the wounds on her hands, before wrapping them snuggly with several clean, sterile bandages.

Wynne shook her head, "That's all." Ignoring her father's glare, "When can I see Caspian?" The doctor looked quickly from her back to her father, a questioning look in his gaze. Her father merely nodded, granting the doctor permission to speak. Wynne frowned, letting her frustration play vividly on her face.

"He needs rest." The doctor began.

"When can I see him?" Her voice lowered.

The doctor sighed, "You can take him his super tonight." He resigned, but quickly held up a cautionary finger, "But, you mustn't stay long, he needs his rest." Simmons repeated, fervently. Wynne nodded but couldn't help the smile spreading on her lips. The doctor quickly bowed and left the room without any further comment. That left her father there, staring at her, in a quiet pensive state. He was studying her, carefully, and it made her nervous under his scrutiny.

"Father, please don't," she pleaded, "if there is something on your mind, just please say it." She cried, shifting under his stare. Her words brought him out of his thoughts, and he quickly shook off the pensive look, but he continued to look at her, strangely.

"You look—"

"Yes, I know—boney, I look boney." She cried, feeling her face flush in embarrassment.

"No!" He cried, laughing slightly while shaking his head, "There is something different about you though. Your eyes," he paused, frowning as he studied her eyes a bit more closely, "They are brighter somehow." Wynne instantly thought to when Caspian had told her the same thing. It had been right after her encounter with Rhymus.

"What happened on that beach?" Her father asked quickly, his own mind working quicker to put all the pieces together.

"Payne found us." Wynne growled, "He was waiting for us on the beach." She winced at the memory of her palms being slit, her hands throbbed beneath the bandages.

"Wynne," he said slowly, folding his arms across his chest, "what happened?" The throbbing in her hands intensified. She hung her head, avoiding her father's eyes. She was afraid to tell him what happened, she had failed and admitting that was not something she wanted to do. Not when it meant she let her mother down. But she knew her father would not take any excuses or stalling. He had a stubborn streak, like her own.

"How did your palms get sliced?"

"Payne did it." Wynne swallowed, "He needed my blood to open the chest."

"Estris above," he swore, rubbing his eyes, "Your mother's essence?" he questioned quickly.

Wynne frowned, "You know about that?"

"Yes, Wynne," he sighed, starting to pace the room, "she told me everything before we were married."

"But the story you told me on the beach—"

"It was the story your mother told everyone else." His throat bobbed, "She begged me not to tell you the truth—she told me there was another destined to tell you, when the time was right." Wynne closed her eyes, Orphia. That was why she had waited for her, met her there, to tell her what her mother could not. Wynne sighed; her mother had known she wouldn't have accepted the truth from anyone involved in the chaos.

"She was right," Wynne whispered, "there was a woman in the cave, she told me everything." Her father seemed relieved that she knew the truth of what her mother had truly been.

"I'm sorry Wynne," her father sighed, "I wanted to tell you. But I was afraid if I told you, it would jeopardize all the plans your mother had put in place." Wynne nodded; she understood her mother had orchestrated many components of everything she had endured. The trust her father had put in her mother, astounded Wynne, but still she admired her father, just as much as she despised him for it as well.

"He got the chest, and he opened it," She whispered, "I failed, I couldn't seal the curse." Her lip quivered. Payne had absorbed some of her mother's essence but was stopped when Caspian had betrayed him. That was what she had felt in him, when she had confronted him, it was why the feeling in him felt so familiar. But, instead of becoming angry, disappointed with her, her father just merely stopped in his tracks, turning to look at her carefully.

"You did not fail." He stated slowly, "You did exactly what your mother wanted."

Wynne frowned, "No!" She cried, "He absorbed some of her essence!"

"And you," her father declared, "absorbed the rest." Wynne stopped, taking a step back. That was the familiar, and yet strange new sensation that she had felt take over her body.

Wynne shook her head, "That's not possible." She muttered, but she remembered the chest lying on the beach, the lid open and a warm golden light glowing inside. She closed her eyes, when she had touched the chest, she inhaled quickly, all that was left she had taken in herself. Warms hand gripped her shoulders, tenderly.

Her eyes popped open, her father was standing before her, a slight smile played on his lips.

"It is possible, and it happened." His voice was low, comforting though amidst the turmoil she felt internally. Wynne, however, tore from his hands and started to pace the room, feeling the panic set in.

"I wasn't supposed to do that at all!" She yelled, "I was supposed to return the chest to Oaran—return mother's birthright—and seal Payne's curse, not absorb her essence myself!" She threw her hands up, her anger flooring her. Wynne wasn't even entirely sure what it even meant that she had absorbed her mother's essence. Her mother had been Oaran's daughter, his prized daughter, a goddess of the sea and now that very essence was inside her!

"Wynne," her father chided softly.

"No!" Wynne snapped, pointing a finger, "Do not try to comfort me—you have no idea what I have been dealing with—what I've become!" Her hands trembled.

"Wynne!" Her father snapped, "Calm down—don't work yourself up."

"What am I going to do?" She questioned quietly.

"You are going to embrace this change, accept it for what it is," He wrapped a sturdy arm around her, "and know that your mother would have been so proud of you."

"She was a goddess, father." Wynne fixed her father's gaze with a pointed look, "And that essence was supposed to be returned to our patron deity."

"Oaran is benevolent, he will understand." Her father replied soothingly.

"You say that like you've met him!" Wynne snapped.

Her father smiled slowly, "Once—after you mother died." Everything in the little room grew silent.

"I didn't see him." Wynne muttered, feeling all her emotions dissipate.

"He wanted to meet you, but he said he would wait till the time was right, when you had the birthright."

"Do you think he'll still want to meet me even when I don't have it?" Wynne snapped, feeling suddenly exhausted.

"Guess there is only one way to find out." Her father mused. Wynne just shook her head, she needed fresh air, she needed space to think, to digest the thoughts running through her mind. She turned quickly, making her way for the door.

"Winnie?"

She threw her hand up, "I need some fresh air." She threw the door open and hurried out of the room, not waiting for her father to protest or convince her to do anything else. Air, she needed air and space to think and to breath. When she had touched the chest, she had known what she was doing, but now—now—she bit her lip. She was an allure by birth, that had been the legacy left to her by her mother, but now that she had absorbed her mother's essence what did that make her? And what's worse, she had nothing to return to Oaran, the god of the sea—her patron deity. Wynne came to the railing and stopped, propping her elbows up on the wood, she peered down at the waves lapping up the side of the ship. Would his rath be kindled because she failed?

Chapter 35

The dinner bell rang, crew members flocked the main deck, making their way to the galley. Some glanced her way as they passed, but none said anything to her. They all knew who she was, who her father was, and no one had any inclination to acknowledge her presence. Which meant some much-needed solitude for Wynne. But, at the sound of the dinner bell, she felt some excitement return, chasing away some of the anxious thoughts that crowded her mind. Caspian would be needing some dinner and she had been tasked with bringing it to him.

She made her way down to the galley, no one questioned her when she grabbed two bowls, and the cook filled them both up for her. When they were full of the stew, Wynne grabbed two helpings of some hard tack and left the galley, slipping up to one of the shipman's quarters. It was the only spot she knew they would keep Caspian. It would be a small, quiet room that would be the safest place for an injured man to get the rest he needed.

"Knock, knock." Wynne cried, rapping on the door before opening slowly, peeking inside. Caspian was lying on the cot, but looked up as she entered the room. There was a slight smile on his face when he saw her. It made her heart throb.

"I brought you some soup." She gestured to the bowls in her hand, as she closed the door behind her. The savory smell of the soup filled the air, tantalizing her nose and mouth. As she got closer, she noticed his face was still quite pale, but he was alive and that's what really mattered. Carefully, she set both bowls down on the little side table, and grabbed the tiny little stool, moving it to be closer to his little cot.

"You came to see me?" His question caught her off guard.

"Of course, I did!" She retorted, "Why wouldn't I come see you?"

He eyed her carefully, "I thought you might still be a little upset from what I did," he paused, "back on the island." His voice was low and somewhat sheepish. It was as if she had expected him to fly here in a fit of rage. She suppressed a laugh, maybe she should have done just that.

"Oh, I am very upset at you for getting shot and stabbed." She declared, "How could you be so senseless?" He laughed, the sound was not his full robust laugh, somewhat stifled and instead of his face lighting up, it turned into a painful grimace.

"Don't make me laugh." He whined, clutching his side.

Wynne chuckled, "I like making you laugh."

"Even when I'm on death's doorstep?" He gasped.

Wynne raised a brow, "You're not at all dramatic, are you?"

"Merely realistic." He grinned, before growing more serious, "I'm sorry." He whispered, "For deceiving you."

Wynne shook her head quickly, "It was for the best." She smiled, "We got Payne in the end." She added, the relief she felt was enough to wash away any past transgressions.

"How are you feeling?" Wynne asked quickly, eager to change the subject.

Caspian shifted carefully, getting a better view of her, "Like I got shot," he chuckled, slightly, "and stabbed."

"That bad, huh?" Wynne questioned, "I thought you were going to bounce back quicker than this." She added, laughing slightly.

He smirked, "I'll be sure to do that next time I get shot and stabbed." Wynne laughed but felt some guilt. He was injured because of her.

"You killed him." She whispered, clutching her hands in her lap, losing her humor, and donning a serious air.

"I had to." He whispered back, "I couldn't let you do it."

"I could have done it." Wynne argued, though she wondered if it had been left to her, would she have really been able to? Ultimately, she was grateful that Caspian had been the one to pull the trigger, but he was the one now confined to a bed, the one who almost died.

"Oh, I don't doubt it," Caspian smirked, "but I didn't want you living with that. Not when you've been through hell already."

She smiled, "Thank you, but you're the one going through hell right now." He smiled, slightly, she knew he could see the gratitude on her face. Even though she wasn't sure she could communicate that with him, she had a feeling he knew.

"Do you want to eat?" She asked quickly, glancing back down at the soup that was now probably colder than it needed to be. Caspian nodded and Wynne moved to help him sit up. Carefully, she helped him sit up and helped him rearrange the pillows behind his back. After a few moments of rearranging, he was sitting up in his cot, looking stronger than he had before.

"Wynne, are you ok?" Caspian questioned, sensing the many thoughts that whirled through her mind.

"I'm fine." She smiled, shaking her head quickly.

"You're a horrible liar." He replied casually, taking a quick taste of his soup.

She chuckled, "You're very perceptive."

"I should be," he laughed, "your face hides nothing."

"What now?" She gestured to the little room, "Where do we go from here?"

His gaze softened, "We go home, and we rebuild our lives, back to normal."

"There is no going back to normal for me." Wynne scoffed. She wasn't even sure what normal looked like anymore. She didn't feel normal anymore. How was she supposed to return to her old life and pretend like nothing had happened, like nothing had changed her? No, she wouldn't be able to do that, and it was unrealistic to expect herself to go back to something she never truly enjoyed.

"What is your plan?" Wynne asked quickly, before Caspian could try to convince her she could indeed return to a normal life.

"I have a ship waiting for me." He reminded. Wynne nodded; she had forgotten about his promised ship. Part of her wished he had forgotten about it too.

"That's right," Wynne sighed, "You have your own adventures awaiting you." Her tone was sad, she couldn't quite help it. He would return to a life of adventure, and what did she have? High society life, filled with individuals who would only see her as a viable option for an advantageous marriage match.

"You know," he said after a few minutes, "no one said normal life means pretending you're someone you're not."

"I know," Wynne groaned, "I just wasn't expecting this to happen."

Caspian frowned, "What exactly?"

Wynne felt her face flush, "I am not ready to say goodbye." She whispered, feeling tears sting her eyes. She had been looking forward to the moment they were off the island, but now that they were, she was dreading the moment when he would no longer be a part of her life.

"Ah," Caspian smiled, "I see." He mused.

"No," Wynne retorted quickly, "you don't! Because you—you— just dropped into my life, quite literally I might add, and just like that my whole world is turned upside down and now I am just supposed to go back to my normal?" She threw her hands up dramatically and grabbed the bridge of her nose, closing her eyes, trying to calm her racing heartbeat.

"I'm sorry," She finally whispered, breaking the tension that had mounted, "I'm having a hard time imagining my life without you. We've been through so much and—and I just—" She couldn't finish, instead she felt her face flush in embarrassment. She couldn't believe she had spoken the words she had buried so deep within her heart. They had been there for some time, but she had pushed them aside, refusing to acknowledge that they even existed.

"Then, why don't you come with me instead?"

"What?" She choked, feeling her ears burn.

He chuckled, "We both know you are not going to fit in with high society once you return," He remarked, "and, it would be a way for you to see the world." He had a point. She had never cared for high society, had never really fit in, and had always had a dream to travel and see the world. It would be nice to do that, without worry about a mad man trying to kill her the entire time.

"There is something I need to do." Wynne replied.

"And what's that?" Caspian questioned quickly.

"I have to return my mother's birthright." Her answer was firm, decisive. This was something she needed to do, needed to finish for her mother's sake.

"We could do it together." Caspian offered. The suggestion made Wynne's stomach light up with butterflies.

But, she shook her head, "This is something, I have to do on my own." Caspian nodded, acknowledging her response, but the look on his face told her that he did not accept her response. He looked like he wanted to protest, but for some reason he kept silent.

"Then you really are saying goodbye." He whispered, a regretful smile on his face.

Wynne frowned, "Not at all!" She cried, reaching out to grasp his hand, "This is not a goodbye, I just need you to know that I have one last thing I need to do before I can give you an answer." Wynne grasped her hand back, tightly, squeezing it gently. She relished the warmth of his hand in her own. Wynne smiled, the very idea of her traveling aboard a ship made her skin tingle with excitement. The fact that Caspian would be there with her, made her heart swell in her chest.

"Just don't make me wait too long for an answer." He chided, giving her his mischievous grin, pulling her closer. She sucked in a quick breath as the distance between them suddenly shrunk. The room was suddenly very hot, and Wynne felt the heat rising in her neck with the sudden thunder of her beating heart. He closed the gap between them and his lips met her own. Fire, electric and sizzling, spread through her as she kissed him back. Then, before she could cherish the taste of his lips, he pulled away, leaving her breathless. He smiled, brushing a thumb across her chin.

"Promise me, you'll come find me when you're done." His voice tickled against her cheeks; her lips still tingled from his kiss. She nodded her head, slowly, trying to bring herself down from the clouds.

"I promise." She whispered, smiling up at him. Slowly, she picked up the soup bowls and forced herself to leave his room. Her legs felt wobbly, the fire that had erupted inside of her was still raging. Her mind still lingered on his kiss; his warm lips pressed to hers. Before the door even clicked shut, Wynne's mind was dancing with the thought of traveling and not returning to her normal life. It was a tantalizing thought, and even more so when she thought of Caspian traveling alongside her. She could do what her mother had done before she had met her father. The idea excited Wynne more than any other idea had. There was no doubt in her mind what her decision would be once she finished her business with Oaran.

The sun had long set, replaced by a pearl moon high in the sky. It was a cloudless night and the stars reigned down from the black sky above. Wynne took a deep breath and closed her eyes, listening to the gentle roar of the waves surrounding them. She felt an ache in her chest, there was something else she needed to do. Her eyes opened, fixing on the horizon before her. This journey was not yet over, and this time she would do what she needed to do, by herself.

Chapter 36

Wynne hung suspended in the dark water. The cold currents brushing delicately around her skin, almost like faint kisses. She could feel the excitement of the water around her, as though the water itself was pleased she was there. The ship was sailing still, far above her, but she was not concerned, it would take no effort at all to return to the deck, once she had finished what she had come here to do. No one had seen her as she lifted herself over the railing and jumped into the water below. She was relieved, the last thing she needed was the entire crew turning into frenzied panic.

Closing her eyes, she settled her mind and calmed her soul. Taking her locket in her hands, she pressed the trident to her lips. Orphia's words echoed in the recesses of her memories.

"Oaran, your child awaits you." She whispered against the locket, praying he would indeed hear her words and would answer her call. She waited, eyes pressed closed, hanging in the water, slowly drifting in the darkness. Suddenly, a thrum of power rippled past her. She opened her eyes and saw the same man she had seen in the ghostly waters, floating before her. Wynne felt her chest tighten, and her breath catch in her throat. It was Oaran, it was really him.

Oaran floated before her, his strong figure glowing slightly in the darkness, illuminating the golden trident at his side. He wore robes of seaweed, that seemed more elegant than any silk garb she had even seen any royal wear. The aura about him was strong and fierce, and yet she felt the calm within, subtle and soothing. His dark eyes searched her face for a moment, before a warm and gentle smile filled his lips.

"Daughter of sea and chaos," his deep voice echoed all around her, "you have returned."

Wynne shook her head, "I failed her," Wynne objected, "I was supposed to return her birthright to you." Oaran chuckled, the deep rumbling sound filled the ocean around them, making the ocean currents vibrate around her.

"And you have." He smiled, reaching up slowly to the locket hanging from her throat, "She accepted the birthright long, long ago—but she wanted to create a life for herself, something different than what she had." He smiled, but his eyes were somewhat sad as he spoke. It must not have been easy to see his beloved daughter want to forge a path on her own, a different one than the one he had intended for her.

"And she did create a life for herself." He beamed, "She learned lessons, fought hard battles, winning some and loosing others. She loved and was betrayed, and she even learned the true meaning of sacrifice."

"My mother's essence—" she began but Oaran held up his hand, silencing her.

"She gave up her essence because it was the only way to live the life she truly wanted. And she gifted you her essence and birthright. Payne was cursed, the moment your mother sacrificed herself." He smiled, reaching out a hand to tenderly stroke her cheek. "It is now yours, as it should be." He declared, his smile beaming with pride she did not think she deserved.

Wynne shook her head, "I don't deserve this!"

"Why?" He turned his head slightly, "Have you not proven yourself worthy?"

"Worthy of what? I am not a goddess!" Wynne cried flushing at the impertinent way she was speaking to her patron deity. But Oaran merely smiled, warmly at her, as though he knew her questions and doubts were valid and worth hearing.

"Because you question your worth does not mean you are not worthy of the title I bestowed upon your mother," he answered calmly, "and, it does not make you any less worthy of being one of my children, if you choose the very birthright I extended to her, it shall be yours."

"I am not my mother." Wynne expressed, somewhat skeptically.

Oaran shook his head, "No, you are not, you are your own person, but" he winked, "you are not all that different either."

"And what if I choose to forge my own path?"

Oaran smiled, "You will forever be a daughter of the sea, regardless of the path you choose."

"What about my father? Caspian? Will I lose them if I choose this path?" She paused, biting her lip, "They are the only ones I have left in this world. I can't lose them."

His smile deepened, "You will never lose the ones that love you and cherish you the most, regardless of the path you choose." His words brought a deep comfort to her. There was no pressure from him, and since no one else knew what truly lie beneath her skin, there could be no other pressure. This decision was hers and hers alone. Her life had never been normal, and there had always been a nagging feeling that something was missing. Now, floating in the depths of the ocean, she felt, for the first time in her entire life, whole. A wave of deep reassuring peace flooded over her, and her clouded mind suddenly lifted into crystal clear clarity.

"Then I shall keep it." She whispered, clutching the locket around her neck, slowly looking up to Oaran. Oaran's eyes lit up, his face beamed with pride and something else she had not seen, joy. Gently, he leaned forward, pressing his lips to her forehead. Wynne felt a gentle warm wave wash over her.

"Welcome home, daughter of the sea."

The End

The port of Whaeldrake was packed with ships of all sizes, each carrying different cargos to be unloaded and eventually transported throughout all Taeren. Whaeldrake was one of the main hubs for imports and exports into the country. She was a fearsome machine, governed by the strictest dock managers, who were responsible for overseeing all the ships coming in and out of port.

The clamor of men's voices filled the air, mixing in seamlessly with the gentle roar of the ocean waves beyond. Crew members busied themselves aboard their respective ships, completing tasks and obeying any orders issued. There was a diligent air that floated about the port, and a general buzz of excitement as new items were unloaded from all the various ships. In general the ports of Whaeldrake offered an excitement that no other part of town offered.

A woman, dressed in a light blue linen dress, weaved her way through the crowds of men scattered along the docks. Eyes followed her where she went, but she did not stop or even seem to notice the gazes as she past. She did not look like she belonged on the docks, but there was something in the way she walked that said she did.

Blonde, curly locks flowed down her back in glistening waves, bouncing with every step she took. Her hair was delicately pinned back away from her face, with a plethora of pearl pins, each sparkling white against the golden hues of her hair. Her eyes, a bright glowing blue, were extraordinary, with a spark of life that caused one to look again. A locket hung from her throat, completing her ethereal appearance. The locket was stunning, with gold filagree along the edges, and in the center sat a gold trident sitting atop of sea of blue jem stones. She was beautiful, a pearl among the dingy bustle of Whaeldrake's ports.

She walked quickly, effortless through the crowd, heading towards the furthest docks. The docks at the end were some of the oldest and smallest. It was not nearly as busy on the outskirts, but the air was just the same. Her blue eyes searched the smaller ports until her eyes found what she was looking for. Her blue eyes fixed on a particular ship, moored on the furthest dock.

This ship was small, but beautiful. Her wooden beams, sparkled like gold in the sunlight, her rigging was pristine and perfectly in place. At the top of the mast, there flew a deep blue flag, with golden trim around the edges. In the center of the flag, there was a bright shining trident. It matched the one found in the center of her locket. She searched the side, looking for the name but found the wooden panels empty. As the woman approached, she noticed the ship's deck was strangely silent. This was the only ship that was void a crew. The woman frowned; a ship void of a crew was vulnerable to any who saw an opportunity to strike.

Carefully she mounted the gang plank, hurrying up to the top deck. A gentle sea breeze swooped across the deck, blowing her skirts behind her in a wave of sea foam. Effortlessly, she jumped down onto the deck, landing gracefully. Slowly, she started her tour of the main deck, her hand traced the wooden rails as she walked to the upper deck. The ship was small, yes, but she was built sturdy. She no doubt would be able to sail the open ocean, just as well as any of the larger vessels.

The woman slowly took the stairs up to the upper deck, smiling as the sea breeze toyed with her golden locks, sending rogue curls across her porcelain face. The upper deck was small, but the helm was well fitted. The woman looked out at the sea, and smiled, open ocean was where she liked to be the best.

"Excuse me!" A man's deep voice called behind her, stopping her in her tracks, "What do you think you are doing?" He demanded. The man was young, with sparkling storm grey eyes. His face was bearded but did nothing to hide the sharp line of his jaw. He watched the woman intensely, his face was a mixture of doubt, disbelief, and hope.

"Your ship is beautiful." The woman called over her shoulder, keeping her back to the man.

"She's getting ready for her maiden voyage." He remarked, moving closer to the woman, hoping to get a better view of her face, but his view was obscured from the curtain of golden curls that flitted in the wind.

"I had a difficult time finding you." She called; a hint of amusement laced through her voice.

The man frowned, "I didn't know anyone was looking for me." He muttered, taking another step closer to her. She suddenly turned to face him, he took several steps back, as if he had seen a ghost.

"Declan Saunders?" She questioned, tears glistening in her blue eyes, "Never in a million years did I think your name was Declan!" She cried, then laughed, "You will always be Caspian to me." The man stood there, shock, covering his face. His handsome face was pale, and his lips trembled slightly.

"Wynne?" He whispered. The woman nodded, letting her tears trickle down her face. She stood there, holding her arms uncomfortably around her waist, her confident air had been reduced to rubble before him. Slowly, he gathered his wits about him and took hesitant step towards her. Slowly, she extended her hand out towards him, her hand shook nervously. Carefully, he reached his hand for hers, and when he felt the warmth of her fingertips touch his, his hand tightened around hers and pulled her in close. He wrapped her up into his warm arms and buried his face in her neck, inhaling her sweet salty scent. He felt her body tremble in his embrace and heard her sobs as she cried into his shoulder. She held onto him tight, her fingers digging into his back. She was real, he breathed deeply, she was indeed real.

"You came back." He whispered, "I thought you were never going to find me!" He cried into her hair.

"I know," she sniffed, "I'm sorry. I have so much I need to tell you." Wynne whispered; the sting of tears continued to flow down her face. Carefully, Caspian held her back away from him, his storm grey eyes searching her face. His hand cupped her cheek, his thumb tenderly rubbed her chin.

"You're here." He whispered, resting his forehead against hers. She moved her arms to wrap around his waist, relishing the warmth of his arms around her.

"I made you a promise." She smiled, looking up into his eyes.

"You took your sweet time fulfilling it." Caspian muttered, a slight smirk flooded his face, filling his storm grey eyes with a mischievous gleam.

She chuckled, "I met Oaran." She whispered.

His eyes widened, "Did you return it?" She inhaled a deep breath, before shaking her head.

"He gave it to me." She swallowed, "And I accepted it." She felt herself trembling, admitting the truth of what she had done. It was the reason why she had disappeared off the ship, Oaran had taken her back to Thalatia. The only person she had let know of her journey, was her father. Her father had accepted her decision without much quarrel, but she had hesitated in telling Caspian. And now, now that she was here standing in front of him, her worry resurfaced.

Caspian stared at her, his eyes searching her face, studying her carefully. Wynne had a difficult time discerning the emotions that played over his face. Was he angry, upset, disappointed in her for the decision she made? Or was he relieved, proud, happy that she had followed her own heart, had made her own decision with letting anyone else sway or convince her to do otherwise. For the first time, she doubted her decision to tell him the truth, to tell him that she had accepted her mother's birthright.

A smile, bright and handsome spread across his face. His storm grey eyes lit up, as the smile on his face beamed down on her. He lifted his hand slowly to her face, tipping her chin up towards his own. Wynne's stomach was jumping in a frenzy of excited butterflies, as she stared up into his face.

"I knew you could do it." He whispered. All the worried feelings that had been crowding her brain, dissipated with those simple few words. Relief swept through her, he was not rejecting her or angry with her, he was proud of her.

"I don't want to live this life without you." She cried, voice trembling.

"And you won't have to." He whispered back tenderly. She met his eyes; they were the same color as the sky get when a storm is about the hit. She had missed those eyes, missed his presence beside her, missed their shared banter and the bond they had shared, even in the hard times. This, she thought, this was what she wanted.

Wynne lifted herself up on her toes, Caspian met her halfway. His lips met her own, drowning her in a fire that she had been longing for. Caspian's arms wrapped around her, pulling her closer to him, she could feel the longing in his kiss and in the way he held her tightly to him. But it was still not close enough, she wanted more.

The kiss was long and deep, with the promise of something more, something that would stand the test of time. No, this is not the life she had expected when she had been captured. She had not expected to make it out alive, let alone find the one person she couldn't imagine life without. But right here, aboard this ship, wrapped up in Caspian's warm sturdy arms, tangled up in his kiss, this was the life she wanted. Wynne felt her heart flutter, this was the adventure she had been dreaming of, an adventure that would rival anything she had ever read in any, simple book.

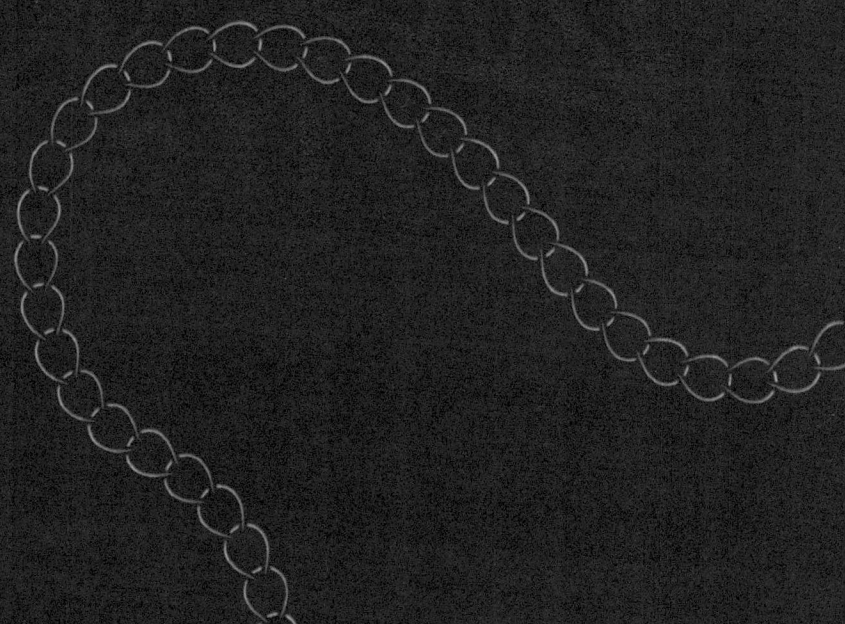

About the Author

A nutrition educator by day and a self-published author by night, Brooke Brauneis has spent the last eighteen years dreaming of the moment she would publish her first book. Her debut novel, *Payne's Curse*, was started when she was twelve years old, going through many, many revisions before finally being completed. Brooke currently lives in Missouri, with her little fur baby Sage and when she is not teaching, she spends her time with her boyfriend, reading and dreaming of everything else she wants to write.